SAFE AT HOME

Jimmy Roseburg is about to have the season of his dreams. In an amazing turn of luck, he and his three best friends from travel all-stars will all play on the same team with the legendary coach Mr. Wells. He can't wait to lead the Dodgers to the league championship before making all-stars. Then he's thrown a real curveball when he finds out that it's no accident. Mr. Wells has selected his team for one specific purpose.

Dominic Lewis has no friends, lives in a dump, and is looked after by his mom's abusive boyfriend…who'd rather spend all day on the couch watching TV than taking care of kids. For him, life couldn't get worse, but often did. Then everything changes when he's given the opportunity to play baseball, whether he likes it or not…

Mr. Wells wants Dominic to play on the Dodgers and it is up to Jimmy to make it happen…without destroying his season. It quickly becomes an impossible task as the season of dreams turns into a terrible nightmare. Only Jimmy and his friends, with the help of unlikely teammates, can save it.
In this exciting baseball adventure, being safe at home gathers a whole new meaning…

Safe at Home

Other Novels by Gregory Saur

Stuck in the Past (with Jack Irish)
Otherworld: Orcish Delight
The Royal Pains & Angels in the Outhouse
Panterror! The Epic Babysitting Adventures of Rachel Pugsley
The Pond Scum Gang
Soccer Star
Diving Catch
Best Shot Forward

<u>*Finding Innocence* Trilogy</u>
Finding Innocence, Book One: Strange Old World
Strange New People: Book Two of Finding Innocence
*Book the Third: Strange Happenings, the Conclusion of
    Finding Innocence*

Safe at Home

Gregory Saur

A Saur & Saur Publishing Project

Safe at Home

ISBN (pb): 978-1-949317-14-5

For any kid who wanted to play a sport but never could.

Acknowledgments

Of course I owe everything to the Creator above who is both loving and forgiving, even after seeing all my errors. But there are many others who deserve my thanks.

Thank you to my siblings and parents, especially to my mom and dad, for putting up with all my writing spells. My dear siblings, I'm finished for now. I promise to act human, until the next book starts. Loving Mom, I simply appreciate everything about you. All my happiness is because of you. Patient Dad, thank you for reading... I know you'd rather read a western.

Thank you also to my many editors. Special thanks especially to Ce-ce Cox of Outside Eyes Editing and Proofreading, for all your hard work and never ending patience. With you on my team, I win no matter what. And also to Diana Cox of Novel Proofreading, stepping up as a closer and finishing off a complete success.

And, finally, thank you, reader, for giving me a chance. I swung for the fences and hope I at least reached first page.

1

The fist pounded into the door like a hammer bent on shattering a nail. The entire frame shook and the door seemed to buckle before holding. The boy on the other side barely flinched. His anger was a tight ball that only squeezed tighter as the pounding intensified.

"Dom!" roared the voice of the monster behind the pounding. "You open this door! Right now, or so help me… Open up! Open up, now!" The door shook as the sharp thud of a foot blasted into its middle. "I swear, you're going to get it!" The angry voice lashed against the door, nearly as powerful as the accompanying hip and fist. "I'll smash your face, I swear it!"

The boy started to waver and his bottom lip quivered slightly, but then the upper lip bit down and he didn't budge. Like the door, he could take it.

Boom! The door shook again. It grimly held on.

The boy's hands clenched the thin blanket under his legs and also held on. His eyes squeezed shut.

Dominic Lewis would not give in. He sat on the edge of the bed with shoulders slouched and his arms tight against his sides. A deep scowl pulled down his round face. His body shuddered slightly as the threats intensified, but his face remained resolute. Like the door, he would stay strong. He hoped.

"Open up!" thundered the deeply savage voice, a storm that promised no mercy.

Dominic cringed as another rattling thump assaulted the stubborn door, the only thing that separated him from a sure beating. If the door broke, his face would be next. But it held. He blinked away a tear. His anger would keep him together.

"I won't open," he whispered so only he could hear it. "I won't."

Lucky for him, whoever had built the door to this room must've been expecting a zombie invasion. Dominic at least could be grateful for that. Everything else about his life? Well, he wouldn't be writing any thank you cards to Heaven anytime soon.

"I mean it, you stupid fat brat!" screamed the voice, growing rough and ragged with rage. "If I come in there, I'm going to bash in your ugly face and kick it through the floor! You'll be eating dirt and worms for your life, boy!"

Blinking away the lone tear, Dominic bit his lower lip harder as he glared at the door. *Let him come in,* he thought. *I don't care. Let him hit me. Go ahead.*

Still, he squirmed uncomfortably. Thankfully the door didn't listen to his thoughts as the hinges rattled from another terrific barrage of fists. Perhaps he'd gone too far this time. He'd been hit before. But never before had Mack sounded so mad. Usually he gave up after a few blows to the door with some curses mixed in with threats. He'd rage a little and then go find the TV and more beer. This time... Another blow rained against the door protecting Dominic.

I hate Mack! Dominic seethed in his mind. *I hate him, I hate, I hate him!*

Mack was his mom's boyfriend...who pretended to be his dad. On his good days. Otherwise, he was a complete monster. Dominic detested Mack with such a passion that sometimes he even scared himself.

Just thinking about this made Dominic's insides burn. Mack shouldn't be in his life. Mack should've been the one killed. Not his dad. But no matter how hard he thought it, Dominic couldn't escape reality. In reality, good guys died and monsters lived. He had yet to figure out where he stood in the mix. Perhaps this would be the day he found out.

His dad had been killed in a car accident when Dominic had barely turned three. They were coming back from the dentist, just him and his dad. A pickup ran a red light and plowed into their car.

At least this is what his mom told him. Dominic had no memory of the incident. All he had was a scar on his right arm—from the broken glass, his mom told him—and a black hole in his heart, full of a lot of pain. The pickup that took his dad had also wrecked his childhood, leaving him with a mental agony that he never could handle. Perhaps that was what made him do it.

In reality, the crash destroyed two lives. Dominic, once a cheery tyke, had become a large, wild beast, or so he'd been told. That was what Mack the Monster called him. A wild beast fit for the kennel.

"I mean it!" screamed Mack again, jerking Dominic back to the here and now. The door rocked back and nearly splintered as a heavy boom thundered against it. *The zombies are coming.*

Mack the Monster Jerk, as Dominic called him, now seemed to be throwing his shoulder against the door. It was only a matter of time.

Dominic's scowl only deepened. Whatever. If he got pounded, who would really care? Not his mom, that was for sure. She was the one who first let Mack into his life and then left him to torment Dominic while she worked all day and most of the night.

Thinking about it, Dominic felt a stab of despair. He really had no hope.

Mack had arrived like a gentle shower on Dominic's life two years before, pleasant but annoying at first. He'd just been a tall, grizzled man who smelled like cologne mixed with smoke and brought Dominic presents, like toy race cars. Dominic really didn't react to the stranger who started staying for weekends. Then the gentle shower intensified until it became a category five disaster. Mack started coming more often and staying longer and longer until one day he'd moved in.

"He's here to help us," his mom told Dominic over and over when he would complain about Mack—his dirty shoes and clothes left everywhere, his dirty habits of drinking beers and leaving his empties laying around, his lazy habit of watching TV all day while demanding everyone else serve him food and fetch more drinks…the list could go on. "He watches you and your sister while I work, honey. Besides, he used to play baseball. Maybe he'll teach you one day."

That day had never come. The toys quickly stopped, replaced by beer and cigarettes. These were not for Dominic. Mack's version of watching the kids involved him lying on a couch surrounded by beer cans and empty bottles, often accompanied by a cloud of acrid cigarette smoke, while watching television. The kids had to stay quiet and had to stay away.

Dominic never adjusted well to this.

Rose, Dominic's six-year-old sister, born a few months after their father died, mostly kept in her room playing with dolls in a make-believe world. While Dominic reacted to life's curveballs with anger, Rose ducked into a fantasy land. Somehow, she managed keep a happy outlook, something that Dominic never could understand.

Their mom worked two different jobs—one in a supermarket during the day and the other as a waitress at an all-night burger joint. She left at noon and rarely returned before 3:00 a.m. Her kids only saw her briefly in the late mornings and on one of her rare days off.

This often left Dominic to fend for himself. Something he was very bad at doing.

On this particular day Dominic had been trying to race his cars across the kitchen floor.

It'd all started ten minutes earlier.

Rosie sat humming to herself in her room with her dolls, while Mack lay sprawled across the couch with a hand dangling next to an open beer can on the floor. Three other cans sat empty around it.

"Okay, Bud racer," Dominic said softly to himself. "Let's see if you can beat Mack this time."

Mack always drove the now dented, severely beat-up blue car—it was the first present Mack had ever given Dominic. Since then it has suffered horrific crashes by being driven off counters, flipped down the stairs, pounded with a hammer, drowned in the bathtub, and even nuked in the microwave for five seconds—saved from a longer stint when his mom had caught him.

Bud was a flashy red car Dominic had gotten from his mom on his last birthday. He named it Bud because that had been his dad's nickname. That was about all Dominic had left of his dad. His mom never talked about him anymore—not since Mack had arrived.

The other cars sat idle—the audience watching the great race.

"Gentlemen, start your engines," Dominic muttered, making engine noises from the back of his throat.

"Shut it in there," Mack bellowed from the sofa in front of the TV. "Can't you kids shut up?"

Rose's humming died as suddenly as it started. Dominic, crouched in the middle of the kitchen floor, froze and instantly his motor sounds died. He faced the TV room, not far from Mack at all. It was impossible to get far from him.

They lived in a small, tight trailer. This was something Dominic could never get over. Everything about it was putrid. Old, with chipped paint, dented walls and peeling siding, perched on a foundation of crumbling cinderblocks, Dominic always thought it resembled an oversized baby's block that had once been painted white and then dropped into a food processor (something he'd tried when a toddler). Sadly, it actually looked better on the outside. The inside resembled the aftermath of a tornado trapped in a box.

After a short flight of crooked stairs made of warped wood, a rickety screen door led to a chipped wooden door that provided the only entrance and exit to the miserable home. The door opened to worn, threadbare carpet the yellowish-green of vomit, complete with the smell. It extended across the main room where the TV sat in front of the old sagging couch. This is where Mack usually parked his fat lazy behind every day, before going out for drinks or cards with his buddies. A small table hidden under empty beer cans, bottles, and dirty dishes was just to the right of the couch along with a floor lamp Dominic's mom had found at the thrift store a year before. This was the main living room.

At the time of the incident, Dominic knelt in the kitchen, just beyond the living room. A small counter stood over his head, well hidden by used cereal bowls, old pizza boxes, and enough spilled food to feed an army of mice. The sink lay covered in food slime and currently held a small mountain of dirty dishes. Everything about the kitchen resembled Dominic's life. A complete filthy mess.

The refrigerator on his right sounded like a kid laboring and about to collapse after running a mile through mud. The outside of the fridge had decorations of encrusted brown stains resembling blood and felt slimy to the touch. Rose had tried taping up her art work, covering the stains, but Mack had ripped them all down, growling about the cost of tape and paper.

At his back was an equally filthy stove holding a dented kettle with a can of instant coffee next to it—the only edible item visible in the miserable room. All the cupboards above the stove were bare. Dominic and Rose had finished the last of the cereal that morning. Their mom promised to go shopping after work…like she'd done the day before. Next to the stove, a small hall led to the washer and then his mom's bedroom…where Mack also slept.

Dominic didn't really care anymore. He was now used to the mess and also used to Mack always growling at him and occasionally walloping him on the side of the head, like he had that morning at breakfast when Dominic took the last of the cereal.

Dominic escaped it all by going to the races with his cars. So, after Mack quieted down, he put all his focus on the opening between the counter and the fridge. His target lay between the kitchen and Mack—the small table used for meals with three mismatched plastic chairs set around it. Mack lay in his usual position, watching a stupid sports show where a group of guys yelled at each other for no particular reason.

Dominic's room was at the far end of the trailer to his right while his sister stayed in the cramped room to the left of his. The two shared a tiny bathroom just outside of Rose's room with a tub, toilet, and cracked mirror. Thankfully there was another bathroom attached to his mom's room. Dominic couldn't bear the thought of sharing such a private room with Mack the Jerk.

All in all, it was a pretty cruddy life. Dominic's clothes always stank and he only bathed once a week, if that. His younger sister endured the same. Both were mostly left alone in school and had few friends…Dominic less than Rose. She at least had a little girl cuteness that teachers adored, and her classmates didn't yet care about her home life. Mack never laid a hand on her. *She* listened and obeyed. *She* wasn't fat, ugly, and stupid.

Don't care, Dominic thought, as he often did. *People are losers.* He never needed friends and didn't want them now. Aiming the cars at the table, he pulled them back.

"Winner of this Trailer Trash 600 wins the Cup of Soda," he mumbled. "Loser gets barbecued in gasoline."

He knelt on the floor with his body hunched over both knees, head close to the floor facing the Bud car clenched in his right hand. Mack's car was crushed in a tight grip in his left.

"Go get it, Dad," he whispered. Then he flung both cars forward, careful to zip Bud first.

Mack's car instantly hit a rut in the floor and did a spectacular flip, landing upside down and spinning crazily into the table's leg. Bud kept going.

"Yes!" Dominic hissed, pushing himself up to his feet. Then his face froze.

Bud zipped under the table and through the legs of the plastic chair he usually sat at and kept going. The small car shot straight into the TV room, straight to where the real Mack lay on the couch. The toy went full speed into the ragged carpet that separated the room from the eating area and jackknifed into the air. It flew over six feet up, right over the couch, and then landed with a clunk.

It had nailed Mack's beer can, knocking it right over before skittering to the side. Suds started gushing onto the rug before Mack could react. Dominic didn't see this, but he knew something bad happened because very shortly after, Mack did react, in a big way.

Jerking back in surprise, he roared, "Hey!" His arms flailed wildly and his eyes bugged out. "My beer!" Then his thick neck whirled toward the kitchen, his eyes striking Dom. "You stupid little—" Then he leapt onto his feet and stomped on the beer can.

The boy heard the crunch and saw beer suds fly up and across the room. The smell of cheap beer mixed with the stench of mold, smoke, and old vomit.

Dominic went still and could only stare.

"Why'd you do that for?" Mack demanded.

Dominic blinked from where he stood at the counter. If he hadn't known any better, he would have thought Bud did it on purpose.

"I didn't do anything," he finally said sullenly. "I was just racing cars. It wasn't on purpose."

"You stupid moron," Mack said in disgust. "You should be out playing with other kids, but nobody can stand you, can they? I don't blame them."

Dominic's face fell and his chin dropped to his chest. He was used to such insults. Mack never missed an opportunity to remind Dominic that nobody had ever invited him to a birthday party, or even to play outside.

It was a sunny spring day in early April. Kids could be heard outside playing a game, but like always Dominic was stuck inside. It felt like prison.

"Why don't they lock you up with the other crazies," Mack muttered. "Oh, yeah," he said sarcastically. "Because you're too young."

"I'm not crazy," Dominic said softly. His gaze remained on the floor.

Mark barked out an ugly laugh. "What's that?" he asked. "That's not what your school says. Don't you have some stupid paper saying you're a certified nutcase? You're crazy, all right."

Dominic only swallowed. He had an ED label. ED meant emotionally disturbed. This much he knew. His mom had gone to his school for some meeting about it. He didn't understand it—just like he didn't understand why he did some bad things. Just sometimes a terrible anger took over his body and made him do them. Now was one of those times. He felt his breath speed up and muscles tighten. His mouth clenched.

"Look at me, fatso," Mack said, his voice rising. He had a nasty tone, even when pretending to be nice. "Look at my face when I'm talking to you."

Mostly Mack left Dominic alone. But when he didn't, things got rough.

A bolt of anger stabbed through Dominic's chest. He lifted his gaze at Mack and blinked.

"That's right, stupid," growled Mack. "You look at me, moron boy."

Mack stood by the couch with an ugly sneer across his grizzled face. Just over six feet, he was a former high school baseball star, or so he claimed. Since then, the years hadn't been good. Pasty white flesh hung from his round, pudgy face, so he looked like a bloated marshmallow covered in soot. Dark greasy strands of hair clung to the sides of his head and slunk to his shoulders like they were snakes trying to escape. A bald spot crowned the top. As if to hide the lack of hair on top of his head, Mack kept his face unshaven until the weekend. Bright blue eyes bore an evil glint as they met Dominic's. His dark eyebrows lifted in amusement.

"So you're not afraid of me, are you?" he purred like a panther about to attack. "I like that. In this world you have to be something to get anywhere." He absently scratched his round gut, hanging below a sunken chest, and belched. "Now go get me another beer. You done spilled mine, you stupid brat."

Dominic knew him to be thirty-five, but he looked ten years older. Wearing a sleeveless T-shirt, stained in breakfast food, and boxer shorts, he looked like an old little kid that never grew up. Only his legs gave evidence of what once had been. Narrow and slim at the calves, they displayed muscle on an otherwise wasted body.

Dominic really, really hated him. Everything about him.

"Why don't you ever get job," Dominic muttered. "All you do is live off my mom."

"What was that, fatso?" Mack asked. His eyebrows instantly narrowed and a flush crept into his cheeks. "You just say something?"

"I said you should be working and not my mom!" Dominic shouted. "You're a stupid drunk!"

Mack threw back his head and laughed. Then he stared at Dominic. "Is that right? Well, I'll go get a job as soon as you get a friend. How about that, moron boy? I can't leave this trash pit because your mom can't trust you not to burn the place down! Without me, you and your snotty sister would be placed in foster homes!"

"We could go live with Sara," Dominic responded.

Mack snorted in disgust. "That stupid girl won't come back here. Not never."

"She will too!" Dominic shouted, feeling the anger grow inside of him. "She promised!"

Sara was his older sister who had graduated from high school the previous year. She'd left the trailer so Dominic could have his own room, so she'd said. Before then Dominic had been forced to share a room with Rose—not great under any circumstances, but Sara had demanded her privacy and claimed to need space for her schoolwork. Now Sara lived in some apartment while going to nursing school and working at a bookstore. While she hadn't visited in several months, she had sent a stack of books for Dominic and Rose just the other week.

"Don't be such a thick moron, Dom," Mack said in scorn. "I tried to get her to stay, but she wants nothing to do with you. Now go get me another beer. Now!"

Dominic stood there with his shoulders trembling for a moment. Then he reached for the nearest object and hurled it at Mack's face. It turned out to be a soggy paper plate holding molding applesauce.

Caught by surprise, Mack stood there dumbly as the plate stuck to his chest, sending spatters of brown gobs into his face. Then his surprise turned into rage.

"Why you—" he shouted. Wiping off the messy plate from his front, he came after Dominic with clenched fists.

Dominic's eyes turned large with fear. Squeaking out a noise resembling a frightened duck, he turned and ran. There was only one place to go. His mom's bedroom.

"Get out of there!" bellowed Mack.

No way was Dominic crazy. Darting past the ancient and dented washer and dryer, he skittered to a stop just inside the bedroom and slammed the door shut, locking it an instant later. The room had the shades drawn and was as dark and gloomy as a grave. Smelling mostly of musty clothes and cheap perfume, it smelled like a grave too. Dominic jumped on the unmade bed and sat facing the door.

The pounding started moments later. It would not end as a good day. And it was only Monday.

2

The ball came into his chest with a small thump and rolled to the mattress next to him.

Jimmy grunted and reached for the ball.

"Nice shot, hotshot," his sister Brittany said from the door.

"Go away, Anything-but-hot," he said lazily. Jimmy Roseburg lay on his bed staring at the ceiling. He tossed the ball up again, this time managing to catch it with his left hand. He was practicing his peripheral vision by playing catch with himself, without taking eyes off the spider settling on the ceiling just over his head.

"Whatever," Brittany said with a flounce of her ponytail. "For your information, your baseball buddies are outside wanting you to play Wiffle ball."

Outside was near ninety degrees with the humidity so bad it felt like stepping into a swimming pool without walls.

Jimmy grunted. "It's too hot to go outside. Our first practice game is tomorrow and I don't want to be burnt out for it."

"Well, they won't go away."

"As long as you go away, I'll be fine," Jimmy promised her.

Then their mom called from downstairs. "Jimmy!" she called. "Your friends want to speak to you!"

"See, I told ya," Brittany said. Then she turned and flounced from the door. Just a year older, Brittany acted like his second mom. Only more sarcastic and doubly more annoying. "I told them you were too busy playing with your dolls."

Groaning, Jimmy rolled from his bed and went to see what idiotic friends he had. He figured it would be Chase and maybe Shawn. Chase lived across the street and Shawn, even though he went to a different school, was Chase's best friend. Though he lived over a mile away, he often rode his bike to Jimmy's house, mostly unexpected, and always with fun in mind.

Jimmy grimaced. Definitely had to be Shawn down there.

Hot, cold, wind, rain, or tornado, they could always count on Shawn making it to Chase's house. Only those two would think about playing something like baseball when trapped in an outside oven.

Sure enough, when nearing the top of the stairs, Jimmy heard Chase's and Shawn's voices. They were trying to explain to his mom that Wiffle ball would be perfectly safe in the heat. Jimmy slowed to a stop. He really didn't feel like baking out there. Not unless he was playing real baseball, at least.

"Mrs. Roseburg, you don't have to worry," he heard Chase say confidently. "We have plenty of water with us."

"Yeah," added Shawn's voice enthusiastically, "and I developed a sure proof system to keep us cool. Guaranteed."

"Well, you're always cool, Shawn," Jimmy heard his mom say teasingly.

"Coolest cat in town," Shawn's voice returned proudly.

Jimmy couldn't help but grin. Then he heard a third boy's voice.

"We'll come back quick if it gets too hot," it promised.

Jimmy suddenly jumped into action and ran to the first stair.

"What are you idiots doing here?" he bellowed.

His three best friends were clustered just inside the door and staring up at him with stupid grins. His mom looked up with raised eyebrows. "Is that how you greet your friends, Jimmy?" she asked.

"These jerks, yeah," Jimmy said immediately.

Chase Stevens, Shawn Dillard, and the third boy, Grayson Daniels, had been friends with Jimmy since t-ball days when they were five. Now five years later, they remained as close as gum stuck under a table. Seriously, they'd been in and out of some pretty sticky and gross places—like Brittany's room during a sleepover, after she'd stolen their sleeping bags and had tried bedazzling them with glitter and pink and purple beads.

Mrs. Roseburg sighed. "Maybe so, but you'd better convince them you're not going out in the heat to play Wiffle ball. Not under my watch."

"But Mom," Jimmy protested, "they're all here! I have to go now!"

Every fall and spring the boys played little league and every year they grew even closer. Now all four of them were on the same team and set to make a run at the league championship. They'd promised on the first practice that if they ever got together, no matter what, they would practice baseball. This was because usually they played on different teams and had to wait for the all-star team before being teammates. This always happened, because, modestly and truthfully, the four of them were all great players.

During league play, the best players were supposed to be divided evenly among all the teams. But this spring they were all Dodgers. How they'd managed to be on the same team was sort of a mystery. Jimmy's dad was one of the assistant coaches, but he refused to explain it. When asked, he only grinned tightly and said they'd see why. Nate Dyson, another friend from the ball field, just not as close, still wouldn't speak to them because he was so mad for being left off the team. A Cardinal, he'd only promised to beat them.

"Well," said Mrs. Roseburg with uncertainty, "maybe for a little while… I know you boys want to be ready this year."

"Definitely," Chase assured her seriously. "We have to win the championship, or we'll never be allowed on the all-star team again."

"Nah," Shawn said in fake disgust, "we *are* the all-star team. We just have to show the others why."

Jimmy put on his sad puppy dog look. "Please, Mom?"

"Oh, I don't know why I had a boy," Mrs. Roseburg said with a sigh. "Girls are so much more sensible."

"What was that you said, Mom?" asked Brittany. She appeared behind Jimmy with her softball glove on and Jimmy's baseball glove held in her throwing hand. In a hard, underhand toss, she sent Jimmy's glove toward her brother's head.

Quick hands caught the glove and Jimmy stuck out his tongue at his sister.

"Um, Brittany, you're not thinking of joining the boys, are you?" Mrs. Roseburg asked. "Surely you're not thinking of doing something that crazy."

Brittany shook her head vigorously. "No way! I thought you and I could go out back and work on my pitching."

"That's where we're going to play, dummy," Jimmy said with a frown.

"Oh, no, Jimmy boy," Shawn said, grinning. "We're going to the field. That's how we're going to be cool." His eyes danced with mischief.

Chase and Grayson smiled widely at Jimmy's perplexed face.

Mrs. Roseburg shook her head in defeat. "Fine. Fine. Just go. Brittany, I'll go get my glove. Later tonight we'll have a talk on how to behave sensibly."

Mrs. Roseburg looked like an older version of Brittany and often the two were mistaken as sisters. Both had slim athletic frames and straight chestnut brown hair. Mrs. Roseburg had played soccer in college, but had converted to softball and baseball since. This was mostly because her husband was all about baseball and managed to sway both children in his direction. If you couldn't beat them…join them.

Friendships were sometimes like that. Jimmy often wondered how he ended up with his three best friends. In truth, none of the boys had much in common in looks or personalities.

Jimmy had light skin just forming a tan and short dark hair the color of midnight, just like his father. Clipped close to his scalp on the sides and slightly longer on top, it resembled bristles when wet. A solid square jaw anchored his wide face that carried his generous mouth and rather broad nose well. When he smiled—which he did often—his deep brown eyes narrowed into slits that often gave him a mischievous look. Even though a straight "A" student, he was not immune to getting into trouble for practical jokes. The only time he was truly serious was during a baseball game. And in baseball, he excelled.

Though he stood slightly below average in height for a ten-year-old and on the skinny side, he had a solid build. Possessing good balance, speed, and terrific coordination, he often played catcher or shortstop. Lately he'd also been working on his pitching. So far he'd only made a few relief appearances as pitcher in all-stars, but he meant for that to change. This year he would be a starter.

On the other hand, Chase towered over most boys their age. Wide shoulders and a burly build with pale skin gave him the appearance of being inactive and overweight. This was not the case. His stocky torso was almost all muscle and he had some of the quickest hands around, as well as deceptively fast feet. Many ball players found this out the hard way when Chase robbed them of base hits at third. His throws to first were always on the money and he proved to be a dominant pitcher when called on.

His solid brown hair hung over his high sloping forehead just above his eyes and was cut short in the back, sort of like a reverse mullet. If any shorter in the front, his head would resemble the shape of an egg, or so Jimmy claimed earlier that fall. Since then, Chase made sure to keep his hair always just above his eyes in front. This didn't stop "Egghead" from becoming his nickname among friends. Only friends could get away with calling him that. His green eyes missed little and he was always ready for a fight if he perceived any injustice thrown his way. He was on the lookout for excitement and had a quick trigger. To date, he was known as the only little league player tossed from a game for arguing strikes.

Now Chase nudged the smaller Grayson aside with his hip and raised his right hand for a high five from Jimmy.

Running down the stairs, Jimmy obliged him by skipping the final two steps in a flying leap to slap that hand with his raised glove. He ended up giving Chase a chest bump in the process and was immediately sent reeling back into the stairs. Hitting Chase was like hitting a brick wall.

"Careful!" Mrs. Roseburg said, wincing, as Jimmy crashed on the final step with his backside striking first.

"Ow," Jimmy said, grinning. "I keep forgetting you're made of metal." He'd lost his glove in the process and Grayson kicked it to his feet.

"Hurry and get your glove," the smaller boy said cheerfully. "We're gonna be late."

Grayson, also known as Gray, stood over an inch shorter than Jimmy and had a slighter build. With boyish good looks, he had skin slightly tanner than Jimmy's and had wavy light brown hair that curled in the back and hung just above his neck. In the front, strands of messy brown settled just over his pair of large blue eyes. His nose was small like the rest of him, and his smooth face, browned by the sun, carried a more serious look. He rarely smiled and when he did, it came out shy and unsure. He only looked confident when on the field.

Jimmy knew better than to think of Grayson as wimpy. A small, scrappy player, Gray could always be counted on to be a fierce competitor to the bitter end. He didn't speak much, but he let the world know he hated losing. Anything from checkers to baseball threatened to bring out bitter tears when he came up on the wrong end.

This especially applied to baseball. Despite this, nobody called him a baby. Seeing him throw his body in front of grounders and sliding cleats proved his toughness. On the field he played any position needed and excelled at them all. Off the field, the three friends, Shawn, Chase, and Jimmy, always looked out for him. Together, they created an inseparable foursome.

Shawn playfully mussed up Gray's hair. They'd all had baseball caps, but had quickly removed them when entering Jimmy's house. Mrs. Roseburg had taught them well—her house meant her rules were to be followed.

"Don't worry, dude," Shawn said. "We got time." He winked at Jimmy. "Soon enough you'll almost be as cool as me. Just wait."

With smooth brown skin and coal black hair buzzed close to his scalp, Shawn stood loose and lean. His dad was ex-Army and ran his own lawn care business. Shawn didn't have to help out just as long as he played some sort of sport with friends. This kept him constantly looking for games to play—especially games similar to baseball.

Inches taller than Jimmy, but slightly shorter than Chase, he had long, thin legs and arms that never seemed to run out of energy. He could play catch for hours and never tire. His narrow face featured sharp cheekbones and a sharper chin. His broad nose and thin lips on his chiseled face only highlighted his good looks, especially when he smiled.

Shawn's white teeth seemed to sparkle and his friendly brown eyes always danced with joy whenever he lit up into a full smile. All the kids liked him, but not all of his teachers. His main problem was his impulsiveness. One of the fastest runners in the fifth grade, he also had one of the fastest mouths. Acting and speaking before thinking often got him into a lot of trouble. He mostly settled on the baseball field, but occasionally his rashness got him into jams, especially on the base paths. Still, when it came to organizing fun, there were few better.

Suddenly curious, Jimmy couldn't wait to be outside with his friends. All the stress of school and the upcoming end of the year tests melted away like an ice cube left on a blacktop. He was a boy with friends, off to play a game he loved. Life was good.

"Come on, guys!" he cried. "Let's go! Last one to the field has to date my sister!"

"Okay by me," Chase said, grinning while flicking hair from his eyes. "Your sister is hot."

Jimmy almost died with puking as he pushed his way past his friends, making sure to step squarely on Chase's foot as he did so.

3

There was an old saying about Eastern Virginia's weather: If you don't like it, wait a moment and it'll change.

Unfortunately, nature seemed to have forgotten this in the last few days. All weekend, and now into the school week, the temperature remained stuck in the high eighties and lower nineties. Storms were on the way to cool things down but were not expected for a few more days, if at all.

Jimmy, like the other boys, wore his Dodgers cap, athletic shorts, and a thin blue T-shirt. Still, by the time they'd hiked the two blocks from his house to the field behind his school, Knox Elementary, he, and pretty much everything he wore, dripped with sweat. His shirt stuck to his back like a second layer of unwanted skin.

The sun blazed as the day slowly started to give way to evening. The temperatures didn't seem to be in any hurry to leave.

"Man," groaned Chase, as he wiped his brow, "I think I smell cooked meat."

"Ah, you're just smelling yourself," Shawn joked. "I'm seriously getting you some deodorant for your next birthday, dude."

"Just shut up, man," Chase grumbled. "Are you sure about this? I'd rather be home playing baseball on my Xbox."

"Trust me," Shawn told him confidently. "This is where you want to be. It'll be cool, dude. Promise."

Grayson, his face glowing with heat, raised his eyebrows at Jimmy and merely shrugged. He looked too tired to talk.

During the whole trip, Jimmy's friends had been hinting about something special ahead, but refused to tell him what to expect.

Now, standing at the chain-link fence separating the infield from the stands, Jimmy was feeling a little more than steamed. Nobody else was in sight and already sweat dripped down his back and into his shorts. Soon his underwear would be melted to his skin.

A soccer field separated the left foul line from a busy road. For a brief moment Jimmy felt the urge to run out in the middle of the field and scream. Only the effort would be too great.

Walking all this way just to drown in sweat promised to be just as bad though, he thought. His best friends were idiots. The next day the Dodgers played the Cardinals in their first practice game. Why not wait until then to stand in the miserable heat?

"Is this fun yet?" he asked, sounding annoyed. "I don't think I want to play catch in the sun. I melt in it, you know."

"Just for a few minutes, dude," Shawn said. He licked sweat from his upper lip. "Let's just do a few minutes of catch and then we'll play Wiffle ball in the outfield."

"Whoopee," Jimmy said sarcastically.

Shawn grinned. "See? I knew you'd come around. It'll be great."

The boys had each carried their gloves. Chase had a real baseball while Shawn kept a plastic Wiffle ball bat and an official Wiffle ball—white plastic with tiny holes on one half of the sphere.

Jimmy stared at Shawn in disgust. He breathed in with his mouth and blew out slowly. "Whatever," he mumbled. "Why do we have to be so stupid?" he asked.

"That sounds like a personal question," Shawn said with a smirk. "How else would I be your friend? Now move back some and see how stupidly you catch my fastball."

Grayson, always quick to join a game, had already backed several feet and began to toss the ball with Chase.

Shawn and Jimmy joined them. Despite his promise of a fastball, Shawn lobbed his throws lightly to Jimmy. All four were smart enough to know the importance of properly warming up their arms. The head coach of the Dodgers was none other than Mr. Ben Wells.

Mr. Wells was a legend among Little League players in Eastland County, Virginia. Tough, but fair, he was one of the few coaches to never raise his voice. Ever. Despite this, he was always heard loud and clear. Nobody wanted to disappoint him, especially his young players. If he ever caught a kid throwing hard without properly warming up…well, Mr. Wells was old school. That kid would probably have plenty of time to think about it while running laps. And then more time to think sitting on the side watching the others. Mr. Wells had one simple rule in all-stars. You don't listen, you don't play. Even without his presence, his players listened.

Surely he would have watched with a smile as the four boys formed a square and began to toss the ball crisply to each other in no particular order.

Every few moments Shawn would glance at his watch. Suddenly he held up his hand.

"Okay, time!" he cried. "Let's start Wiffle ball in the outfield!"

Jimmy paused in mid-throw and glared at him. Despite the heat, he found himself just getting into the groove.

"Why do you want to go all the way to the outfield?" he demanded. "Why not just play in the infield?"

The field at Knox Elementary didn't have a pitcher's mound, but was well kept for softball. They would have to go another half mile to reach the Little League baseball park, which sported four pristine ball fields. This they only did for real games.

That being said, the well-raked clay infield of Knox would be much more suitable for Wiffle ball than the green outfield grass with no markings. At least the infield had foul lines. Usually they played that any ball hit out of the infield still in the air counted as a home run.

Shawn only grinned and shook his head. "Not today, Jimmy. Remember, today we're going to be cool. Right, guys?"

Chase laughed and tossed his glove into the grass. "Shoes and socks off," he said in response, reaching down for his sneakers. "Last one to center field has to lick my feet!"

Without blinking, Grayson, his eyes glinting with excitement, kicked off his shoes and hopped on one foot as he started peeling off a sock.

Shawn quickly joined the race to bare his feet.

Looking at his friends like they were nuts, Jimmy sighed and dropped his glove. "You guys are all idiots," he mumbled. He started untying his laces.

"Of course we are," Grayson yelled over his shoulder as he dropped one sock and hopped on his opposite foot to grab the other. "Why else would we let you hang out with us?"

Jimmy kicked his first sneaker at his friend's backside and soon sent the second after. Both missed and Grayson happily kicked dust on top of them. Then, barefooted, he raced for the outfield.

Chase and Shawn followed seconds later, leaving Jimmy standing in his socks choking on dust. Air-conditioned cars whizzed by as their occupants rushed to get to their destination and out of the heat. A few slowed when seeing the crazy boys running in ninety-plus heat. None of the cars' occupants seemed to have nearly as much fun.

Jimmy certainly didn't think it very fun at first. "Hey, guys!" he cried. "What are you doing?" Peeling off his socks, he gave chase as his friends only laughed like idiots.

By the time Jimmy reached the three in the middle of center field, his flushed face dripped with sweat and he struggled to breathe normally. "What is this all about—" he began.

Then he heard a faint click at his feet.

"Now!" shouted Shawn. "It's started!"

"Huh?" asked Jimmy. Suddenly a sharper sound clicked under him and a gush of water exploded, right up his shorts.

"Aaaieee!" screeched Jimmy, jumping back. The entire front and back of his shorts were completely soaked. Water continued to spray up into his stomach.

Grayson and Chase also got caught in the sudden deluge from down under and danced back. Only Shawn managed to jump back in time to avoid the surprise water.

"I knew it!" he crowed. "The sprinklers come on at five every night!" He laughed like a maniac and then jumped into the spray.

"You could have told me, idiot!" Jimmy shouted. "That scared me!"

This seemed to crack Chase up to no end. "So much you wet yourself!" he sputtered.

Grayson laughed so hard he ended up on his back as the water droplets fell over him.

"I hate you all," Jimmy muttered. Then he grinned. "You're really a bunch of idiots. So are we playing, or what?"

"Wiffle ball in the water!" yelled Shawn. "I told you it would be cool!"

Jimmy kicked water toward him, but laughed. Behind him another sprinkler sputtered to life and soaked his back. It felt good. Real good.

Across the entire outfield, a series of sprinklers popped up from their hidden homes and started lacing the green grass with spouts of water. The boys were quick to throw themselves in the cooling liquid arcs.

Laughing and sometimes slipping in the wet grass, the boys eventually started the perfect game of Wiffle ball on a hot afternoon. Shirts were soon discarded and became bases. Home, Jimmy's soaked shirt, was placed just under the first sprinkler. This made hitting extra difficult because often the ball would be shot down by a stream of water before reaching the plate. The other bases were also carefully placed to be soaked by water. Whenever a boy did manage a hit, they made sure to slide at every base possible. Slipping and sliding, they played the game with wild abandon.

In no time their stomachs were covered in grass and shorts streaked with mud. None could keep from falling in fits of laughter. So caught up in the game, they failed to realize they were being watched.

At the same time the boys arrived at the field, Dominic sat against the side wall of the trailer with his knees up near his chin. Hugging them tightly, he stared at the ground intently.

A jumble of ants ran back and forth in a panic. Their home had been smashed and smeared by Dominic's feet minutes before. At the time it felt good. Now looking at the ruin he'd caused, Dominic only felt sick. Sharp pain echoed off his back from where Mack had slapped him repeatedly after busting open the door. More bruises to hide, that's all they were. Mack, even in his rage, had taken care to make sure all his hits and slaps struck where Dominic's clothes would hide them.

The physical pain didn't bother him as much…not as much as the terrible feeling filling his empty belly.

"I'm not like him," he whispered as he stared down at the carnage he'd made of the ants. But inside, he knew better.

Bitter laughter welled up in his head. *You're like him, Dom. Only worse. You're stupid, fat, and ugly. Nobody will ever like you.*

His thoughts were interrupted by the rumble of gravel being driven over by a car. The trailer park was just off the main road and consisted of over twenty decrepit trailers set up in haphazard rows.

It'd been named Queen's Garden Park, probably by somebody with a sick sense of humor. None of the trailers featured a garden and nobody who lived there ever claimed to be queen. Trees lined the border of the park, mostly to keep it from being too visible to passing cars, but little else grew once inside. Gravel roads led to each trailer and were hard to distinguish from the dirt yards in front. Patches of crabgrass grew with clumps of weeds, but little else. Dominic's tiny yard consisted mostly of dirt and broken toys.

Often when he was bad at school, Mack would take one of his toys, break it, and then toss it in the yard. To teach him a lesson. "Do a bad thing, get a bad thing," was one of Mack's favorite sayings. Everything Dominic did was bad, so there was no surprise so many bad things happened to him.

He watched the car entering the park with idle curiosity. Few visitors ever came, and he knew most of the cars by sight. Mostly they were old secondhand junkers and pickups. This one he saw to be a black Mercedes with glistening wheels.

Probably a drug buyer, he thought. He knew there were drugs around. Everyone in the park knew it. Bobby Wayne and Dill Coose were two high school dropouts who made no secrets of their new profession. Nobody cared, and if they did care, it was most likely because they were a buyer.

His eyes grew wide when the Mercedes took a left and aimed straight at his trailer. He got to his feet warily. Then his knees quivered when the car stopped a few feet from the front door. Dominic's insides clenched. Nobody had ever visited Mack before. Mack always went out when he wanted to see somebody. And for a car this nice to come, he knew it meant trouble. He stared at the front door and wondered if he could make it inside before the driver got out. His best chance would be to go hide in the back. He'd just started backing that direction when a cheerful voice hailed him from the car.

"Hello there!" a man's voice called in a friendly greeting. It sounded pleasant and older.

Confused, Dominic stopped and swallowed as he stared at the car. In any case, it was too late to run now. Whoever had spoken had to be speaking to him. Nobody else was around.

"You wouldn't be Dominic Lewis, would you?" asked the man, still sounding cheerful.

No doubt about it. Dominic swallowed hard and blinked rapidly. His mouth opened and closed, but made no sound. All at once his tongue felt as big as a frog and completely clogged this throat. His head barely moved as he tried to nod.

"I take that as a yes. Mind if I come out?" Without waiting for an answer, the driver's door swung open and Dominic watched an older man unfold himself before him.

He looked to be much older than Mack, but at the same time almost younger. Short gray hair grew thickly around his deeply tanned face. Though wrinkles lined his forehead and creased his eyes and mouth, his face held a youthful look. Rosy cheeks and square chin were placed firmly under bright green eyes that looked at Dominic with more curiosity than malice. His wide mouth curved into a friendly smile. But what really made him appear youthful was the way he moved. Like a cat on the prowl—not on a hunt, but more like on an adventure.

Loose khaki pants and blue buttoned shirt couldn't hide the broad shoulders and slim waist. He moved easily and energetically. Stepping lightly toward Dominic, he stretched out a hand.

"Name is Ben Wells," he said smoothly. "Your mother sent me."

Dominic never trusted grown-ups and shuffled another step backwards. He didn't take the hand. "I didn't do nothing," he mumbled.

"What was that? You didn't do what?" Ben Wells stared down at Dominic shrewdly. His smile narrowed, but didn't totally disappear. He had to be at least Mack's height if not a little taller. Drawing back his offered hand, he raised it up and scratched the back of his head. "Never mind. You don't know why I'm here, do you?"

Dominic shook his head slightly. Curiosity started to win over his fear.

"Dominic, I coach baseball. Does that help?"

Immediately Dominic's body stiffened and his head jerked up. He'd told his mom that he'd wanted to play a sport several weeks before. Earlier that morning she'd promised to call one more time to see if she could get him on a team, but admitted it was probably too late. She'd filled out several forms, but all the leagues were full by the time Dominic had turned them in…without the required fee. It cost money to play on a team. Dominic remembered the conversation vividly that morning.

Mack had snorted when Dominic's mom promised to call one last time. "Too late for that fat kid do anything athletic," he'd said. "Should've started years ago. I know you already called the soccer league three times. Face it, Mary. Nobody wants a fat psycho playing on their goody-goody team." He'd then belched and had laughed when Mary, Dom's mom, had told him to shut his face. "Don't listen to him, baby," she'd said to Dominic.

Now he couldn't help but remember Mack's words. Did this guy come out all this way to tell him to his face he couldn't play? That didn't sound right. So why'd he come? He knew from school that baseball season had already started weeks before and he'd long missed the tryouts. As if pulled by an invisible anchor, Dominic's chin drooped until it pointed at the ground.

Not being able to bear any more pain, he stared down at his feet. He'd run from the trailer soon after Mack had beat down the door and then slapped his back. He'd gone so fast that he hadn't put on any shoes. Looking at his filthy socks full of holes, Dominic couldn't help but feel like he was staring down at his own life. He was like an ant whose whole life had been smashed and trampled by an uncaring bully.

At school Dominic always sat by himself at a desk separated from the other students and could be counted on to be kicked out of the classroom at least once a week. Already he'd been suspended from school twice—once for throwing his shoe at the teacher, and another time for running out of the cafeteria when the monitor yelled at him for flicking peas across the table. Adults never understood him—except for his mom. And she always worked. That left only jerks to look after him. This man could be nothing but another jerk.

"I don't play baseball," he muttered.

Ben Wells's smile turned to a frown. "Look, son, I got a call from your mom several weeks ago. She promised me you were interested in playing. Well, I've been working behind the scenes for a while and got you a place on my team. I tried calling several times, but I haven't been able to get through." His voice turned suddenly gentle. It slowed so it came out like small drips of cool water on a hot burn. "Dominic…is everything okay? I mean, you're not hurt, or anything…"

Dominic flinched and shook his head vigorously. "I'm fine. My mom's cell phone ran out of battery. We lost the charger."

"Oh. Well, is it okay if I speak to her?"

Again Dominic shook his head. "She's working all night."

"Then who's looking after you?"

"I'm ten," Dominic said quickly.

"I see. But don't you have a little sister?"

Almost on cue, the door of the trailer banged open and Mack stepped out like a bear awakened during his hibernation. At least he'd put on a pair of jeans. He'd tried to wear a menacing sneer with them, but was caught by the sun and ended up blinking rapidly.

"Who's this?" he said with an undertone of anger. "We're not buying anything today."

Ben Wells stepped back at the intrusion and surveyed Mack coolly. "I'm not selling anything, Mr.…"

Mack frowned. "Name is Mack," he said thickly. "Who are you?" He eyed the car nervously and scratched his round belly sticking out from a dirty sleeveless T-shirt. Rich people only came to the trailer park for two reasons: to buy something illegal, or sell something—likely also illegal. "Did this little punk cause trouble again?"

Ben Wells shook his head and frowned deeper. "I'm a baseball coach."

Mack swallowed a laugh. "No kidding? Then why'd you come here? None of these kids can play baseball any more than they could hit a toilet when—"

"That's enough, Mack," Ben Wells said softly, but with a flinty tone. "I came to offer Dominic a spot on my team. I've just been telling him how I tried contacting him earlier."

Mack stared incredulously down at the stranger. "How'd I know you're who you say you are?"

Ben Wells had been holding a packet of papers in his left hand. Pulling them out of a large envelope, he walked over to hold them up to Mack. As he passed Dominic, he patted the boy lightly on the shoulder. To Mack, he said, "These are copies of the forms Dominic's mother filled out. On top is the letter I write to all the parents. If you'd like, I can show you my driver's license. I've been a coach for years."

Mack's eyes narrowed. "Wait just a sec. You're that Ben Wells, aren't you? I remember your name... You used to always win the championships. I played baseball before."

"Not on my team, you haven't," Ben Wells replied flatly.

"What do you mean by that?" asked Mack.

Ben Wells shrugged and said, "Just that I'd have remembered you. I remember my boys."

Dominic watched it all with wide-eyed wonder. He'd never seen somebody stand up to Mack like this. Even with Mack standing two feet above, it'd looked like Ben Wells had stared him down.

Mack chewed on his lower lip furiously. Then he shoved the papers back. "Take the kid with you. He won't be any good. He can't even run."

Ben Wells nodded as he took the papers. "We'll see what he can do." He turned to Dominic and grinned. "How about you and I take a walk, Dominic," he said. "You already missed the first practices, and tomorrow we have our first practice game."

Too shocked to feel anything, Dominic dumbly nodded.

Mack went back into the trailer and slammed the door. "Be back in half an hour," he yelled. "Supper won't wait!"

Dominic didn't bother fetching his shoes, especially with Mack in the trailer. He ripped off his socks and tossed them on the ground. Ben Wells made no comment as he watched.

So Dominic, almost in a daze, walked with the tall mild man who'd just taken Mack down a few pegs. They passed through the trailers in silence. It was about suppertime and all the kids in the park had gone inside so only the two of them remained. At the edge of the trailer park they'd reached a thicket of trees where a well-worn path began.

"Do you know where this path goes?" Ben Wells asked, breaking the silence.

Dominic nodded. "It goes to the school," he said glumly. "I take it when I miss the bus."

"Excellent," Ben Wells said with no surprise. "On my way here I noticed some boys playing ball there. Why don't we go and see if we can find them. I think I recognized some of them from our team. We're the Dodgers, by the way. I have a cap and shirt for you in the car. Uh, you do have a glove, right?"

Dominic pursed his lips and nodded. "My dad had an old one... I just have to find it."

Mr. Wells patted Dominic's shoulder lightly. "I know about your father, Dominic. Your mother told me. I'm sure he was a good man. You must miss him."

Dominic stood still and then roughly pulled away. "Let's go," he said huffily. "I don't even remember him."

Ben Wells stopped to turn back to the nearest trailer and wave at a woman watching from an open window. "We're going to the school for a few minutes," he called loudly. "Don't worry, we'll be back soon."

The woman made an ugly face at him and quickly slammed the window shut before covering it with a curtain.

Dominic couldn't help but stifle a laugh. Mrs. Burgot was the nosiest lady he'd ever known. In no time the whole entire park would know about Dominic and baseball. His shoulders grew straighter.

For a moment he felt a surge of happiness. His mom hadn't forgotten and had come through. He'd made a baseball team! His heart started beating wildly. Outwardly he walked with his head still hung low and his face blank. He didn't want his new coach to see him too excited. Really, he didn't know what he wanted…or what to think. Everything was happening in a blur and he figured the best way to deal with it was to watch and wait to see what happened. That was how he dealt with Mack…until his anger took over.

On the path, the two fell into silence again and only a few birds were heard. The trail before them twisted and turned around trees and clumps of thorns before abruptly exiting just behind a tall chain-link fence bordering the back end of the soccer field at Knox Elementary. On their right, cars whizzed by from the main road. From where they stood they could plainly hear the excited shouts and laughter of kids coming from beyond the field to their left.

"Now what are those boys up to?" Bens Wells muttered, mostly to himself, sounding a little worried. With a sigh, he quickened his step, but almost immediately stopped. Turning to Dominic, he smiled and said, "Oh, and you can call me Mr. Wells, or just Coach." He nodded at the fence blocking their way. "Uh, I've never entered the school from the back way before. I don't think I can climb very well. Which way to get to the ball field?"

Dominic grunted in response. Hearing the boys caused his legs to falter and head sag. Fingering the fence, he kicked at the dirt. "I want to go home," he finally said.

"Oh." Mr. Wells sounded surprised. "What about meeting the boys? I think some of them go to this school too, you know."

Biting his lower lip, Dominic kicked the dirt again with his bare toes. "Fine," he said, almost as if sighing. "We go this way." Shouldering past the coach, he led the way along the fence to the left.

It curved around the soccer field, shot in a straight line to reach the softball outfield before curving again in a slow arc to form the home-run fence. When reaching the curve, Dominic abruptly stopped and dropped to his knees. Mr. Wells nearly plowed into his back and barely held up in time by leaning over the boy and grabbing the fence.

"Ouch," he hissed. "Everything okay?" he whispered.

The shouts of the boys were louder now, but none were directed at the new arrivals. Both Mr. Wells and Dominic were still mostly hidden among the trees just outside the fence and got a good view of the field without being seen.

"What are they doing?" Dominic finally asked.

"Uh, good question," muttered Mr. Wells. He wiped his eyes with the back of his hand. "Water polo and baseball combined? Do you know any of them?"

Dominic grunted. "Yeah, I see Chase. He's in my class. And I think the kid he's pushing in the mud goes to my school."

"That would be Jimmy," Mr. Wells said with a frown. "I just hope nobody gets hurt." He looked down at Dominic and grinned. "Want to join them?"

Dominic could only stare.

Four boys were out there—all bare-chested and wearing nothing but shorts. Dom could see bony ribs sticking from skinny chests on a couple. Fit and trim kids with no worries in the world. Their eyes were full of laughter and mischief as they wrestled and slid under a series of sprinkles. It looked like they were having a ball…

Dominic's shoulders flinched and he suddenly started shaking his head. "No, I want to go home," he said. Ignoring Mr. Wells's attempts to pat his shoulder, he crouched down and crawled backwards on his hands and knees. When in the tree line, he abruptly stumbled to his feet. Without a look back, he raced back along the fence and toward the trail leading back to the trailers.

Mr. Wells made to call out to him, but then thought better of it. Scratching the back of his head, he sighed.

"This," he muttered to himself, "is going to be an interesting season." Then with a low whistle, he continued his walk along the fence, making his way toward the four best players of his ball team. The ones intent on drowning themselves in the outfield of a softball field on a bright, sunny evening.

4

The trouble with good friends, they never knew when to stop. Jimmy was having the time of his life. It turned out Shawn had been watching the field for a solid week to learn just when the sprinklers turned on to water the grass. The new system of sprinklers had been installed the year before and had gone largely unnoticed until now. The Wiffle ball game had quickly broken down into a mixture of water wrestling and dodge ball and dodge bat.

Then Chase started playing king of the sprinkler. Standing over Jimmy's soaked shirt, used as home plate, he challenged anybody to move him. The sprinkler shot a steady stream of water into the back of his shorts. Of course all three had charged him at once. Grayson ended up being flung into the next sprinkler, while Shawn flipped over Chase's shoulder before crashing into the mud behind the bigger boy. Jimmy nearly had Chase in a headlock, but ended up being grabbed around the middle, squeezed tight, pulled down in Chase's arms, and then drop-kicked like a football in the backside. He ended up face-first in a mud puddle. Chase promptly jumped on his back and shoved his face back in the mud.

"I'm king!" Chase shouted in triumph.

"I'm drowning," choked Jimmy, lifting his head up and spitting out water and a mouthful of grass. "Get off, man."

"Not until you admit I'm king." Chase grinned when he said it, but firmly kept Jimmy pinned in the mud.

"No you're not!" cried Grayson. Having gotten to his feet, he'd raced back into the fray carrying the Wiffle bat. This he used to pepper Chase's unprotected back in a series of not so gentle taps. "Give up and I'll let you free."

"Ouch! Stop it!" Chase cried out and twisted away. Before he could go after Grayson, Shawn beat him to it.

Attacking the smaller boy from behind, Shawn brought him down with a textbook football tackle—shoulder planted just above Grayson's thigh while wrapping both arms around his waist. Both boys went down with a muddy splash.

Soon all four boys were rolling in the soaked grassy field quickly filling with mud puddles. Before it could go any further, a loud cough sounded from the fence.

"Time," said a familiar voice. It came out calm but strong.

Immediately the four boys stopped what they were doing and sat up straight.

Grayson rolled off Shawn's lap and the boys sat side-by-side in a puddle, both wiping water from their eyes. In front of them, Jimmy and Chase had gone straight to sitting crossed-legged and were staring at their laps as if deeply interested in how all the water and mud had gotten there.

A sprinkler behind them rained water over their shocked heads.

"C-coach?" stammered Jimmy. "Is that you?"

Mr. Wells leaned against the wrong side of the fence behind the deepest part of center field. It was like he appeared there by magic. "Who do you think it is?" he asked without cracking a smile. "Boys, any of you care to explain yourselves?"

Jimmy shot to his feet and wiped mud from his forehead. "Uh, we were just, uh, trying to get cool, Coach."

"Injured is more like it," Mr. Wells said coolly. "Don't you boys know we have a game tomorrow? Shawn, help Grayson up and don't hit him like that again. We're a baseball team, not a rugby team."

"Yessir," Shawn replied, leaping to his feet and turning to pull Grayson up with him.

"I'm fine, Coach," Grayson muttered. Still, he winced slightly when standing. He couldn't help but crack a grin at Shawn. "You jerk," he whispered.

Shawn grunted and slapped the back of Grayson's shorts, dusting off clinging grass. "Punk," he whispered back.

"Um, it's my fault," Chase said. He moved to stand next to Jimmy. "I started the wrestling stuff. We were just playing Wiffle ball when the sprinklers came on. We, uh, then got a little sidetracked."

Mr. Wells nodded. "I see. They came on all by themselves, right?"

"Uh, yessir," Chase said, ducking his head.

"And," their coach continued mildly, "you boys just happened to be out there when they did, right?"

Shawn licked his lips. "Something like that… I, uh, kind of scouted the place first, Coach. I came up with this, uh, idea."

Their coach nodded wisely.

The boys were so surprised at seeing him that they never stopped to think what he would be doing behind the fence. They stood dripping wet as the sprinklers continued to beat over their bodies.

Their coach all at once sighed and relaxed his shoulders. "Boys, I actually came to speak to you, not to yell at you. So come closer and listen up." He nearly cracked a smile, but kept his mouth firm. "It's hard to lecture boys while they're under the sprinkler. Even if it's a sprinkler meant to keep the outfield grass intact…and not turned into a muddy swamp."

Exchanging worried looks, the foursome quickly trotted to the fence. They stood in a ragged line facing their coach.

None had shirts and their browned backs dripped with mud and water and were covered in bits of grass.

Jimmy wiped droplets from his eyes. "What's up, Coach Wells?" he asked. "Is, uh, my dad here?"

Mr. Wells looked at Jimmy and allowed a small grin. "Don't worry, Jimmy," he said. "He's not here to see you like this. And no, I wasn't meaning to spy." Mr. Wells moved his gaze to the other boys and he licked his lips. He always did this before saying something important. The boys knew this and they immediately stood up straighter without even thinking. "The fact is, boys, I was just visiting our newest player. You see, I need to ask you all a favor. A big favor."

"Anything for you, Coach," Shawn said. "Even if you do tell our parents on us." The others nodded. They meant it.

Mr. Wells smiled again. "I know I can count on you… But don't worry. My lips are sealed." Then his face grew serious. "Boys, you're probably wondering how and why you were all picked for the Dodgers. The fact is, it was for a special reason. A very special reason." He cleared his throat. "You see, there's this boy who wanted to play ball this year. But nobody wanted him."

Confused, Jimmy exchanged glances with Chase. The larger boy shrugged, equally befuddled.

"Who is he?" Jimmy finally asked.

"Oh, you probably know him," Mr. Wells said mysteriously. "He goes to your school."

"Huh?" asked Chase. "Who?"

"Dominic Lewis," Mr. Wells said, nearly wincing when he finished.

Jimmy twisted his mouth in deep thought and then his face cleared. "Oh, I know him! He was in my class two years ago! He's always getting in trouble, right?"

Chase meanwhile groaned and clapped a hand over his eyes. "Are you kidding? That guy is in my class! He doesn't just get in trouble, he lives in trouble!"

Grayson and Shawn stared dumbly at each other. Neither boy had to deal with Dominic in their school. They didn't know how many times Chase's class had to exit the room while Dominic went off on a rampage, ripping papers and throwing stuff. Jimmy saw it from a distance, but Chase saw it every day.

"That kid is the definition of crazy," Chase said as if almost a wail. "How did he get stuck with us?"

Mr. Wells didn't raise his voice, but his eyebrows lifted. "Because I chose him. So stop there, now. He's your teammate, for better or for worse. You boys were handpicked by me to be on his team, you know." He nodded sadly when all four boys stared at him with surprise. "Not one team, minor leagues or major leagues, wanted to touch him. Finally, I said I would take him if I could pick my players to be around him. I chose you four first. I know how close you are. Boys, I coach baseball because I love the game. I coach kids because I know they'll love the game if given a chance. This is one kid who needs a chance and I'm afraid we're all he's got."

"Does he want to play?" Chase asked suddenly. "I mean, he never plays with anybody at recess…when he doesn't lose it for being stupid."

Mr. Wells wiped back his gray hair with both hands. "Look." He kept his tone even. "You boys love the game more than most kids. If anybody could make a stranger feel welcome, it's you four. I won't go into details, but Dominic isn't a happy kid. He doesn't always know what to do, or even how to act, especially in baseball. I don't know if he wants to play, or not. Why, he might never show for a practice. But the fact is, he asked to play and we need to give him a chance. I'm counting on you four to welcome him like a teammate and make him a part of the team. Okay? Go out of the way for him. It won't be easy, but in the end it'll be worth it. It'll bring our team closer and that's what matters. Got it?"

"Yessir," the four boys chorused.

Mr. Wells nodded his approval. "Great, boys," he said. "I knew I could count on you. Now go rinse off one last time and run a lap. No lagging tomorrow, or I'll make you run ten more!"

"Yes, Coach," Chase said. He slapped Grayson in the bare back. "That's for the bat attack. Race you around the field!"

"Idiot!" Grayson screeched, arching his back in pain. "That stings!"

Chase already took off running. "Don't forget, last one kisses my feet!"

"Not if I trip you first, Egghead," Jimmy yelled after him.

As the boys took off, Mr. Wells watched with a frown. He stared at the fading handprint on the lower side of Grayson's back and scratched the back of his head. Dominic, he thought, may be in more trouble than anybody realized.

By the time the four boys finished their lap, Mr. Wells had vanished. The four were left dripping in front of the sprinklers, all bent over from exhaustion.

Breathing heavily, Shawn looked over at Jimmy. "What now?" he puffed. "It's getting late and we have school tomorrow."

Jimmy, still bent over his knees, looked up and managed to wiggle his eyebrows. "Did I mention my parents filled my pool yesterday? It's ready for the first swim of the year. If you guys are interested in getting wet."

"Are we?" Chase asked, straightening. "Lead on."

Laughing and joking, the boys retrieved their soaked shirts and then their gloves, shoes, and socks.

They were just exiting the field when two tall figures stepped from around the school. They were coming from the basketball courts located to the left of the school and headed their way. Both looked to be in their mid to late teens. Loose, baggy clothing hung from their broad frames.

"Hey!" called the larger of the teens. He had a chest as wide as a small car and perfectly straight blond hair that rose from his head like it'd met a bolt of electricity. A lot of hairspray and gel had been wasted that morning. His eyes were large and dominated a hard but handsome face. Only his cruel sneer ruined it. "You guys from the trailer trash?"

His companion, shorter and of a slightly darker complexion, shouldered him. Long black curls hung over his shoulders and a faint moustache lined his upper lip. "Not them," he said loud enough to be heard. "Look, I recognize one. Isn't that Mr. Daniels's son?"

Grayson bit his lower lip next to Jimmy. His dad taught English at the high school and made no secret of using his son in his PowerPoint slides. Poor Grayson had his picture plastering many slides next to Shakespeare and the great Romantic poets of Europe. This could be one reason why he rarely smiled.

The taller teen peered intently at Grayson and then barked out a rude laugh. "Hey, it is! It's the famous son of the worst teacher in Eastland High! Hey, kid, you're a baseball star, right? Can we have your autograph?"

"Shove off," Chase muttered, putting an arm around Grayson's shoulder.

The two high school teens laughed nastily. They were still several yards off, but were getting closer.

Grayson clenched his hands into fists. His shirt and glove were tucked under his armpit and his eyes flashed with anger.

"Leave it," Shawn warned him. "I recognize the big lout. He played football and is said to be meaner than a snake with a knot in its tail."

Jimmy stepped in front of Grayson and Chase. He nodded his head toward the opposite side of the school away from the teens.

"Let's just go," he said. "They're not worth it."

"Yo, little Daniels!" called the larger teen when seeing the boys heading off. "Tell your dad not to fail us, or you'll regret it. Tell him Kelvin Michelle and Richie Jollster better pass English and graduate…or else."

Grayson's face darkened. A small tear formed in the corner of his eye.

Shawn suddenly stopped and turned around to face the hecklers. "You serious?" he shouted. "Isn't Michelle a girl's name?"

"Come say it to my face and I'll pound your face in!" the large teen yelled back.

Jimmy grabbed at Shawn's arm. "Uh, remember when you said to leave it? Well, now I think we should just better leave. Come on, man."

Shawn shook him off. "No wonder you guys can't pass English!" he hollered back. "You idiots can't even speak it!"

"Shut your face, kid!" hollered Kelvin. "If it wasn't so hot, we'd come over and pound you to the ground!"

Richie stuck up a finger in a rude gesture.

Grayson swallowed and shook his head. "Jimmy's right," he said. "Let's go."

Chase growled. "Not yet. Why don't we moon them?"

Jimmy's eyes widened. "Why don't we not moon them. You're crazier than our new teammate. I'm going home. Coming, Grayson?"

Grayson nodded once and after a moment Shawn and Chase followed. None of the boys wondered or cared where the teens were headed.

Kelvin and Richie were left laughing to themselves as they strolled toward the trailers. Both lived in large houses and drove air-conditioned vehicles. Still, for some reason, they'd chosen to walk in the heat. As they did, they walked as if they owned everything they touched. Maybe in their minds they did.

By the time the foursome reached Jimmy's house, they were again hot, a little sweaty, and very tired. The two teenage jerks were long forgotten as the boys quickly hosed off in the front yard and then ran around to the back to jump into Jimmy's pool. Still in wet shorts, they didn't worry about bathing suits. It was the first swim of the year and anything went.

Built into the ground for swimming laps, about half the size of the community pool, it went up to eight feet deep and even had a small diving board and short hoop for water basketball. Brittany appeared in her bathing suit and jumped into the fray.

After a bit of horseplay, Jimmy pulled himself from the water and rolled to his stomach at the side of the pool. Shawn and Grayson were playing horse at the diving board. They took turns trying to come up with the craziest dive while trying to make a basket in the process. Poor Grayson already nailed a few belly flops, but no baskets. Brittany and Chase were racing each other on the far side. As much as Jimmy hated to admit it, his sister took to water like a fish. Even a great athlete like Chase had trouble keeping up with her.

For a moment Jimmy was left alone to think. His thoughts settled on his favorite subject: baseball.

Tomorrow the games would begin… He smiled dreamily as he imagined himself at the plate facing Nate Dyson, the Cardinals' best pitcher. A fastball across the outside of the plate ended up a home run over the right field—

A large splash over the wall nailed him in the face and erased his dream.

"Hey, sonny boy, what're you thinking about?" Chase asked from behind a second splash, again nailing Jimmy in the face.

Brittany giggled behind Chase. "About time my brother had a shower," she said. "Next time I'll bring soap."

Jimmy covered his face and grimaced. "The last of the soap was used on the carpet where you sat down last night. It's still stained."

"You little creep," shouted Brittany. She lunged for the wall and pulled herself out. For a moment Jimmy was sure she would kick him. Instead she rushed past and disappeared into the house.

"What's with her?" Jimmy asked slowly.

"Well, you were a little rude," Chase replied. "How old is she? Isn't she in the sixth grade?"

Jimmy stared at his friend. "Really? No way. Don't tell me you're actually interested in my sister. If you are, then you're definitely crazier than Dominic Lewis. Just don't go there."

"Hey, I'm just asking," Chase said easily. Then he bit his lip. "You know, I was held back in the second grade. I should be in the sixth grade. She's eleven, right?"

Covering his ears, Jimmy got to his feet. Then with a loud yell, he leapt over Chase's head and smacked back first into the water, sending a large wave in Chase's surprised face.

The boys ended up having supper at Jimmy's house. Grayson's and Shawn's parents were called and happily agreed to pick up their sons later. Sure, it was a school night. But it was also a baseball night. That made it a great night. And nothing could ruin it.

Farther away, Dominic got ready for bed alone. It was just another miserable night for him. Perhaps tomorrow would be better...

Earlier that evening, just before departing the rundown trailer park of Queen's Gardens, Mr. Wells had left behind a Dodger cap and dark blue jersey, with the team name scrawled on the front in bright white and the number thirteen plastered on the back. Both were folded neatly and carefully placed on the front step of the trailer.

Dominic had missed the coach's departure and never knew about the uniform as he closed his eyes for sleep. Embarrassed after returning from the field, he'd rushed straight to his room. He had only left to eat a quick supper of canned spaghetti he had to prepare for himself and Rose. The siblings had eaten in silence while Mack snored from the couch. Though young, Rose had learned the importance of keeping Mack quiet. When finished, Rose had slipped back to her dolls, leaving Dominic to load the crowded sink with their dirty dishes. They'd used paper plates, which he crammed in the overflowing trash bag under the sink. Then he'd retreated back to his room to sulk until drifting off to sleep.

Much later, in the very early morning, the jersey and cap were hand delivered straight to his room when Mrs. Lewis returned from a long shift of work. Tears were in her eyes when she left her son's room.

Dominic woke up to find the hat and jersey waiting by his bed. Not bothering to get dressed, he nearly fell out of his bed in excitement. Grabbing up the jersey, he hugged it tightly to his chest. Then, putting it back on his bed, he ran to his closet.

Before rushing to the bathroom, he emptied the tiny closet of all his toys and most of his clothes to finally uncover the old baseball mitt that'd once belonged to his father. And the guy yesterday had said there would be a game that day.

The sun barely peeked over the horizon when Dominic raced into the kitchen wearing his new Dodgers jersey with an old pair of jeans and his Dodger cap. He also wore the large glove on his wrong hand. His face held its familiar scowl, but his heart beamed and danced with a new excitement he had thought long gone forever.

For once in a long, long time, he was excited about the future. He would do it—he would play for the Dodgers. Now he only needed to find baseball pants…and a baseball.

5

An hour before dawn in another household, Grayson woke up to his father shaking his shoulder.

"Time to get up, Gray," Mr. Daniels said gently. "It's just past six fifteen."

Groaning, the boy rolled over before curling up in a ball. It was a daily ritual. Before heading off to work, Mr. Daniels woke his son up early so they could eat breakfast together. Usually he had to literally carry his son to the bathroom and apply water to his face to get him awake. This time Grayson blinked and then snapped his eyes wide open.

"Coming," he mumbled.

"What?" asked his father in mock surprise. "My son getting up on his own this early?" He smacked his son's thigh lightly. "What? Is it the last day of school or something?"

Grayson rolled his eyes and yawned as he sat up. "Just don't leave until I get down there," he said sleepily.

Mr. Daniels ruffled his hair and solemnly promised not to go anywhere until his son was checked over by a certified doctor. After all, never before had his son appeared so eager to get up on a school day.

Grayson swung his feet to the floor and stood unsteadily in his pajamas. "Dad?" he asked. "What grade do you teach English to?"

Mr. Daniels stopped at his door, just in front of the large Bryce Harper poster hanging on the wall. "Now I'm seriously worried. You're taking an interest in my teaching? Gray, what's wrong?"

Scratching his stomach, Grayson frowned. "Daaddd, I'm serious. Do you teach seniors?"

His father frowned before answering. "Well, yes, I do. Why, are you planning to skip a few grades next year?" Mr. Daniels walked over and clapped both hands on his son's small shoulders. "First, I advise you to eat more and grow a few feet. Some of my students could walk on you without knowing."

"I know," mumbled Grayson. "That's what I'm afraid of."

His father had already left humming and didn't hear the last part. Sighing, Grayson pulled off his pajamas and quickly got dressed. After a quick stop in the bathroom, he rushed down to the kitchen table.

His dad whistled when seeing him. "This has got to be a record. But come here and let me do something to your hair. It looks like you combed it with a stick of dynamite. Here, I'll dab it with orange juice. Or do you prefer coffee?"

Grinning, Grayson avoided his dad's attempts to grab him and sat across the table where an empty bowl and spoon awaited him. Sugary cereal and milk sat in front. Mrs. Daniels wouldn't be down for another half hour and wouldn't have time to remind Grayson to only eat healthy food in the morning. Her idea of breakfast consisted of eggs and whole wheat toast. Grayson poured chocolate cereal in his bowl. The milk also happened to be chocolate.

His father winked from the other side of the table. "Our favorite, right?" he asked. He lifted a spoon full of chocolate cereal dripping chocolate milk.

It was their secret tradition to eat only chocolate breakfasts on big game days. So his father hadn't forgotten Grayson's first game of the season. He never did.

"Will you be there today?" Grayson asked as he carefully poured the milk.

"Well, guy, I have some papers to grade, but I'll try to make sure I'm done early. I wouldn't miss the first pitch for anything."

Pleased, Grayson nodded. Then he looked up casually. "Uh, Dad, do you know anybody named Kelvin Michelle, or Richie Jollster?"

It was like he slapped his father across the face. The spoon fell with a clatter and Mr. Daniels coughed hard as he tried to breathe while choking on chocolate. Finally, he managed to regain control and he stared at his son with wide eyes. "Where did you hear those names?" he demanded.

Grayson swallowed hard, his face full of alarm. "I, uh, just heard somebody say them."

"Oh…" Mr. Daniels took a deep breath and relaxed. He gathered up his spoon and stirred it into his coffee. "As a matter of fact, I do have two students that go by those names. They, uh, happen to be causing me some trouble."

"What do you mean?" Grayson asked, trying to keep his voice calm. "What are they doing?"

"Oh, nothing much. That's the problem." Mr. Daniels smiled without humor. "Kelvin's father works for the school board. He even hinted to me that he plans to run for an office in the local government next year." Mr. Daniels winced and lifted his coffee cup. "In any case, Kelvin and his pal Richie seem to think this makes them entitled to free grades. They feel like they don't have to do the work to pass."

"Well, um, do they?" Grayson asked.

His father shot him a hard look. "What do you think? You play baseball. If you don't work hard, are you going to make any outs and get some hits? Of course not. Remember. Hard work gets good results. Unless they get their act together, Kelvin and Richie are in for rude awakenings when graduation time comes. They need my class for their diplomas and so far they've blown off pretty much every assignment."

Grayson nodded thoughtfully. His dad was tough, but fair. He pushed Grayson to always be his best and never settle for less. If Kelvin's or Richie's father tried to cross his father, they'd be sorry. He didn't have to worry. His dad would take care of things.

He quickly finished his cereal and yawned. "Okay, Dad. I think I'll go lie down and sleep a few more minutes."

Mr. Daniels was left alone at the table with his mouth hanging open. "I'll never understand boys," he muttered. "And I'm supposed to teach them…"

He bit into more chocolate cereal and crunched down loudly.

The school day passed by quickly—end of the year tests were rapidly approaching. Teachers did their best to cram a year's worth of information into their students. The students did their best to eke out as much fun as possible while within the confines of a brick building, designed to keep them too bored to do anything else but learn. Neither side won. For the most part it was a stalemate.

But in a certain fifth-grade classroom, a certain student named Dominic Lewis had to be escorted to the office early in the day. He'd been biting pencils in half and when asked to stop he'd spat the chewed bits at the teacher.

When watching it all, Chase had covered his face with his hands. "Is he really a Dodger?" he muttered aloud.

The girl behind him, Sally Walker, clicked her tongue. "Our teacher sure isn't a dodger. Dominic nailed her right in the nose."

Chase only shook his head. How could he deny it? The whole school pretty much knew it—Dominic had shown up wearing his Dodger shirt and cap. Nobody could make him take the cap off and finally the frustrated staff let him wear it.

Chase made sure to sit as far away as possible from him at lunch. The school made all the students sit with their classmates, so he couldn't be near Jimmy. Instead, he watched in disbelief when Jimmy stopped by the table to slap Dominic's back.

"Nice hat," he said loudly in plain view of the cafeteria. "I'll see you at the field. The game's at 5:30, right?"

Dominic's mouth was full of hamburger and ketchup—more ketchup than burger. But he nodded and perked up his shoulders.

Later, when Chase got up to throw away his trash, he sidled by Jimmy's table. "You seriously being nice to that freak?" he hissed. "If you get too close, count your fingers. He'd probably bite them off."

Jimmy only waved him away. "It'll be fine. See you at the game!"

Chase snorted. "Yeah, sure. Just hope we don't see Dom," he muttered.

The game was scheduled for 5:30, but the players were expected no later than 5:00. Mr. Wells wanted a good warm-up before batting and fielding practice.

Jimmy arrived before five. With his dad being one of the assistant coaches, he always made sure to be first to greet any early players. In the car ride over, Mr. Roseburg made it very clear that he'd hoped *not* to greet one particular player. Chase wasn't the only one hoping a certain player would skip the game.

"This Lewis kid," he said, glancing sideways at Jimmy, who sat up front next to him in the minivan, "do you think he'll show?"

Jimmy shrugged and twisted his mouth. "Not sure," he replied. "I think he got in trouble at school today."

"Yeah," his father said with a grunt. "I heard all about it. He was eating pencils. Man, I sure hope Mr. Wells knows what he's doing. I'm glad we don't use wooden bats."

The two were alone. Jimmy's mom and sister would join them later—they were at Brittany's softball practice. Mrs. Roseburg had the sleek silver Toyota Camry—usually Mr. Roseburg's car. The minivan, he said, was his baseball car. In the back now were a bag of bats, extra batting helmets, a bucket of baseballs, catching gear for Jimmy, and a cooler of Gatorade and water bottles. Father and son were ready for the new season.

"What do you mean, Dad?" Jimmy asked, staring out the window at the passing trees and houses.

"I'm going to be honest, son. I wanted nothing to do with this kid. I think he's trouble. Now don't you go blabbing this to anybody, but every coach thinks Mr. Wells is, well, crazy. Mr. Wells thinks everyone deserves to play, and I get that, but from what I hear, this kid is a piece of work. I just hope it works out for him, that's all. And I hope the kid decides to stay home, because if he tries any stunts in the dugout, I'm not sure what we can do. I don't want to go chasing some wild maniac in the middle of the fifth inning."

Jimmy shrugged again. "I'm sure it'll be fine. He wants to play baseball."

"I hope so." Keeping one hand on the wheel, Mr. Roseburg reach out and slapped Jimmy lightly on the knee. "And I hope you do everything in your power to make him feel welcome if he does come out, got it? I'm counting on you. You're the leader, Jimmy. It's up to you to keep him happy."

"Sure, Dad. So, where do I hit in the lineup today?"

Instantly the conversation turned to baseball. Mr. Roseburg and Jimmy had a tight bond—both shared the same passion for the sport.

As they pulled up at the stadium, they were in the midst of discussing the best way to get a hit on Nate. Not surprisingly, they were one of the first cars in the lot.

"Why don't you grab your glove and take a short jog around the field," Mr. Roseburg said as he parked the van. "I'll grab your bag and gather some balls for the team."

Making a face, Jimmy nodded. He hated running. As he slid the side door open, his father's voice stopped him.

"Hey. I know you'll have a great year, Jimmy. Just do your best with the Lewis kid if he shows up, but don't let it hurt your game. Remember. When you're at the plate, focus on one pitch at a time and swing only at the good ones. The bad ones, leave for the catcher to fetch."

Jimmy grinned. His father always gave advice like this before a game. "Sure, Dad," he said. "Race you to the field!"

Mr. Roseburg sighed as he exited the van and watched his son run across the parking lot. A few inches below six feet, he wasn't a tall man, but was still stocky and solid. Jimmy inherited his looks, but had yet to get his muscles. With a square jaw and similar facial features as his son, Jimmy's father carried a set of broad shoulders and a thick chest. One day his son would grow into it, he hoped. His dark hair hid under a Dodger ball cap and he wore a Dodger jersey and tan shorts. His arms and legs bulged with muscle.

Few parents ever gave him trouble, but his face rarely showed any emotion except pleasantness. Taking the cue from Mr. Wells, he never raised his voice when coaching the boys and always spoke calmly. Almost always, at least.

If that Lewis kid showed up with an attitude, he meant to squash it fast. This year the Dodgers were loaded and primed to win the league championship. But only if they stuck together. One bad player wouldn't make much of a difference on the field, but one bad attitude could ruin the best of teams.

Dominic stood in the dingy bathroom adjusting his cap for the tenth time. He'd been in this position for over five minutes. Should he wear it tilted to the right, or left? Or should it be pushed back to show his hair? No, it should definitely be pulled low.

A heavy fist pounded on the door.

"Hurry up in there," barked Mack's voice. "Your sister needs the potty! I'm sick of her whining!"

Rose's tiny fists also hit the door. "Yeth!" she shrieked. "I need to go! Get out!"

Dominic bit his lip. His sister was just over six years old, but sometimes acted like a princess with Dominic as her servant. Something that Mack encouraged. He blinked as he took one final look in the mirror.

His new Dodger jersey now had a ketchup stain on the front and dirt smudged his cap from where Mack had thrown it outside earlier in the afternoon. Still, it looked good on his otherwise drab body. He tried to smile, something he rarely did.

At seeing his stained yellow teeth, his mouth drooped low. One of his front teeth was chipped. Ever since the accident with his father, he'd hated dentists and hadn't been in over a year. Nothing about his appearance thrilled him.

Dominic had a husky build and pale complexion. Mack liked to call him a blubbery whale out of water. He blinked his brown eyes, dull and sunken into his long sallow face. Baby fat rounded the edges of his cheeks and chin. His small mouth and broad nose gave him a pinched look, as if he was always in pain.

Stepping back from the mirror, Dominic got a good look at himself from head to knees. Round sloping shoulders led to a bulging stomach and thick legs. Mr. Wells had left him a shirt too big for him so it at least hid most of his girth.

Licking his upper lip, Dominic pulled off his hat and brushed his thick bushy hair furiously. He hadn't washed it in a week and it itched like crazy. The color of mud, it curled up at the front and flowed backwards to hang over the back of his neck like a tidal wave. He wished he could get a haircut, but his mom always claimed to be too busy either working or sleeping to give him one. Sighing, he jammed the hat back in place.

Reaching behind him, he grabbed his father's glove and put it on correctly. Earlier that day, Mack had laughed himself silly when seeing him wearing the glove on his right hand. "It goes on the left, stupid! You throw with your right!" he'd howled between fits of laughter.

Dominic had to admit, it felt much more comfortable on his left.

Mack again pounded on the door. "Don't make me do this again, Dom!" he shouted. "If I have to come in there, I'll do much more than slap you! Then you definitely won't be seeing any baseball for a while!"

"Fine!" Dominic yelled in the mirror. Turning, he jerked the door open and brushed past Mack. "I need to go to the game," he said.

Mack ignored him as he guided Rose into the bathroom and closed the door. Then he turned to Dominic and sneered down at him. "Go do your homework," he said.

"I don't have any homework. I need to go to the game."

Mack raised his eyebrows mockingly. "Do you really think that rich fancy coach wants you there? Just be happy he gave you a shirt and hat." He snorted. "Enjoy it while you can. I'm sure he'll send the bill in the mail." Then he walked to the couch before plopping down in front of the television. The news had just started, which meant it had to be just past five.

Instead of feeling angry, Dominic just felt tired. Nothing ever worked out for him. He walked slowly behind Mack and sat at the table. His mom had managed to stop at the store for food before work. His dinner had been a frozen meal that he'd eaten cold. Mack hadn't let him use the microwave. She'd promised him before school that Mack would take him to the game on time. He hated Mack.

Suddenly he shot to his feet and ran to the door.

"Hey!" shouted Mack. "Where are you going?"

"The game!" Dominic yelled back as he left the trailer. If he couldn't get a ride, then he'd just have to walk.

All the county's Little League games were played at the Eastland Sports Park. The vast park, complete with outdoor basketball courts, nature hikes, and a large indoor gym, boasted six separate baseball diamonds and three softball fields on one end and six soccer/football/lacrosse fields on the other. Needless to say, it was the hub of all major sports in the county and often attracted regional and even state tournaments.

On the day of the practice games, the Dodgers played the Cardinals on the field closest to the parking lot, which made it easy to find. Other preseason games were being held at the other fields and it was difficult to know who played where. Poor kids in different uniforms dashed from field to field in desperate search for their team. Being an unofficial opening day, the stands were nearly packed full of parents. Excitement filled the air. Rain had washed away the only other scheduled practice game. For almost all the teams in the league, this would be the final tune-up before the regular season.

For the Dodgers, everything started off great. When Mr. Wells arrived precisely at 5:10, he found nearly his entire team going through throwing drills in the outfield. Jimmy's dad had them all partnered up and kneeling in two rows facing each other. Each pair lightly tossed a ball back and forth. The Cardinals were still organizing at the side of the field and had yet to gather nine players.

Jimmy knelt beside Chase and tossed to Grayson. On his left a kid named Will Evans threw with Shawn. The boys bantered lightly back and forth, mostly about the Major Leagues and who would win it all that year. Nobody mentioned Dominic Lewis.

"Jimmy," called Mr. Wells as he walked onto the field from the dugout, "grab your catcher's mask and warm up Grayson. He's pitching first."

Jimmy's partner lit up and he instantly hopped to his feet. They were the home team that day and would bat second.

"Can I pitch next, then?" Jimmy asked Mr. Wells as he rose to his feet, dropping the ball behind him. He and his dad had worked on his pitching all winter and he was anxious to show off how much he'd improved.

Mr. Wells scratched the back of his neck absently. "We'll see," he said cryptically. "We'll see."

Grayson had a smooth delivery and a sharp fastball. None of them were allowed to even try throwing curves or sliders at their age, but most experimented with different ways to throw an off-speed pitch. Grayson's personal favorite was a knuckleball—something he only tried during practice. Often it never reached the plate and rarely did it come off without a spin. Still, he had fun trying and after a few hard throws, Jimmy encouraged him to throw it during warm-ups.

They were set up in the "bullpen" on the side of the right field fence—in reality it was just a pitcher's mound facing a home plate backed by a fence. Grayson bit his lip on the mound while Jimmy opened his glove wide.

"Let's go, Gray," he called. "Let's see the knuckle."

Nodding, the smaller boy gripped the ball in his glove and threw from the stretch.

The secret of the knuckleball was throwing it like a normal fastball, only instead of releasing the ball with your hand you pushed it forward using just your knuckles. Done right, it came out slow and without any rotation, dancing and darting in all sorts of directions. Trying to catch it was like trying to catch a butterfly. You had no idea where it would end up until too late and it got away.

The first knuckle spun lazily and landed several feet in front of Jimmy.

"Not quite what I had in mind," Jimmy said ruefully as he got up to retrieve the ball.

Grayson grimaced and angrily snatched the return toss with his glove. He rarely spoke when pitching. His body language said it all.

The next pitch came out clean and had no rotation, but also fell short.

"It's coming, Gray," Jimmy said as he fired another crisp toss back. "One more."

"One more of that and you'll both be on the bench," snapped a hard voice from behind Jimmy. Mr. Gordon acted as the third coach of the Dodgers and took it upon himself to oversee the team's pitching. His son, Phil, claimed to be the best pitcher on the team. Jimmy had his doubts, but still felt Phil had good stuff.

Phil's father, on the other hand, just had a big mouth. Unlike the other Dodger coaches, he felt more talk meant better coaching. He stood watching the boys with his large belly pushed forward on an otherwise skinny frame. With both hands behind his back and Dodger hat firmly on his head, overseeing a clean-shaven face with a bulbous nose, he resembled a blue-billed duck.

"You boys stick to good pitches only," he said sharply. "Do just what I showed you, Grayson. Stand up straight, push off with your body and follow through with your arm. You got this now, you hear?" He waited for Grayson to nod and then focused on Jimmy. "And you, Jimmy, you're a catcher, not a coach. Understand?" Mr. Gordon walked back to the dugout before Jimmy could respond.

Jimmy sighed. In nine-to-ten-year-old little league, the good pitchers only needed good aim. A well-located pitch anywhere near the strike zone often went for a strike. Most coaches didn't want any experimenting with pitches. Rear back and fire, was their motto. His dad said this was great for now, but not for long. As soon as a kid learned to hit a fastball, then what did you throw him? Mr. Roseburg always let the boys practice new pitches, just as long as they threw them properly without any spins. Doing so at their age could mess up their arms for good.

"All right, Gray," Jimmy called. "Let's aim for the outside corner."

Grayson wound up and fired a fast one, right down the middle.

From across the field, Nate and the other Cardinals were warming up in the batting cage. The clinks of their bats striking the ball sounded like musical bells to Jimmy. Of course, the greatest sound in baseball had to be the crack of lumber striking the ball squarely. But a solid clink of metal was music to a Little Leaguer's ears.

Like Jimmy, Grayson had arrived early and the two of them already had their batting practice with Jimmy's dad. Nate had also come early and had joined them. He'd heard about Dominic Lewis, but since he went to a different school didn't really know what this meant.

"I heard he was big," he'd told Jimmy after they were through hitting into the net.

Jimmy had looked at him and had grinned. "Compared to you, Nate, everyone is big," he'd joked.

Nate stood even shorter than Grayson. But quick like a cat, his athletic prowess more than made up for his size. Low to the ground, any ground ball hit his way was easily gobbled up. He also possessed a strong arm and was known as one of the best pitchers in the league. He also tended to get the most walks.

"I doubt he'll show," Grayson had then said. "My dad said kids like him don't like being around other kids too much."

Nate had shrugged. "Well," he'd said seriously, "if he does come, I'll strike him out like I'll do to you two."

"Big words from a little guy," Jimmy had fired back. "See you on the field, Nate. Don't forget your booster seat for when you hit."

"Can't today," Nate had replied over his shoulder as he left to join one of his just arriving teammates. "Grayson has it!"

Grayson had grinned tightly through narrow eyes. "I got a fastball for you, that's all I got," he'd said.

That had been nearly thirty minutes earlier, but the way Grayson threw now, Jimmy doubted he'd forgotten.

"Hey, Gray," he said nonchalantly, "save some of the fire for the game, hey?"

Grayson nodded seriously and threw a slower pitch. The two were battery mates for each other when on all-stars. When Grayson pitched Jimmy caught, and then they switched when Jimmy pitched.

At their age in league play, each pitcher could only throw two innings before having to switch positions. This kept their arms fresh and allowed multiple pitchers a game. It also meant the coaches had to be careful on who to pitch when. Many made the mistake of putting their best pitchers in early, only to suffer from poor pitching late.

On the flipside, waiting to put the best pitchers in late could be even more dangerous. In the fall, league rules held a five-run limit per half-inning. Once a team scored five, they automatically switched to the field. Since the games were six innings, a big lead early often led to victory. If a team led by more than five after five innings the game would end since the other team had no chance for coming back.

In the spring, the baseball got more serious and the five-run limit was lifted. However, if a team led by ten or more runs after four innings, the game would end in a mercy rule. Coaching and playing Little League at this age took a lot of strategy. Later, in the all-stars, this rule would also go away and the pitching rule would be relaxed. In the summer all-stars, a pitcher could throw up to seventy to eighty pitches before being pulled. But all of that would come much later...

Thankfully, the Dodgers wouldn't have a pitching problem to worry about. They had an overabundance of good pitching. Grayson always proved to be reliable and Phil and Chase each had big arms. Then there came Jimmy. His arm always had been strong. Only, sometimes on the mound, he had trouble focusing on the catcher and got a little wild. His father said it happened because he forgot to push off with his body and used his arm too much. This made him tire too fast and overthrow his pitches. Jimmy wasn't so sure, but he'd worked hard to follow the mechanics of pitching that off season and felt confident he'd figured it out. He'd hoped to prove it that day against Nate.

Only time, and Mr. Wells, would tell...

6

As Grayson wound down his warm-up tosses, the rest of the team gathered in the dugout to receive the final instructions from Mr. Wells.

The old coach waited patiently for the boys to settle. He stood in the center of the dugout like a general addressing his troops. Mr. Roseburg and Mr. Gordon stood on his left. As soon as Grayson and Jimmy slipped in and took a seat, the coach licked his lips. Immediately the eleven boys went silent and sat up straight. Mr. Wells swept his gaze over the boys and nodded in approval. He never needed to yell to be heard.

"Boys," he said calmly, "this isn't our first game. This is just a practice. Remember that. Whatever happens, it's just practice. It's okay to mess up, just don't give up."

From the other dugout, the Cardinals were also receiving their final instructions. Unlike Mr. Wells, their coach was a screamer. He could clearly be heard telling his team to keep their focus and play with heart.

Mr. Wells waited a moment before continuing his talk. "Remember what we told you to do at our first practices. Take your time at the plate and keep your head in the game on the field. Let your body do the work and always play together. And remember," he said, breaking into a smile, "it is a game. Have fun out there."

Jimmy listened and nodded with the rest of the team. He'd loved playing for Mr. Wells. Usually this never happened until the all-star team. A former military man and father of three grown children, after his wife died from cancer, he devoted his life to coaching baseball. Mr. Wells never berated a player individually. If he offered criticism in public, it was always to the whole team. Otherwise he pulled individuals aside and spoke to them privately. Usually he did this in such a way it sounded like encouragement more than anything else. When he spoke it came out soft and sincere. And the players listened and obeyed. Each one would follow Mr. Wells anywhere. They did their best to make him proud. A quick pat on the backside from Mr. Wells was the ultimate reward for a good play. A cool measured look from him served just as well as a sharp tongue lashing.

After the small speech, Mr. Wells gave the batting lineup. Grayson would lead off with Shawn hitting second in the order. Jimmy was due up third. Chase would bat cleanup. A tall gangly kid named Mike Khol was due to follow him, and then came Phil, and the rest of the team. A short freckled kid with bright red hair named Liam McKinney, a chubby boy named Tom Stallings who wore glasses, Draymond King, a burly power hitter with dreadlocks, Will, with his bleached blond hair, and finally, Xavier Rhodes, a football star trying baseball for his first time, made up the rest of the Dodgers.

Dominic Lewis, his name in pencil, had been scheduled to hit last…if he ever showed. League rules had it so every player had to hit and play at least two innings in the field. With Dominic not showing, it meant the Dodgers only had eleven players. Two would be on the bench when they took the field.

Then, just as Mr. Wells started to call out positions, Mr. Roseburg coughed loudly. Mr. Gordon was much less subtle.

"What in the world is that boy doing?" he demanded loudly, not bothering to hide the deep groan in his voice.

Every player in the dugout turned to look where the two assistant coaches stared. The dugout was actually just a long, covered, wooden bench in a narrow fenced in area. They all got a good view.

Dominic Lewis, his face bathed in sweat, ran towards them with his eyes downcast and arms straight at his side. An oversized glove was on his left hand and looked about ready to fall off at any moment. But he wore his royal blue Dodger cap and shirt and didn't look to be stopping anytime soon. The whole time he moved he mumbled to himself, too low to be heard.

With his jersey and cap, he wore stained jeans with holes in the knees and dirty sneakers. His sweat-stained face glowed a deep crimson red from sun and heat.

"Who is that?" Phil asked with scorn. He sat in the middle of the bench and could be clearly heard by all.

Chase, sitting next to him, sighed. "That, gentlemen, is our new star. Dominic Lewis. I'd hoped he forgot to show up…or had been arrested."

Hearing them, or perhaps sensing their eyes on him, Dominic abruptly drew up and stared into the dugout. Suddenly his eyes widened and his mouth opened. He looked like a giant dog caught in the headlights of a truck. His eyes didn't focus on one particular person as they blinked rapidly.

Before anybody else could speak, Jimmy shot to his feet.

"Dominic!" he called loudly. "You made it! Over here, come this way, the door is here!" Getting to his feet, Jimmy grabbed Grayson by the arm and dragged him out of the dugout to the door behind the backstop. "Come on, Gray," he whispered while pretending to clear his throat. "Help me out."

Grayson swallowed and managed a shy smile. "Uh, hey, Dominic," he said. "You, uh, missed warm-ups."

Shawn quickly caught on. He stood and grinned. "Come on, man! We almost started without you!"

Dominic had shuffled toward them, but still looked ready to bolt. Reaching the fence, he grunted. "I, uh," he stammered, clearly befuddled. "Where do I go?"

Jimmy swung open the gate and ushered Dominic inside. He stepped on Grayson's foot with his spikes, careful not to do it too hard, before leading the way. Dominic followed him like a lost lamb trying to find a safe pasture. Inside the dugout did not look safe to him.

Eyes fully of curiosity and hostility greeted Dominic. Then Mr. Wells took over.

"Dominic," he said excitedly, reaching out his hand. When Dominic didn't respond, the coach clapped the hand on the new arrival's shoulder. "It's great to see you! I'm really glad you made it. Take a seat. I'm just about to go over where everyone is playing."

Dominic ducked his head and plopped down between Jimmy and Grayson.

Mr. Gordon wandered off to the back end of the dugout with his head staring up at the ceiling. Jimmy's dad swallowed any emotion, but he nodded approvingly at his son.

The other boys waited to see what would happen next. They'd been told about this new player, but no one expected it to be like this. They played in the majors. Everyone in the dugout had played ball of some sort since they could walk. Kids like Dominic belonged in the minors, if anywhere on a ball field.

"He's wearing jeans," hissed Phil softly.

Chase grunted at his side. "Just take a look at his shoes," he whispered. "Think he got them from the garbage on his way here?"

Phil stifled a laugh. Then they both sat up as Mr. Wells licked his lips.

Staring at the paper in front of him, the Dodger coach suddenly crumpled it and slipped it into his pocket. Funny, but he also wore jeans and sneakers with his Dodger jersey and cap. Smacking his hands together in front of him, he breathed out slowly.

"Coach," called the umpire from behind home. "Your boys need to take the field."

"Right. Sorry," Mr. Wells told him. Then he gave out the assignments. "Grayson, you're on the mound. Xavier, get the catching gear. You're behind the plate."

Jimmy had already started to get up to get his padding. Now he abruptly stopped and stared up in confusion. He always caught when Grayson pitched. Xavier, a new kid to the league, was supposed to be the backup catcher. He didn't have any relationship with Grayson, or the other pitchers. Jimmy heard nothing else Mr. Wells said about the positions until the very end.

"And," said his coach without looking up, "Jimmy you're in center."

"What?" he burst out. "I never play outfield."

Mr. Wells leveled his cool green eyes on Jimmy. "Today you do. Help Xavier get ready and grab your glove. You have to warm up Dominic. He's in right."

Jimmy blinked and then sat down with a thump. His dad walked over and rubbed his hand on top of his son's head. "Sorry, kid. We planned this last night, in case, uh, well, in case we needed to."

Jimmy nodded dully. He always played in the infield. Catcher, shortstop, sometimes third, and sometimes pitcher, those were his positions. He hadn't played in the outfield since t-ball. Few kids hit out there and the team needed his arm and quick fielding where it mattered most. Then he looked up and saw Dominic standing on the other side of the dugout looking lost.

"Hold on, Dominic," he said, getting to his feet and hiding his disappointment with a cheery voice. "Wait for me."

"Uh, okay," Dominic said, blinking at him. "Where do I go? What's right field?"

Jimmy's face fell. It would be a long game.

Nate Dyson made any team he played on good. But he wasn't the only player on the Cardinals. They had other stars, some Jimmy knew nothing about. The worse part, he could do nothing about it but watch.

The game actually started out promising. Grayson looked focused on the mound and came out firing a good fastball. Xavier proved adept at catching and made sure to get the signal from Mr. Gordon on ball placement before each pitch. After four pitches, Grayson had a strikeout and the Dodger parents were making some noise.

Then a tall, stocky batter entered the box.

Jimmy recognized him from school. Joey Carter, new that year, had moved from Texas and spoke with a heavy southern accent. Big and friendly, he also proved to be good at baseball. Grayson's first pitch was a fastball down the middle. Joey eyed it and then bashed it down the third baseline.

Shawn never had a chance to react. The scorching grounder burned by him and sizzled toward the fence by the time he turned to see what flew by him.

"What do I do?" Dominic's voice asked as Jimmy started trotting toward the infield.

He stopped and turned to the hapless right fielder. "Nothing," he muttered. "We do nothing."

In left field, Liam retrieved the ball and threw it in to Chase, who, at shortstop, served as the cutoff man. Joey had an easy standup double. Kicking the dirt, Chase threw the ball to Grayson.

"Good pitches!" hollered Mr. Gordon from the Dodger dugout. "We want good pitches!"

Jimmy sighed. He'd seen the pitching sign. Mr. Gordon had called for it down the middle. When he played catcher he never felt out a new player this way. He would have had Grayson start with an outside pitch to see how Joey reacted. Then he would've gone in and tried to tie him up.

Meanwhile the Cardinals coach started talking it up.

"That's the way to swing!" he bellowed. "Good job, Joey! You started the hit parade! Let's keep them coming! Go ahead, Nate. Knock Joey in!"

Jimmy arched back his head and squeezed his eyes shut in frustration. Nate Dyson batted next. He was a smart hitter and would keep the ball out of the air. This would force a decision to either throw him out at first or hold Joey on at second. With his speed, Nate could easily beat a slow throw to first.

Blowing out his breath, Jimmy slapped a hand into his glove. He just hoped Grayson remembered their earlier conversation and would bear down with good pitches near the inside of the plate. If only he'd at least played shortstop! Then he could at least talk to the pitcher.

"What do I do when the ball is hit over here?" Dominic asked him.

Turning with surprise, Jimmy saw that Dominic had left his position in right and had wandered to centerfield.

"Go back," he said in alarm. "That way!" He gestured at the wide-open right field. "If the ball is hit in the air, catch it. If not, get it and throw it to Will."

Dominic stared at him in confusion. "Who's Will?" he asked sullenly.

Jimmy swallowed his frustration. "He's at second base. The little guy in the middle, okay?"

Dominic nodded. "Okay," he said. Then he shambled back into right.

Shaking his head, Jimmy turned back to the plate. He tried to focus on the play.

Grayson had seen the exchange and had stalled on the mound with his throwing hand on his hip. Now he turned to the plate.

The Cardinal coach kept up his yelling. "Hit it hard, Nate!" he cried.

Grayson wound up and fired a fastball in the dirt that Xavier just managed to keep in front of him. Joey feinted toward third, but then retreated to second.

"Good eye!" shouted the Cardinals coach. "Make him pitch to you proper!" The other coaches at first and third also added their encouragement. Then the Cardinals' dugout joined the chatter.

"Nate, Nate, Nate!" they chanted. "Nate the great!"

Jimmy sighed from centerfield. Heckling wasn't allowed in Little League, just supportive chants for teammates. And Jimmy hated chants. They sounded corny and were more annoying than helpful. Especially when the other team did them.

The next pitch was outside and again Nate held back.

"Ball two," called the umpire.

"Come on, Grayson!" barked Mr. Gordon. "Focus!"

Nate grinned and waggled his back. Being short meant he walked often, but not when Grayson pitched. Being of small stature himself, Grayson had good ability to find the smaller strike zones of short batters. He just had to keep his focus.

Then things fell apart.

Grayson had stepped off the mound to get Xavier's return toss. Distracted by Mr. Gordon, he turned his head. Then Xavier, who was still not used to Grayson's short stature, threw the ball high.

The short pitcher saw it too late. He jumped for it with his glove outstretched but came up empty. He landed on the seat of his pants, turning in horror.

Chase had his focus on watching Joey at second and Will was also distracted by Mr. Gordon's yelling. The wayward throw landed just in front of second and skittered into the outfield.

"Run!" screamed the Cardinals coach. The third base coach already waved Joey forward to go home. The fans on both sides screamed—some in alarm and others in triumph.

Jimmy had been playing deep to keep any fly ball in front of him. For a little guy, Nate had good power. Now he charged from center. Leaning forward, he kept his glove low. He reached the ball as it continued to roll. From the corner of his eye, he saw Joey reach third and turn for home.

Jimmy never hesitated. Still on the run, he smoothly snatched up the ball with his glove. Then he pretended to stumble. This would ensure that Joey would dig for home. In reality, he was already priming his throw.

Sure enough, the yelling coaches and fans let him know Joey sprinted to score. Setting his feet, Jimmy reared back his arm and leapt into his throw, putting all his force behind it. Grayson had gotten to his feet and promptly ducked under the throw. It sailed straight over his head and made a line straight for the plate.

Joey was caught a clear two feet from the plate when the ball smacked into Xavier's glove, right on the mark. The Cardinal runner tried sliding, but Xavier had already applied the tag.

"Safe!" yelled the umpire. "Catcher dropped the ball!"

The Cardinals' dugout went wild.

Jimmy smacked his glove in disgust. Xavier, in his hurry to apply the tag, had moved too quickly and hadn't secured the ball. It was an easy mistake to make. He'd done it before in the same position. Still, it let in a run. The Cardinals had struck first.

It would not be their last.

7

The Cardinals' fans went wild as the entire Dodger team, minus their right fielder, sank their heads in shame.

"Wake up out there!" hollered Mr. Gordon. "Come on, boys! It's like you're in t-ball all over!"

"We'll get it back, boys," Mr. Roseburg called out calmly. "It's just a run. Now the base paths are clear. Gray, put it behind you. Focus on the next pitch."

"Hey, pitcher!" yelled a Cardinal fan. "I got a stepladder in my truck if you need it!"

His face clearly burning with anger and shame, Grayson caught a new ball from Xavier and fingered it in his glove. He looked for the pitching sign, first from Mr. Gordon, and then from Xavier. With Xavier being a new catcher, he trusted the coach more. Then with his glove in front of his face, he stared toward the plate.

At the plate, Nate grinned and crouched into his batting stance.

"Come on, Gray," Jimmy muttered to himself. "Throw a strike."

Grayson shrugged his small shoulders and then fired a fastball from the stretch. It hit the dirt for another ball.

That day, like the one before, stayed hot and sunny. As the sun sank lower, the temperature seemed only to rise on the field…at least on the Dodgers' side it did.

A pitch later, Grayson walked Nate. The next batter, a kid Jimmy didn't know, strode to the plate with a smirk. He would remember him, though. He lined Grayson's first pitch over Chase's head and into left field. Jimmy rushed to back up Liam and managed to save a triple when the redhead mishandled the sharply rolling ball. Jimmy corralled it before it reached the fence. His strong throw to Chase held the runner at second. Nate, meanwhile, crossed the plate for another Cardinal run.

"One out!" yelled Jimmy in frustration, as if to remind his team they'd done something good that inning. "Play's at first!"

Chase echoed his call.

"We still got this," Shawn then yelled. "Come on, Grayson. Just keep throwing and we'll help you out."

Grayson looked pained on the mound. Wiping his eyes, he kicked the dirt. Xavier called for time and trotted out to meet him.

Jimmy groaned from centerfield. He saw Grayson do this many times and knew crying only helped the pitcher. When Grayson got mad, sure he cried. But he also focused and played better. Xavier trying to calm him down wouldn't help matters. It would make it worse.

Sure enough, Grayson lost his control and walked the next batter. Then his next pitch sailed well over Xavier's head and hit the backstop. Both runners moved up so they were at second and third.

Grayson slammed the ball in his glove and stalked back to the mound. Really angry now, he fired his next three pitches straight into Xavier's glove. The hapless batter struck out swinging, but Xavier mishandled the last pitch. It bounced off his glove and toward the Dodger dugout.

Jimmy groaned in frustration as Xavier raced after it. The catcher yanked off his mask like Mr. Wells taught them to. Keeping it on made it harder to see and move.

Grayson rushed from the mound as the Cardinal runner from third charged home.

Picking up the ball, Xavier spun wildly, but managed a strong throw to the plate. It came low and behind so Grayson slid across the plate with one leg extended to catch it in his glove. His other leg bent under him, he caught the throw and rolled to his left, desperately flinging out his hand for the tag. The runner sent his cleats straight into the seat of Grayson's pants and pushed the small player back so the tag fell short. The small pitcher ended up lying flat on his stomach, choking on dust and writhing in pain.

Xavier hurried over to him and patted his back in consolation.

The umpire called for time, but ever the ball player, Grayson quickly got to his feet. After sucking in wind, he showed the umpire he felt fine and smacked Xavier's arm to let him know everything was okay between them.

Jimmy kicked the grass, but sighed with relief. It was a good thing this was just a practice game.

Grayson only got mad at himself. Dusting himself off, he returned to the mound with his head low. Xavier put his mask back on and banged his own glove in frustration. Watching him, Jimmy knew he would make a good catcher. New to baseball, he was still getting used to the sport. Also, he just didn't have the practice with Grayson.

Mr. Gordon didn't see it that way.

"Come on, guys!" he bellowed. "This isn't the minors! Get your heads in the game! Xavier, no more passed balls! And Grayson, let's get your focus!"

"Two outs!" Jimmy called, raising two fingers. "Two outs and we're done."

Chase called from shortstop. "Play's at first."

Grayson gathered himself and delivered another strong fastball. They were near the bottom of the batting order and the batters lacked the power and skill. Still, this one managed a sharp grounder between first and second. It headed straight at Will. The second baseman stopped to wait for it only to watch as the ball took a crazy hop straight over his glove. Now the ball rolled into the outfield in right.

"Get it!" Jimmy yelled at Dominic. "Get the ball!" He'd instinctively started to run behind Dominic to serve as backup. He quickly changed direction as he sprinted to the slow-rolling ball.

Dominic, standing still in deep right, had failed to react at first contact. Now he started forward at a stumbling run.

At the last minute, Jimmy saw Dominic only gaining speed instead of slowing. He pulled up and slid to the seat of his pants, watching Dominic fall over the ball before reaching back and picking it up with his glove. On his knees, with his back facing the bases.

Wincing, Jimmy lunged to his knee. "Use your bare hand, it's faster," he said. "I mean next time," he hastily added when Dominic promptly dropped the ball and then picked it up with his other hand.

"What do I do now?" Dominic asked. He sounded scared.

"Turn around and throw it," replied Jimmy glumly. "Just throw it."

The batter had seen the mishandling and already headed for second. At least he would be held there.

Then Dominic took two steps in, cocked his arm, and launched the ball high and far toward home plate.

Jimmy's eyes widened. "What did you do that for?" he asked without thinking. "You're supposed to throw it to second!"

"You did that last time," Dominic said accusingly.

Jimmy blinked but could think of nothing else to say. "Well, nice toss," he finally managed.

The ball arched like a long fly ball and finally landed in Xavier's glove. By this time the Cardinal runner had moved to third. Another run had scored and the Cardinals led 4-0.

One batter later the score moved to 5-0. Grayson's final pitch was knocked weakly to shortstop. Chase charged it, but bobbled the pickup and his throw drew Phil off the base.

"All right!" yelled the umpire at second. "That's five runs. Since this is just a practice game, we're playing fall ball rules. Switch it up!"

Jimmy tossed his glove up with a sigh as he trotted to the dugout. He caught it on the way down, but didn't raise his eyes. They kept pointed down at the grass. Letting in five runs and getting to bat a mercy rule felt like a failure and a definite embarrassment. It meant you couldn't even get the other side out. You couldn't play real baseball.

Coach Wells greeted the players as they trudged off the field.

"Hey," he said calmly, patting each player on the head or shoulder. "Keep your head up. It's our turn to get some runs, now. Remember what I told you. It's practice."

Grayson came off last. Mr. Wells greeted him with a head pat and light smack across the shoulder blades. "No doubt you don't want to sit just yet," he said with a small grin. "I bet the back of your pants are burning right now."

The small pitcher had his head down to his chest. Lifting it, he blinked back tears and managed a pained smile. "Yeah, I really got spanked out there," he said.

Mr. Wells pulled him close to him and knelt beside him. "You did fine, Grayson," he said firmly. "They're a good team and we were just practicing. Got it?" Grayson nodded and the coach slapped the back of the boy's knees. "Now go get a helmet and do some batting practice of your own."

Meanwhile, as Jimmy found his own helmet and batting gloves, he could hear the Cardinals coach loudly praise his team.

"Everyone said the Dodgers couldn't be beat," the coach crowed enthusiastically. "They were supposed to be the best this year! Well, you guys just drove them off the field with five runs! Now let's drive them off again with three quick outs!"

The Cardinals took the field like a conquering force returning home from a victory. They moved with excitement and purpose. In contrast, the Dodger team looked like attendees of a funeral. They had all heard the Cardinals coach. Heads were hung low and spirits were lower.

"Okay, boys," Mr. Roseburg said, turning from where he'd started his position as first base coach. "Don't let me see you guys hang your heads like that. Look up. It's still a sunny day out. You're playing baseball, act like it! You boys look like you're doing homework or something."

Jimmy grinned. "Yeah, guys," he said. "I mean, losing a practice game is still better than homework."

"Depends on what the homework is," Shawn mumbled. But he said it with a grin. Everyone cheered up after that. Almost everyone.

Dominic scooted to the far end of the dugout and sat by himself with his head staring at the glove in his lap. Nobody spoke a word to him.

Mr. Wells always sat on an overturned bucket just outside the dugout. He usually only stood to grab a bat left by a batter or to greet a player coming off the field. Now he turned to look at Dominic. Swiveling on the bucket, his eyes next found Jimmy and he raised his eyebrows expectantly.

Jimmy ducked and pretended not to notice. Putting on his batting gloves he only thought about what he would do at the plate. Nate warmed up on the mound.

Grayson batted first. After a few practice swings, he stepped into the box and hunkered down. He looked eager to turn his day around. Instead, Nate turned him around. Throwing a mixture of fastballs and arching changeups, Grayson was called out on strikes. He left the box in tears and refused any encouragement. Slamming into a seat on the bench, he pounded his fists against his thighs.

Shawn had a little better luck. He hit a sharp grounder back to the mound. Any other pitcher would have dodged it, or misplayed it. Nate, though, calmly backhanded the ball before jogging toward first then delivering a soft toss for the second out.

Jimmy went to the plate next. The Cardinal fans were ecstatic and their coaches kept up their hollering.

"One more, boys!" yelled their head coach. He was a middle-aged man with graying hair and a tanned round face that matched his body. Large ears stuck out on either side of his cap and Jimmy thought he resembled a bulldog. He certainly had the bull part down.

Once at the plate, Jimmy settled and forgot everything but finding the ball. Smoothly bringing the bat to his shoulder, he spread his legs shoulder-width apart and bent his knees slightly. Licking each corner of his lips, he watched for the first pitch.

It came out a falling changeup and Jimmy backed away.

"Ball," the home umpire called.

The next pitch was delivered in a hurry and just missed the outside corner.

"Strike!" yelled the umpire.

Jimmy backed out of the box and swung his bat in frustration. Umpires in Little League were well known for wide strike zones. This was great when he pitched, but not when he hit.

"Jimmy!" called Mr. Gordon from third. "Watch my sign!"

Jimmy nodded and glanced his way. He already knew the sign. Hit away. With two outs, nobody on, what was he supposed to do? Back in the box, he dug in.

The next pitch came low and hit the dirt in front of the plate. With no base runners, it bounced harmlessly to the backstop. Two balls and one strike.

All of Nate's pitches were low so far. Nate knew Jimmy loved pitches belt high. What Nate didn't know was Mr. Wells's teachings.

On the first day of practice Mr. Wells had the entire team take turns hitting off several tees, each at different heights. At first he gave no instruction and balls were hit all over the place. Pop flies and grounds had scattered the outfield. Then Mr. Wells told them the secret. You swung on top of the ball for high pitches and under the ball for low pitches. This gave the best chance for solid line drives and made it less likely to ground out or pop up. "Then," the coach had said, making sure every player listened intently, "when you're at the plate stare straight at the ball. Ignore the pitcher completely. Find the ball and watch it come in slowly. You want to not just see the stitches, you want to count them. Then once it's inside your wheelhouse, bust it out."

Jimmy, already a good hitter, listened and found, as usual, that Coach Wells knew what he was talking about. No, he never could count the stitches in a baseball, but he could see them slow enough to hit them.

He watched Nate wind up and fire in the next pitch, another low one, but over the plate. Jimmy didn't wait for it. Stepping forward, he swung the bat low and was rewarded with solid contact.

With a sharp clang, the ball shot off down third and went over the baseman's head. It landed in front of the left fielder and Jimmy had the first Dodger hit of the game.

"Hey!" yelled Mr. Gordon from third. "Watch the signs! I called for a bunt!"

Jimmy's dad congratulated him at first. "Good swing," he said.

"Thanks, Dad," Jimmy said, pulling off his gloves. "When do I steal?"

"Be patient, kid," his dad told him, grinning.

Leading off wasn't allowed at their age. Stealing only happened if the catcher missed the ball, or the pitcher wasn't on the mound with the ball.

Joey played first base. He nodded at Jimmy and grinned faintly. "You got lucky," he drawled. "If I were pitching, I'd put you down with a high fast one."

Jimmy smiled. "Can't wait for it to happen."

"Me neither," Joey said, smiling wider. Then he moved toward second and crouched low.

Chase now batted. Nate knew about Chase's power and would have to throw carefully. That meant he wouldn't be watching Jimmy at first. He started with a slow diving pitch for a ball. His next pitch went high and fast, one that Chase, well, chased. He caught only air.

"That's it!" roared the Cardinal coach. "That's what I'm talking about! Two more!"

Jimmy shook his head. "Don't your ears hurt after a while?" he asked Joey.

"Not as much as your rear end is going to hurt when we're done kicking it," Joey shot back in his drawl.

"Good one," Jimmy said, grinning.

"Easy, son," Mr. Roseburg said from first. Then he tapped Jimmy's left shoulder two times and smacked the back of his pants. It was their secret signal. The next pitch he was going to run for second. He couldn't start until after the ball crossed home plate and would have to be ready if he hoped to make it.

Like his father, Jimmy had been watching the catcher after each pitch. He only looked at Nate, never once checking the runner at first. Hopefully he'd be caught napping.

Jimmy never got the chance to find out. Nate missed with his next pitch. Instead of another high fast one, it went over the plate belt high. Chase crushed it with a mighty swing. It finally landed over the left field fence for a two-run home run. Suddenly the Dodgers' power was back on display.

"Yeah!" shouted Chase, pumping a fist. "That's how I like it!"

Joey and Nate ducked their heads and said nothing as the Dodger fans and players roared their approval.

Mike struck out four pitches later. The teams switched and the fans settled down.

Mr. Wells caught Jimmy on the way out to the field. "How's it going out there?" he asked, nodding to the outfield. The only change he'd made was to put Phil in to pitch, moving Grayson to second and Will to first. Jimmy still played in center with Dominic in right.

"Oh, um…" Jimmy stammered to reply. "Well," he finally said, "Dominic isn't quite ready yet…but he's got a good arm."

Mr. Wells nodded. "So I saw," he muttered. "Just not a good baseball one yet. He doesn't know how to read the game yet."

Jimmy hoped the coach would tell him it would be the last inning for him in center, but instead he waved him along.

Jogging to centerfield, he tried to engage Dominic in a game of catch. It quickly turned into a game of fetch. Dominic missed all of Jimmy's throws and none of his own came close to Jimmy.

At least I still get infield practice, Jimmy thought as he raced to his right to scoop up another bouncing toss from Dominic.

The second inning went better than the first. Phil and Xavier seemed to bond quickly and only gave up a single hit. Chase threw the first batter out with a strong throw from short and, after a single between third and second, Grayson finally had something go right when he made a diving stop at second to rob the next batter of a hit. The fourth batter struck out.

The game settled after that and the only other excitement came in the bottom of the third. Dominic was scheduled to hit second, but after putting on his helmet and taking up a bat he froze in the on-deck area.

Jimmy, who'd helped him with his helmet and bat selection, stood nearby and heard everything. The on-deck batter always took his swings just outside the dugout behind the backstop. The fence separating the fans was low and a lot of parents liked to stand there to watch the pitches come in. So did a lot of kids.

A couple of older kids from middle school hung over the fence when Dominic stepped out. Immediately one of them put a hand to his nose. "Ew, what's that smell," he said, frowning.

"I don't know, but there's something rotten in the state of baseball," said his friend. Then they both looked at Dominic and started laughing.

"Jeans in baseball?" the first asked. "And what's on his feet? Road kill?"

His friend started to choke. "Oh my gosh, the smell, it's him!"

A parent finally shooed the two away and they ran of laughing.

Dominic never looked at them, but stood with the bat in his hand by the dugout. When his turn came, he didn't budge.

"Let's go, Dominic," Jimmy said. "You're up."

Mr. Wells turned and waved him on. "Go hit, Dom," he said.

Dominic flinched. Lifting his head, he looked up at Mr. Wells. "No," he said firmly. "I don't want to." Then he flung his bat into the backstop and stomped back into the dugout.

Nobody knew what to do or say. Finally, Mr. Wells gestured at Grayson to go hit, but the umpire already decided to call an out for skipping a batter…and throwing a bat. The inning was over. So was any resemblance to peace in the Dodger dugout.

Dominic refused to go out to the right field and he ignored any attempt from Mr. Wells to talk to him. Anytime somebody approached, he kicked his feet out and shook his head vigorously.

"What's up with him," Chase asked with a frown. "He's such a jerk sometimes." He stood with Jimmy, Grayson, and Shawn at the edge of the infield between home and first. Mike warmed up on the mound with Mr. Gordon catching. Grayson was supposed to be catcher, but he couldn't get his gear just yet. It was in a bag next to Dominic.

Jimmy grimaced. He was certainly glad it was just a practice game. More like a circus. "Look, I don't know what's wrong," he said, "but coach needs us to help."

"With what?" Chase asked sarcastically. "Taking him for a walk? Did you bring a leash?"

Shawn grunted and elbowed Chase in the side. "Leave him alone, man. You heard those jerks at the fence."

Chase scowled. "Yeah, well, they didn't exactly lie."

"Hey," Jimmy said sharply. "He's on our team now." Then he sighed. "Look, guys, we have to do something."

"Well, what do you suppose we do? I mean, really?" Chase asked, crossing his arms.

Only Chase met Jimmy's eyes. Grayson and Shawn both kicked at the grass.

"Um, let's start with being friends with him," Jimmy said.

Chase snorted. "Good luck with that."

Jimmy suddenly brightened. "No, I'm serious! I got it. We take turns sitting by him in the dugout. Every inning we switch."

"What's that going to do?" Shawn asked. "Somebody always sits by somebody in the dugout."

"No," Jimmy said eagerly, "I mean we sit next to him like we want to. Whoever has the turn has to say at least two things nice to him."

Chase lifted his eyebrows. "Really?" he said.

But Shawn nodded slowly. "Hey, not bad. We can do that."

Chase rolled his eyes. "What about you, Gray," he asked the smaller boy who'd been silent the whole time. "You want to do this?"

Grayson shrugged. "I guess. It'll help the team."

"Fine," snapped Chase. "Who's first?"

They ended up doing paper-rock-scissors to decide and Grayson ended up losing, er, winning first. This made Jimmy even happier.

"I've got my catching gear in my bag just by the door," he told Grayson as the smaller boy's face fell. "Why don't I take your spot and you sit an inning out with Dominic."

Grayson bit his lip, but nodded miserably. "Yeah, I guess." He turned to the dugout like a man going to his funeral.

Chase whacked his backside his glove. "Go get him, tiger," he said. "I hope you got all your shots."

Grayson jumped sharply. "Ow!" he cried. "Don't you idiots remember what happened?"

Shawn smacked Chase's own backside with his glove. "See how you like it, man!"

"Hey!" barked Mr. Gordon from where he crouched behind the plate. "You boys playing ball, or what?"

"Let's go!" called the home umpire. "Two minutes!"

Jimmy rushed for his gear, calling for his dad.

Mr. Wells and his dad were busy trying to talk to Dominic and at least get him to give up the catching gear for Grayson. They both turned to see what Jimmy wanted.

At hearing Jimmy's plan to play catcher and have Grayson stay on the bench with Dominic, Mr. Wells frowned, but then nodded. Mr. Roseburg quickly helped Jimmy put on his gear and the game resumed.

As it did, Dominic slouched lower in his seat. Grayson, after sitting quietly in the center of the dugout for a minute, slowly rose to his feet and walked near Dominic. Offering a faint smile, he gingerly took a seat a few feet away. The other Dodger players in the dugout, Will and Tom, both sat as far away as possible from them.

"Hey," Grayson said.

Dominic didn't look at him.

"You have a strong arm," Grayson tried, but Dominic still didn't look at him. Sighing, Grayson rubbed his left ankle with his cleat. "So what's your favorite baseball team?" he asked. He still got no response. "Well, um, have a good day."

Feeling as if he said two nice things, Grayson moved away from Dominic and joined Will and Tom. The three practiced tossing baseballs toward the ball bucket. None of them bothered with watching the game. By this time the score was 9-3 in favor of the Cardinals.

It would later end after six innings with the Cardinals winning 13-6. It wasn't until the team started gathering for their usual post-game meeting that somebody realized Dominic had gone missing.

8

"How did he even get here?" Mrs. Roseburg asked her husband. She stood at the gate to the dugout and looked worried. Having arrived with Brittany soon after the second inning, she'd witnessed Dominic's humiliation.

"I have no idea," her husband said, shaking his head. "By the looks of him, I think he walked."

His wife sucked in her breath. "Oh, dear," she said. "Listen, honey. I think you'd better find him."

"But I have the team—" Mr. Roseburg started to say, but was cut off by his wife's glare.

"That boy is part of the team and he's missing," she said fiercely. "Take Jimmy with you and find him. I'll get somebody to put all the gear in the van. Once you find him, drive him home. Okay?"

Nodding his head in agreement, Mr. Roseburg gave his wife a quick hug and kiss. Then he called Jimmy and set off searching. Jimmy didn't mind missing the postgame meeting…there was nothing good to hear there.

After a few minutes of wandering the sports park, they found Dominic walking on the side of the maintenance road leading off into the woods. He acted surprised that anybody was looking for him. More surprisingly, he gave little resistance when offered a ride. Barely speaking a word, he followed with his shoulders slumped.

Jimmy looked up at his dad as they headed for the van with Dominic trailing behind them. "Is this a 'windows down' ride?" he asked ruefully.

His dad snorted. "You bet it is. You stink, kid. As soon as you get home, stay out of the pool and get into the shower. I don't want to pollute my backyard."

But when they'd reached the van, Mr. Roseburg turned to Dominic and stopped. The boy walked with his head so low it looked as if he were trying to eat his shirt. His arms hung stiff, straight at his side, with his oversized glove hanging limply off his left hand like a giant cow pie ready to be dropped and stepped in.

"You know, son," he said after a deep breath. "Before we head home I think we need to stop at a store."

Jimmy gave his dad a look. "Why?"

"Because," his dad answered, "if I don't do it now, your mother will make me do it later. Come on, I need you on this one."

Jimmy sat in the front with his dad while Dominic settled in the back with the baseball supplies. All the windows that could be rolled down were rolled down and the air still went full blast. This did little to dull the strong stench of unwashed boys.

Before stopping at the store, Mr. Roseburg hit a burger joint and went through the drive-through.

"Want anything?" he asked Dominic. "My treat."

The boy looked so startled that he had a hard time to answer at first. "Well," he finally said, "I am hungry."

Mr. Roseburg didn't have to ask Jimmy. He ordered three large combos with Cokes.

Once the food came, Dominic didn't waste any time. He tore off the burger wrappings immediately and started shoving it in his mouth like it was an antidote to poison.

Jimmy lifted his eyebrows watching in the rearview mirror. After a moment, he started on his own burger, but left the fries. Moments later he offered them to Dominic. They were accepted without a word and chomped down quickly after.

As they continued driving, Mr. Roseburg reached over and rubbed his son's head. Then he shared his own fries with him. Father and son finished their meal long after Dominic had devoured his. He'd even eaten half of Jimmy's burger.

They'd swallowed the last bite just as Mr. Roseburg pulled into a large sporting goods store at the mall.

"What are we doing here?" Jimmy asked.

"Didn't you want oil for your glove?" his dad asked innocently.

Jimmy frowned. He started to say, "Well, there's still some left at—" but then he saw where his dad gestured. Dominic, stuck in his filthy holey jeans and sneakers, licked ketchup from his dirty fingers in the back. Stains of red and brown covered the entire front of his shirt.

Jimmy shrugged and said. "Uh, okay…but I also need new baseball cards and sunglasses."

His father grunted in response. "Don't push your luck, kid," he said.

Jimmy and his dad had been to the store countless times before. But it was the first visit for Dominic.

The larger boy stepped through the doors and stopped with wonderment filling his face. "Look at all that stuff," he said. "Do they sell everything here?"

"Everything to do with sports," Mr. Roseburg said absently. "Say, I, uh, got a coupon for this place that's about to expire. Why don't you help us spend it? What size pants and shirt do you wear?"

Dominic had no idea, so Mr. Roseburg sent Jimmy with him to the bathroom to find out. Then they went shopping. Jimmy got baseball cards, but not the eighty-dollar sunglasses. Dominic got new gleaming white baseball pants, a pair of Dodger blue baseball socks, black baseball cleats, and three new T-shirts, each with a different baseball logo on the front.

He also got a baseball cup. Jimmy had to explain the use of it on the way back to the van.

Looking dazed, but like a kid on Christmas morning, Dominic climbed into the van excitedly. "Thanks for everything," he said to Mr. Roseburg as he buckled his seatbelt. "I really need the shirts and stuff."

Mr. Roseburg waved him off. "You're part of the team, so you need to look like one of us. Oh, we have one more stop before taking you home. Jimmy has an old glove at home. I think you can use it more than him. Right, kid?"

Jimmy shrugged. He didn't care. If Dominic had to be a Dodger, then he should look like one. Maybe now no more kids would make fun of him and things would be all right. He certainly hoped so.

Dominic had a hard time falling asleep that night. After the stop at Jimmy's house, he left with a baseball glove that fit and a small paper bag full of stuff baseball players "got on their first day," as Mrs. Roseburg explained. Apparently ball players needed a lot of soap and deodorant.

Mack had barely greeted him when he returned. He did raise his eyebrows when seeing all the bags Dominic carried. Then he went back to playing a video game with zombies and vampires.

Dominic did his best to stay up until his mom returned. He wanted to tell her all about the game. He could hardly believe it. He was really playing baseball. Jimmy's dad told him there would be practice at the elementary school in two days and the opening game of the season on Saturday.

Mr. Roseburg offered to pick him up for both, but he declined. He didn't want Jimmy to see his trashy house in the daylight. He could walk…or maybe his mom would be free on Saturday and she could take him…

His last thought before drifting away into darkness was of him hitting a home run in front of his mom. The homer sailed off his bat, high in the air before crashing down straight into Mack's face, turning him into a zombie…

He awoke with the happy feeling still bubbling inside as sunshine filtered through the lone window in his bedroom.

"School time, honey!" his mom's tired voice called from the kitchen. "Let's go!"

He jumped out of bed and immediately started dragging out all his new stuff so his mom could see. He didn't have his Dodger shirt. Mrs. Roseburg told him she served as the team's laundry mom and had him take it off the night before. He now wore one of his new shirts. He would get his jersey back next practice.

Seeing Dominic coming out of his room loaded with shopping bags, Mrs. Lewis frowned. "Where did Mack get all the money to buy you *that* stuff," she demanded.

"He didn't buy it," Dominic said. "I got it from playing baseball."

His mom slammed down her coffee cup. "What?" she said sharply. "Did some stranger buy that stuff for you?"

Dominic's lower lip jutted out. "He wasn't a stranger. Jimmy's dad did it. He said he had a coupon for it all."

Giving off a disgusted snort, Mrs. Lewis sank into a chair at the table. "I just bet he did. I work my fingers to the bone and can barely pay the bills. What right do these people have? Oh, I hate being poor!"

Dominic swallowed and dropped the bags. "They're stuff I need for baseball…but I can take them back. I don't care."

His mom shook her head. "No, don't do that… I'll just have to save up money and pay for it all. You tell Jimmy's father I'll pay him back, you hear?"

"Yeah. I'll tell him." Dominic wiped his nose with the back his hand and stared at the dirty floor. He never did ask if she had Saturday off.

His mom's eyes were puffy and thick with tiredness. Still a woman under forty, she had deep lines on her face and a drawn look of perpetual worry.

Dominic vowed to never bother her again. Grabbing his book bag, he trudged to the bus stop without bothering with changing. He still wore the same jeans from the night before.

School passed in a blur. Everyone was used to Dominic there. Seeing him in smelly old jeans was nothing new. Sure, some kids made snide comments, but never to his face. They were too afraid to see his reaction. Chase made it a point to stay as far away from him as possible.

At first Dominic thought maybe Chase didn't recognize him, but that was impossible. Then he tried sitting across from Chase at lunch. Chase immediately got up and took his tray to the opposite end of the table. Dominic didn't care too much. He was used to kids doing stuff like that.

At least Jimmy had greeted him. He was in Mrs. Lupps's so they only passed each other in the hall. Dominic tried going to the bathroom several times in hopes of finding Jimmy in the hall, but finally got yelled at for trying to skip class.

The only kid he managed to talk to in the bathroom turned out to be Rufus Cliner. Rufus had once been in class with Dominic back in the first grade. They'd even been friends for a while. Many times they'd gone to the principal's office together. There was the one time in the third grade when Dominic went into the bathroom to find Rufus drowning cockroaches in the sink. He wasn't laughing, but merely watching with interest. Since then, Dominic stayed away from Rufus.

On this day, Rufus nodded and headed into a back stall. He'd failed a grade at some time and was closer to twelve. Already with a deepening voice and the fuzz of a faint mustache, Rufus strode the halls with little fear. Tall for his age, but as thin as a broom, he had long dark hair tied back in a ponytail. On this day he wore tight black jeans and a black shirt at least two sizes too small. The teachers made no secret of loathing him. Just that fact alone helped create a bond between the two.

"Heard you were playing baseball," Rufus's voice said from the stall.

Dominic grunted. "I just started," he said.

Rufus abruptly exited the stall without flushing and stared at Dominic. "You guys practice here, right?" he asked.

Dominic nodded. "Yeah, I think so. I know there's practice here tomorrow. There's a game on Saturday."

"The game is here at school?" Rufus asked, lifting his eyebrows.

"No, not here." Dominic had an uncomfortable feeling and suddenly wanted to leave. Rufus had no interest in baseball, but certainly acted interested in something. He turned to the sink without even using the bathroom. "It's at the big fields."

Rufus grinned tightly at hearing the news. "Oh. Well, maybe I'll see you around some practice."

Rufus walked out jauntily, leaving Dominic standing at the sink wondering what had just happened. Dominic didn't ask to use the bathroom the rest of the day.

After school Dominic took his new glove from Jimmy and tried playing catch with himself. He never did get a baseball, so had to use one of Rose's large blocks for a ball.

Mack caught him in the back behind the trailer. At first he laughed, but then surprisingly turned around and went off. He returned minutes later with a glove and worn ball.

"Told you I played," he said when seeing Dominic's astonishment. "Now let's see if you can play."

Minutes later, Mack sauntered back in the trailer. After berating Dominic for every mistake, he'd left the boy seething in anger kicking at the dirt. The ball was somewhere in the woods. Dominic had thrown it there after Mack had called him a fat whale with a ball glove.

By the time Thursday's practice time arrived, Dominic hated baseball.

9

As usual, Jimmy arrived early to practice. He dragged his heavy baseball bag from the van and settled it on his shoulder. Stuffed with catching gear, two bats, five balls, his fielding glove, batting gloves, and bottles of extra water, it had to weigh nearly as much as he did. Years of practice carrying a school book bag prepared him to carry it.

His father trotted ahead of him to a small shed by the basketball courts. This was where the team stored extra balls, batting helmets, and other supplies.

In reality, the league owned everything. Most of it was left over from years ago—there were even shelves of wooden bats. Since only the Dodgers practiced at Knox Elementary, the shed became their own unofficial storage space. Mr. Roseburg wanted to find a helmet big enough to fit Dominic. The others had barely made it over his head.

When Jimmy reached the grass from the parking lot, he heard some voices. Turning, he saw a group of teens and kids around his age hanging around the side of the school. One of them saw him and pointed. Quickly the group turned and rushed away, heading toward the far end of the school. Nobody looked back and soon they were out of sight. Jimmy frowned, but then shrugged. The older teens had all worn large puffy jackets and beanie hats, even in the warm weather, and he didn't recognize any of them. He'd recognized one of the kids from his grade, though. Rufus was his name…

Seeing no sign of them as he approached the ball field, he put them out of his mind.

Grayson arrived moments later and the two started a game of catch. Jimmy always enjoyed catch with Grayson. The two never needed to speak a word as they let their arms and gloves do all the talking. While not showing off, they both liked to stretch the other with throws to the side or snap catches—snapping the ball out of the air at the last second. The best thing about Grayson, all he cared about was playing. Everything else came second. The two fell in an easy rhythm that wasn't interrupted until Chase appeared with Shawn right behind him.

"You guys alone?" Chase called out as he lugged his heavy gear from his mom's car. Shawn, as usual, rode his bike and only carried his hat and glove. He only brought his heavy bag with bats on game days.

Jimmy threw a high, lazy throw to Grayson and called back to Chase. "What does it look like?"

"I just want to make sure the freak isn't here," Chase said. "I hope he doesn't show up today."

Jimmy grimaced and ignored the comment. He plucked Grayson's return thrown and smoothly transitioned the ball from glove to hand before firing a low, hard throw towards Grayson's knees.

It was a perfect throw to get out a sliding runner. Grayson responded by laying his glove low, gathering in the ball, and applying a sweeping tag on the imaginary runner, almost in one motion.

"Out!" shouted Chase from where he watched.

As Grayson stood back up, Shawn yelled for a throw. Grayson turned and fired a long, high one that Shawn had to run and catch near the soccer field. "Bryce Harper, eat your heart out," he crowed as he made the catch on the run.

Soon the three friends gathered at home, waiting for Chase to put his bag with Jimmy's on the dugout bench. Mr. Roseburg still puttered around the shed and hadn't returned.

Trotting to join them with his glove, Chase cut straight to the, well, chase. "What's up with you and freak kid," he asked Jimmy directly. "How come you talk to him in school?"

Shawn frowned and looked away. Grayson pretended to have something wrong with his glove.

Jimmy stifled the urge to laugh in Chase's face. "What are you talking about?" he said. "He goes to our school. He's on our team. Why wouldn't I talk to him?"

"Because," replied Chase hotly, "the kid is going to wreck our season! Seriously, you saw what he did the other day!"

Jimmy shook his head. "Come on," he said with more certainty that he felt. "We'll be fine. You heard what Coach Wells said. It was only practice. I mean, I played centerfield most of the game."

Shawn scratched the back of his neck. "Yeah, because you had to babysit that Dominic kid."

"That freak, you mean," Chase said.

Jimmy frowned at Chase. "Lay off him. He just hasn't played before."

"Yeah, but he's playing now, for us," Chase reminded. "We're in the majors, not some special club team. He's going to make us lose."

"What if he does?" challenged Jimmy. "We have the all-stars. That's what counts."

Grayson and Shawn now stared at him.

"You mean you're willing to throw games?" demanded Shawn.

"Yeah," added Chase, "for that guy? And for your information, if we stink up the field, how are we even going to make the all-stars, huh? I mean, we should walk our way to the championship, and if we don't, we're going to look pretty bad."

Jimmy sighed and rolled his eyes. "Look, I didn't mean it like that. I'm just saying this is Little League. It's fun. We'll make the all-stars. We always do."

Their conversation was interrupted by the arrival of other players and coaches. Nobody wanted to be caught standing around when Mr. Wells showed up.

As Jimmy jogged back into the outfield with Grayson, he couldn't stop a frown from forming. What if Chase was right? Could one or more of them lose their spot on the all-star team if they had a bad year? Joey on the Cardinals certainly looked all-star worthy...

Then he saw his dad coming from around the school carrying a bucketful of balls. "Just focus on your game and don't let the outside world bother you," he'd told his son that morning. "Baseball is like life. When you're distracted you make mistakes. So learn to push it all out when it matters."

Jimmy quickly felt better. After all, Mr. Wells and his dad had a lot of pull with all-star selections. All he had to do was play hard and he'd make it. The others could do the same.

When Dominic did appear, walking across the soccer field towards them, he wore his new baseball gear and carried Jimmy's old glove. Chase blinked in disbelief when seeing him.

"Wow," he said grudgingly. "He at least dressed the part. Where'd he get those cleats?" he wondered aloud. "Now if he could only act the part."

Ignoring Chase, Jimmy immediately went out of the way to be extra nice to Dominic. This plan backfired later when he got chosen to pull Dominic to the side and give him extra pointers on fielding and hitting with Mr. Gordon. The rest of the team played situational baseball with Mr. Wells and Mr. Roseburg—the coaches would make up a situation, put the ball in play, and see how the players reacted. It was one of Jimmy's favorite games. Still, when seeing Chase glance his way, he put on a big smile and showed Dominic how to properly position the glove to receive a throw.

When practice ended, the players gathered around Mr. Wells to hear the game plan for their season opener. It would be against the Yankees at the same field as their practice game debacle.

"Come ready to play," Mr. Wells said, looking over his players. "If you show up, you're playing, so be ready. Show up early and we'll have the regular warm-up drills. Otherwise, I'm confident you guys know what you're doing. How about it, you guys ready?"

The team immediately responded with cheers. Getting to their feet, they gathered around their coach and started a Dodger chant. Jimmy did so halfheartedly. Dominic was the only player not to participate at all. He stood in the back watching with a wistful expression. When it ended, he immediately started for the soccer field, but was called back by Mr. Wells.

"Jimmy," Mr. Wells said. "Why don't you get your catching gear on. I want to see something."

Most players headed for the cars where their parents waited. Shawn remained. After a hard look and shake of his head, Chase left.

"I'll see you Saturday, man," he called to Shawn. He completely ignored Jimmy.

Grayson also remained, more so because his dad was late picking him up. Mr. Daniels almost always came late on practice nights. He used the time to plan lessons and grade papers at the high school.

With his dad's help, Jimmy quickly got on his catching gear and set up behind the plate. Mr. Wells, meanwhile, had Dominic standing where the mound should be and spoke to him softly. There was an artificial mound available in the shed, but it required a lot of man power to move it. Mr. Wells only used it for weekend practices. He knew most of the kids pitched on the side with their dads at other fields with real mounds. "I just want you to throw the ball to Jimmy's glove," he was saying. "Don't think about anything but that, okay?"

Dominic nodded and took the ball from the coach's hand. Without hesitating, he turned to Jimmy and threw the ball. It came out lazily and wide. Jimmy had to stand and move to his right to catch it. He tossed the ball back to Mr. Wells, who caught it barehanded. He handed it back to Dominic.

"Good," said Mr. Wells. "Now do it again. This time aim at the glove and hit it. Pretend Jimmy isn't even there. Just his glove."

Dominic proceeded to do so. At first his throws were hesitant, as if unsure. Then they settled and came harder. Jimmy returned each toss to Mr. Wells, but after the fourth throw the coach moved back off the mound and crossed his arms.

Sighing at first, Jimmy threw instead to Dominic. The first return throw Dominic dropped. The second, he bobbled. Each time he had trouble, Jimmy moved closer before tossing the ball. Soon the two worked out a system. And suddenly Dominic started throwing hard, fast, and straight.

"Wow!" called Jimmy as the ball popped into his mitt. "That one hurt!"

Shawn whistled from where he stood next to Grayson near third base. "Dominic," he said, "where did you learn to throw like that?" he asked, his admiration unmasked.

Dominic blinked and stared up as if caught by surprise. "Uh, I don't know," he stammered. Then after a moment's thought, he added, "It's fun."

Mr. Wells clapped his hands. "All right, that's enough. Dominic, I suspect you walked here. Come with me and I'll give you a lift home. Boys, thanks for staying, but now go home. Oh, and keep this under your hats. All of you. Dominic, you have an arm, but you're not a pitcher. Not yet." He smiled wide. "But you will be. See you on Saturday, boys."

It turned out they'd left just in time. Just as Jimmy reached the parking lot, Grayson's dad showed up, the sky started rumbling and dark clouds rolled in. Finally, the hot spell would break.

"Hey, Shawn," Jimmy called. "You need a ride?"

"Nah, man," Shawn yelled as he pedaled past. "I can beat this storm!"

"Yeah, good luck with that!" Jimmy yelled back.

His dad had the back of the van unlocked and opened so he could dump his bag in. Climbing in the front seat, he waited idly for his dad. Mr. Roseburg stood at Mr. Wells's car talking.

When his dad finally climbed in the driver's seat, he wiped his brow and glanced at his son. "So, how was catching with Dominic?"

Jimmy grinned. "My hand still hurts. He can really throw."

"Yeah, there's no doubt that he's strong… I just hope he can stay in control." Mr. Roseburg grimaced. "I saw some scratches at the shed door today. Looks like somebody was trying to break in." He grunted. "I just hope it wasn't our friend."

Jimmy frowned. "Dominic? Why would he do that?" he asked.

"Well, for one, to get baseballs. I doubt that poor kid has anything not given to him from a stranger. And most of what is given probably isn't in his best interest. Not enough good role models in his life, I'm thinking."

Jimmy squirmed in his seat. He couldn't imagine a kid reduced to stealing old balls from a shed just to play baseball.

As the van left the parking lot, the sky opened up and a deluge of rain fell. Poor Shawn probably didn't make it.

The rain continued deep into the night without let up. Dominic climbed into bed that night listening to the drops pounding against the thin roof of the trailer. It sounded like cheering. In his mind they were cheering for him—new ace pitcher for the Dodgers.

He grunted as he rolled to his side. *What a mixed-up world,* he thought. Before practice he'd decided that he hated baseball. Now it had to be his favorite thing in the world.

Especially when standing on the mound and throwing hard. He could do that for hours. And every time he threw he imagined aiming at a face. Instead of seeing Jimmy's glove that afternoon, he'd only seen Mack's big ugly mug. Oh, yeah. He could throw at that for hours, all right.

When Friday finally dawned, the rain had slackened to a light sprinkle. The sun came out before lunch and started its work in drying the fields. The best news, though, the temperatures never made it out of the seventies. Perfect weather.

Chase showed up at Jimmy's house that afternoon after school. Looking sheepish, he asked if Jimmy wanted to play Wiffle ball.

"Sure. We can hit against my house," Jimmy responded.

Even if mad at Chase, Wiffle ball against his house was too good to pass up. Jimmy had invented the game with his sister, but had perfected it with Chase. The right side of Jimmy's house went up two stories and had only a few bushes growing next to the foundation. It was also covered with several windows. The top two belonged to Brittany.

The game consisted of one hitting toward the house from about fifteen feet while the other pitched slow, regular pitches. Each part of the house meant something different. A ball striking a window meant an automatic hit. The first-story windows went for singles. Brittany's left window went for a double, while her right window being struck meant a triple. A home run occurred if the ball went over the roof. If the ball missed the window, and struck the wall, the pitcher had the chance to catch the rebound for an out. Otherwise it went down as a foul. Any groundball also meant an out unless it got stuck in the bushes. Then it would be a foul.

Neither Chase nor Jimmy aimed for the bushes. They always went for Brittany's windows. Combining baseball and annoying his older sister all at once made it one of Jimmy's favorite Wiffle ball games.

Jimmy hit first. It didn't take long. After a few fouls, he rocketed a shot that banged into Brittany's left window.

"Double!" Jimmy yelled.

Seconds later, the window jerked open and Brittany's head appeared. "Stop that, you moron!" she cried. "I'm trying to study! Do it again, I'm going to tell Mom!"

"Quick!" Jimmy yelled at Chase. "Throw another."

Chase hesitated. "Hey, maybe we should move somewhere else…"

"Just one more pitch!" Jimmy pleaded.

Chase shrugged and threw. Jimmy tore into this one too. It went straight at his sister's face.

She screamed, but at the same time instinctively raised both hands and caught the ball. "There!" she shouted. "You're out!" Ducking back inside, she slammed the window shut. The ball stayed with her.

"Wow," Chase said after a moment. "That was some catch."

Jimmy frowned. "Still counted as a double," he mumbled. "Want to go to the pool?"

"Okay," Chase said, not sounding too eager. "It's a little cold for swimming, but we might as well."

The two never ended up in the water. Instead they lounged on chairs and discussed their favorite players in the real major leagues.

Shawn found them there shortly after. Having ridden his bike to Chase's house, he'd guessed where he'd find his friend. Joining in the conversation, the three passed the time until Mrs. Roseburg poked her head from the back door to announce dinnertime for Jimmy.

"You guys want to stay over?" she asked when seeing Chase and Shawn.

Jimmy grinned mischievously. "I know Chase does. He wants to sit next to Brittany."

Chase immediately kicked Jimmy in the leg. "Shut it!" he snapped.

Shawn laughed and said he would be happy to stay over. "I need to chaperone," he said innocently.

Chase and Shawn were a common sight at the Roseburg's dinner table. Both sets of their parents worked and weren't always home until late. Shawn had older sisters who looked out for him, something he took great pains to avoid, and Chase had his grandmother who liked to watch old TV shows and sip sodas while eating pretzels. He'd always rather be with his friends than participate in that.

Mr. Roseburg nodded at them as they came in and sat at the table. "I'm going to adopt whichever one of you makes it to the Major Leagues first," he said gruffly.

"That would be me, Coach," Shawn said. He pretended to grab at the chair next to Brittany, but at the last moment backed away.

Chase, his face turning red, was forced to take it. Jimmy sat across from him with Shawn on his left. Jimmy shot Shawn a look with raised eyebrows and then shook his head. His friends were real idiots.

As they sat down to a meal of hot lasagna, string beans, and garlic bread, the conversation steered toward their Little League team, the Dodgers.

"You know," Mrs. Roseburg said as she got up to bring more orange juice to the table, "after the game on Saturday, you boys should come here for a swim. The temperature is supposed to go up tomorrow."

"That would be awesome," Shawn said enthusiastically. "I need to work on my tan." He pretended to flex his slender brown arms, batting his lashes at Brittany.

Chase coughed and tried to drown himself with orange juice. Then he ducked his head toward his plate and worked on the lasagna.

Mr. Roseburg also liked the idea. "I can pick up some steaks and we can have a barbecue." It was no secret that he loved burning meat on the grill.

Brittany snorted. "What if you guys lose?" she asked cruelly.

"Then," Jimmy told her, "we'll throw you on the grill."

Glaring, Brittany aimed a kick under the table at her younger brother, but he saw it coming and moved his legs back. She ended up kicking Chase in the ankle.

Coughing louder, Chase nearly spit out his pasta.

"Oh, dear, are you all right?" Mrs. Roseburg asked in alarm. "It isn't too hot, is it?"

"You mean her?" Shawn asked innocently. "Huh, Chase?"

This earned a sharp kick from Jimmy. Shawn yelped and busily stared at his bread.

"Everybody okay?" Mrs. Roseburg asked, eyeing her son carefully.

"Of course," Jimmy said innocently. "Shawn just had too much spice."

When things settled, the plans for the barbecue were set. Jimmy would invite Grayson, Mr. Wells, and Phil the next day.

Then Brittany opened her big mouth. "Why not invite Dominic too?" she asked. "I mean, I'm sure he has nothing else to do after the game."

Mr. and Mrs. Roseburg exchanged worried glances. The boys put down their forks and looked toward them, almost in fear.

"Well," said Mr. Roseburg after a moment, "I'm not sure we're, well, he's not..." he sighed. "We'll see," he finally said.

Blinking as if dazed, Chase couldn't help staring at Brittany as if startled. The whole meal, even when kicked by her, he avoided looking anywhere near her direction. "Wh-why?" he spluttered "I mean, why do you want him here?"

Brittany tossed back her hair and grabbed her juice. "I want to grow up to be a teacher and help people. The best way to do that is to understand them first. I bet I can get Dominic to talk if I listened." She sneered at her brother. "Did any of you ever try and do that? I didn't think so." Then she turned and smiled at Chase. "That's all he needs, somebody who understands him."

Chase nodded slowly. "That actually…sounds like good advice."

Shawn and Jimmy both looked at each other, their eyes wide. This did not sound like the Chase they knew just the other day.

Brittany blushed and nodded. "Yeah, well, somebody in this family has brains."

"Uh," said her mother, "maybe we'll talk about this later. Who's ready for ice cream for dessert?"

"Yeah," mumbled Jimmy. "We need to cool things off around here." He was surprised when he saw not only Chase blush, but also his sister. "Good grief," he groaned. "I'm so doomed."

Shawn only laughed and banged his back with his hand. "I saw this one coming, dude. Win or lose, we'd better have that pool party."

10

Game day arrived bright and sunny. The grass had mostly drunk in the excess water and baseball was given the go.

Dominic woke up to heavy banging on his door. He lay in a tangle of sheets in only his boxer shorts.

"Get up, Dom!" he heard Mack yell from the other side of the door. "Your sister wants you!"

"Rose?" Dominic asked blearily, sitting up in bed. "What did she do? Wet the bed again?"

"No, stupid. Your other sister. The ugly one!"

"Sara? Sara's here!" Dominic immediately swung his legs over his bed and thumped down to the carpet. His room was narrow and cramped. Overbalancing, he crashed into the wall and caught himself on the closet door.

"That's what I said when I saw her too," Mack's voice said from behind the door. "Tell her she can't stay unless she moves back in."

Dominic ignored him. Most of his clothes and toys were still scattered over the floor from when he'd searched for his dad's glove. The nearest clothes he found smelled ripe with sweat and mildew.

"Ah, heck," he said, tossing aside a damp T-shirt smelling like an old trash bag. He hadn't seen his older sister in a long time.

Running to the door, he was about to burst from his room wearing only his boxers. Then he remembered. The Dodgers played that day.

Whirling, he looked at where his freshly cleaned Dodger jersey rested on top of his roughly folded baseball pants on the foot of his bed. The jersey had been given back to him by Mr. Roseburg after the last practice. Waving his hands wildly, he rushed to his bed and quickly struggled into his baseball uniform. Unfortunately, his pants hadn't been cleaned, but they weren't too bad. His baseball socks…they smelled, but not awful. Minutes later, he crashed from his room and immediately dashed for the bathroom. Emerging, he was finally ready.

His older sister stood just outside the trailer door with an unlit cigarette in her mouth. Tall and slender, she had the same features as Dominic, but slimmer and more feminine. Her hair, the color of honey, hung down to the middle of her back without a curl. Currently it hung in a tight ponytail. Her face, though, had the same drawn, pinched look of constant harassment as Dominic's.

At seeing her little brother in his baseball uniform, her frown immediately went upside down as she lit up in a rare smile.

"Dominic!" she cried. "It's true! You really are on a team!"

"Sara, what are you doing here?" Dominic asked, flinging open the door. He threw himself into his sister's open arms.

"Hey!" yelled Mack from the couch. "Close the door and keep it down! Your mother's sleeping here! Somebody should care about her." Then he belched.

Sara made a face and pulled Dominic down the steps. "I've come to see you, Dominic. Mom called me the other day when she was at work. She told me about you playing baseball." She kept her cool hands around Dominic's back the whole time. Many hours she'd once held him like this on her lap. When Dominic was younger and smaller, she was the only person who could make him stop crying and throwing tantrums. Dominic missed those days.

"Yeah," Dominic said excitedly. "I have a game today." He grinned up at his sister, displaying his chipped tooth.

"No kidding?" Sara ran a hand through Dominic's thick hair. "Maybe we can go see you play. Say, why don't you get your shoes and we'll go out to breakfast first?"

Dominic literally jumped in her arms then, nearly bowling her over. "Really? Mom's coming too?"

"Mom? Oh, no, sorry, sweetie. I meant Rick and I."

Dominic's face immediately fell. "Who's Rick?" he asked.

"That would be me, mister," said a cheerful voice from the front of the trailer.

Sara stepped back and raised a hand toward the voice. "This is Rick, Dominic. He's my boyfriend. He's studying to be a doctor."

A tall, stocky man stood in front of the trailer dressed in a light blue suit with a bright orange tie. Thick, dark-brown hair was parted neatly to the side and his freshly shaven face glistened with cleanliness. He grinned widely, displaying white, crooked teeth. Raising his hand, he waved at Dominic. Then he gestured them forward.

"Come on," he said. "The chariot is waiting." Behind him, a dark red sedan sat with two doors open.

Dominic continued to frown. "Does Mom know he's there?" he asked.

Sara sighed. "Dominic, Mom doesn't care much or know much about me these days. Listen, Rick drove me here to see you. He wants to meet you. Trust me. You'll like him a lot." She pushed him toward the trailer. "Go get your shoes and anything else you need for the game. Rick and I will take you to eat and then straight to the game."

"What time is it?" Dominic asked, sounding unhappy. "My game is at 10:30."

"It's not even eight, mister," Rick said cheerfully. "We have plenty of time."

"See?" hissed Sara. "You two will get along great! Now hurry!"

Dominic didn't get along great with Rick. But he'd at least gotten a good pancake meal. They went to a small diner and found seats in the back. While Dominic wolfed down a stack of syrupy cakes, Rick tried telling funny stories about when he played sports as a kid.

"I wasn't the fastest guy on the court," he said at one time, "but I was tall. When the kid tried to shoot over me, I stood up straight and blocked the shot with my head! With my head," he repeated when Dominic didn't laugh. "Well, my coach said I did a great job using my head."

Sara laughed much too loudly and clapped her hands. "So were you a good baseball player?" she asked.

"Huh?" Rick asked, giving her a funny look. "No, I played basketball. I never touched baseball."

Dominic tuned him out soon after. Licking his plate clean, he looked up. "Can I get more?" he asked.

As Dominic ate his pancakes, Grayson had trouble swallowing the last of his chocolate cereal. His lean stomach gurgled and jumped around like a kid on a trampoline. He couldn't wait to be on the field and wished time could move faster.

"Slow down there, guy," Mr. Daniels said in an amused tone. He sat opposite his son at the small kitchen table, pretending to read the newspaper.

In reality, he was just as jumpy. Grayson had three older brothers but was the only one left at home. Two were in college and the eldest had already married and now lived in Kentucky. Grayson, the baby of the bunch, had benefited by receiving all their attention. Each of his older brothers had played ball and each passed on their knowledge to their kid brother. Eric and Sam, the two in college, would be home in another couple of months. They'd both called the night before to wish Grayson luck and to promise to be there for the championship game. They all wanted to see him win. Still, neither were bigger fans of his than their dad. And Grayson wanted to do everything possible to win for him.

The night before, he'd heard his parents talking. Thinking Grayson was busy playing one of his video games in the living room, they'd sat over cups of coffee in the kitchen discussing Mr. Daniels's job. Apparently, Kelvin and Richie were still making trouble. They were now turning in work, but Mr. Daniels was pretty sure it wasn't their own. Not only that, but he'd been getting pressure from his principal to just pass both students and to stop worrying about it.

"I don't want Grayson to think people can get through life by cheating," Mr. Daniels had said angrily. "If I find proof Kelvin and Richie have cheated, I'm failing them. I don't care. They can have my job if they like!"

"But honey," his mom had said, "then what would you do?"

"I'd find something else," his father had firmly stated. "Those guys are the two most disrespectful, rude, and obnoxious students I've ever dealt with. They think they can bully their way to do anything they want. If I don't teach them anything else, I at least want to teach them a lesson in humility and honest work."

Grayson had been playing his MLB video game, but had paused the game when hearing the names of the teens. He'd sat in front of the television listening to the discussion, deep in thought.

When his father had walked in moments later, he'd glanced down at Grayson and had frowned. "You heard us?" he'd asked.

Grayson had nodded. "Can I do anything to help?" he'd asked.

"Yes," his dad had replied seriously. "You can play ball the right way tomorrow. That would be a big help." Then he'd smiled. "Now let me give you a hand up and send you off to bed. Don't worry about my job or anything else. Just worry about the plate tomorrow. Okay? I'll be there with my camera. I'd love to put up a picture of you scoring the winning run to show what a true champion looks like."

Now in the morning, Grayson hadn't forgotten his father's words. He meant to play the right way, all right. He meant to win the game so his father could shove it in Kelvin's and Richie's faces. Only it was still over an hour before they had to leave.

"Dad," he asked. "Can we go early and play catch?"

Mr. Daniels put down the paper and blinked. "Why would we do that? Don't you want to clean your room this morning or something?"

Grayson just gave him a look with chocolate milk dripping down his chin.

Father and son left for the ball field soon after. Dirty rooms took backseats to baseball games and catch between father and son.

The sun sent brilliant rays down on Eastland Sports Park and a cool breeze blew from the north. The official opening day, when all the teams met for a ceremony and speeches, for whatever reason, wasn't scheduled until the following Saturday. This was a shame, because the clear blue sky promised a perfect day for baseball.

Only a handful of teams from the nine-to-ten-year-old major league were to play that day. In all, the league had eight teams. In the regular season, the teams would play each other two times. Then they were seeded based on their records for the playoff tournament. The top four teams played the lower four and the winners advanced until only one remained. That team would be crowned champion.

When Dominic finally arrived at the sports park, his stomach felt ready to burst. Worse, after riding in the back of Rick's car listening to Sara and Rick talk nonsense, he felt queasy.

"I'm not going to barf," he told himself softly as the car finally stopped in one of the few open parking spaces left.

"What's that, mister?" Rick asked from the driver's seat. "You say something?"

"I'm late," Dominic said, reaching for the door.

"Well, don't forget your glove," Sara said, turning in her seat. "Rick and I will be in the stands watching, so play good out there, little brother."

"You bet we will, mister," Rick said with a grin directed more at Sara than Dominic.

Dominic grabbed his glove and escaped into the fresh air. Rushing through the crowded parking lot, he headed for the field. Already several Dodger players were on the outfield doing pop fly drills. The Yankees, wearing uniforms a different and darker shade of blue than the Dodgers, were practicing on the infield.

Dominic didn't know where to go and slowed to a walk when he reached the area behind the backstop. His stomach did some flips and the eight pancakes he'd eaten started to settle like a load of bricks.

Just then a lady came rushing to him wearing a large smile.

Instantly Dominic froze and stared at her. The only grown-ups who smiled at him usually were teachers that got him in trouble shortly after. Then he relaxed as he recognized Mrs. Roseburg, Jimmy's mom.

"Dominic," she said in greeting. "I'm so glad you made it! Are you here all by yourself?"

He shook his head. "My, um, sister brought me. She and her boyfriend."

"Really?" Mrs. Roseburg stopped a few feet from Dominic and gave him a new look. "I didn't know you had a sister! You'll have to point them out to me."

Dominic turned and spotted Sara and Rick coming from the parking lot. They were holding hands. "Uh, they're right there. She's in the jeans and white shirt. He's the guy wearing the ugly suit."

"Wow, Dominic," said Mrs. Roseburg brightly. "They make a nice couple. Here, you go join the team. Just go to the same dugout you were in the last, well, the last time you were here…" She hesitated. "After the game…maybe you'd like to come over with Jimmy. He and some of the boys are having a pool party. You and your sister, and, uh, Rick, would be very welcome."

Dominic started to nod, but suddenly froze. "Uh, you'll have to talk to my sister about it. I, uh, have to go." He stiffly walked away.

"Okay," called Mrs. Roseburg. "I'll do that. Good luck today!"

Dominic didn't look back. The pancakes and syrup were really making a mess of his stomach. Worse, though, was the thought of going to Jimmy's pool party. Mack had delivered another thump to his back the night before. No way could he take his shirt off for swimming. Not only that, but he didn't even own a bathing suit that fit. And besides, he didn't know how to swim.

As Dominic entered the visitor's dugout, the rest of the team started heading towards him. He'd missed all the warm-ups. Putting his head down, he then noticed the clumps of sticky syrup clinging to his shirt. This was not a good way to start baseball. A sudden jolt from below let him know it would be worse. The pancakes wanted a fast exit from the back way.

Dominic got his chance for relief shortly after.

The players started filing into the dugout. They had trotted in from the outfield laughing and joking together, but fell silent when seeing Dominic.

"Sit down, boys," Mr. Wells said, walking from the home plate area where he'd been talking to the home umpire. "Just relax."

Dominic moved to the far end of the bench and slumped down, but did little relaxing. The other players also sat, but almost none glanced in his direction. Then Jimmy practically dragged Grayson down the bench and shoved him next to Dominic.

"I did it last time," hissed the smaller boy. "Remember?"

"Yeah," Jimmy whispered back, "but we haven't decided who's next, so you still have to fill in until then." Jimmy batted the front bill of Grayson's cap and quickly retreated back to the other side of the bench to sit with Chase and Shawn.

"Hey, is there a bathroom in here," Dominic whispered to him.

Grayson frowned and didn't look in Dominic's direction. He adjusted his hat and sighed. "No," he finally muttered.

Dominic made a face and knew he was about to be in big trouble. Then Mr. Roseburg came to the rescue.

"Before Coach Wells goes into positions and lineups, everyone do a bathroom check," he called loudly. "We don't want you boys to have to go in the middle of an inning, or when you're batting."

This caused several of the players to crack up.

"I'm serious," Mr. Roseburg said. "If you have to go, go now."

Dominic stood and looked down the line of players. Mike and Will were up and heading out the dugout.

"Where are they going?" he asked Grayson.

The smaller boy looked up at him and sighed again. "Come on," he said. "I'll show you the bathroom."

Grayson got up like he had to go to the dentist. As he led Dominic from the dugout, the other boys averted their eyes. That is, until they reached Jimmy and Chase. Chase snickered and smacked Grayson's thigh with his glove as he went by. Grayson made sure to step on Chase's foot with his cleats.

Jimmy nodded at Dominic and then turned to Chase and Shawn. "Paper-rock-scissors time," he said.

11

The bathrooms were in a large brick building across from where concessions were sold. It stood in front of the parking lot midway between all the baseball fields. The smell of cooking burgers and hot dogs hung in the air. It made Dominic feel even queasier. Both his hands were clutched to his stomach as he rushed to keep up with Grayson.

Mike and Will were just leaving the restroom when Grayson and Dominic made it. They greeted Grayson and ignored Dominic.

"See you on the field," Mike called to Grayson as he raced Will back to the dugout. Grayson looked as if he wanted to join them, but instead pointed his head toward the restroom.

"You'd better hurry," he said. "The game starts soon."

"Aren't you going?" Dominic asked. They were standing at the wall next to the boys' restroom.

Grayson shook his head. "I'm going to buy a bottle of water for the game." He knelt down and reached into his right sneaker before extracting a five-dollar bill. Looking up, he saw Dominic staring at him. "Uh, I can get you a bottle, too."

"Hey, how about hooking me up?" asked a voice. "Can I get something?"

A boy their age stepped from around the far corner of the building and sauntered their way. Dominic recognized Rufus Cliner immediately.

"It's not your money, Rufus," he said, momentarily forgetting his bathroom needs.

Grayson, still kneeling, eyed the boy carefully. Going to a different school, he knew nothing about Rufus.

"I know it's not my money, Dom-Dom," Rufus said rudely. "That's why I'm asking nicely." He looked down at Grayson. "Any more in your shoe bank?"

Grayson stood slowly. "Not for you," he said levelly. He stared Rufus in the eye. Even though he was several inches shorter, he didn't back down. Dominic moved to stand by Grayson's shoulder.

Rufus looked away first. "Whatever, baseball stars," he said sarcastically. "Go have yourself a ball." He turned and stalked away.

"That was Rufus," Dominic said when the bully had turned the corner. "He goes to my school. He's a jerk."

Grayson gave Dominic a wan smile. "What grade?" he asked. "Kindergarten?"

"No," began Dominic, "he's in—" Then he stopped and smiled. "Yeah, kindergarten." Then his face contorted. "Uh, I got to go."

Grayson said he would wait with the water, but Dominic didn't hear him. Nature wasn't calling. It was screaming.

Grayson bought two bottles of water and leaned against the wall next to the restroom to impatiently wait for Dominic. Mr. Wells would already be handing out positions by now.

He glanced at the field nearest the restroom. There the Cardinals and Blue Jays were just about to get started. He was just about to turn and tell Dominic to hurry when he spotted two teenagers walking towards him. Kelvin and Richie. Between them walked the Rufus kid who'd asked for his money. The trio walked slowly and looked to be in deep discussion. None of them appeared to have seen him.

Frowning, Grayson wanted to keep it this way. Backing slowly to the restroom, he opened the door and slipped in.

"Um, Dominic?" he said. Nobody was in sight. Then from the far stall he heard Dominic's voice answer.

"Yeah?"

"Are you almost done?"

"It's going to take a little longer…"

Grayson breathed out slowly. "Well, I'm going back to the field. The game's starting."

"I'll be there," Dominic assured him.

Grayson left just as the two teens and Rufus reached the building. He had no chance to duck them, but didn't really care. After listening to his dad, he wasn't afraid of them.

As it turned out, the three completely ignored him. They filed in the bathroom as Grayson scampered back to the Dodgers.

Dominic had just finished and was about to flush when he heard the main bathroom door open. Rufus's harsh laugh entered, followed by voices. From the sound of the deep voices, there were at least two older guys with him.

Dominic sat back down and kept very quiet. The last thing he needed was for Rufus to catch him with his pants down. Kids like that were as mean as skunks. Rufus wouldn't forget Dominic standing up to him. From now on, they would be enemies.

"So," said one of the older voices. "Where are they? You said they'd be here." The voice sounded accusing.

Rufus's voice came out whiny. "They'll be here, you'll see."

"They'd better, for your sake," the other older voice said in almost a growl. "We didn't get up this early and come to this park for nothing. There're too many people here."

"Don't worry," Rufus said, sounding a little nervous, "the guys found a perfect place for now on. Nobody will suspect it."

"I hope so," muttered the first voice. "I hate going to the trash trailers."

Then the door opened again and Rufus heard the sound of cleats clacking against the hard floor. Immediately the voices went silent. After a short while a toilet flushed and the clacking retreated back out the door.

"The little punk didn't wash his hands," laughed the second older voice.

"Neither do you half the time," his companion scoffed.

Then the door opened again.

"Hello in there," said a new deep voice. "Anybody home?"

"You guys waiting for us?" asked another voice.

Dominic's insides lurched. He recognized both voices instantly: Bobby Wayne and Dill Coose—a couple of teenage dropouts from his trailer park. What were they doing in a little league bathroom on a Saturday morning? Dominic felt his body tighten. He was glad he'd just emptied his stomach.

Rufus and the other guys sounded glad to see them. Then things got serious.

"Look," Bobby's voice said soothingly. "You'll have to trust us. We didn't bring anything today because there's too much of a, shall we say, parent presence. But," he continued quickly, "we have it. You'll have to meet us on Tuesday. Little Rufus here found us the perfect place and perfect time."

Before they could continue the conversation, the door opened again and a father escorted two little kids in.

Immediately Bobby coughed loudly. Dominic heard the door open and the sound of exiting feet. He relaxed, thinking the teens were gone. Sure enough, in moments, all he heard was the father telling his boys not to miss.

Jimmy frowned when seeing Grayson return to the dugout alone.

Chase, on the other hand, looked relieved. He'd lost the latest paper-rock-scissors round.

"Did the fre—I mean, did Dominic go home?" he asked Grayson hopefully.

Shaking his head as he entered the dugout, Grayson put two bottles of water on the bench and went to retrieve his glove from his bag.

"Then where is he?" Jimmy demanded when the crouching boy said nothing. He wore his catching gear and stood with Chase in the on-deck area. "He's supposed to play right field this inning."

"Yeah," Chase added grumpily, "and I'm supposed to be in centerfield to cover for him."

Grayson, glove trapped in his thighs, looked up and frowned as he zipped up his bag. "He's, um, taking, well, he'll be back soon."

"Dominic is taking a number two," Chase said, rolling his eyes. "That's great."

Shawn called from the infield. "Hey, you idiots!" he shouted. "We have a game to play!"

Jimmy pulled on his mask. "Well, you're pitching, Gray. We'd better warm up."

When the game began Dominic still had yet to show up. Liam took his spot in right. Chase got his wish and went to shortstop, moving Shawn to third and Phil to center. Grayson started on mound. Behind the plate as catcher, Jimmy had every bit of confidence the game would be a breeze. There were five potential all-star players on the field. He looked toward the dugout where his dad gave him the sign for the first pitch. Mr. Gordon had been sent to look for Dominic.

See? he thought. *Dominic was good for the team after all!* Jimmy much more preferred his dad to Mr. Gordon giving the signs.

"Play ball!" announced the home umpire.

A second umpire stood behind second base to make the calls on the field. Both were big, burly men and just about dared anybody to argue with them.

With the crowd clapping and whistling, Jimmy signaled the first pitch—fastball over the inside of the plate.

"Steee-rike!" yelled the ump.

The season was under way.

Dominic returned with a red-faced Mr. Gordon shortly after the first out. The tall assistant coach practically shoved the boy in front of him as they entered the field area. Water droplets soaked the front of his Dodger shirt so it looked as if he spat all over himself.

Mr. Wells stood from his bucket and lifted his eyebrows as a way of greeting. Dominic brushed by with slumped shoulders. He took his usual seat at the far end of the bench. Will and Xavier, the two other Dodgers not in the field, totally ignored him.

"I found him playing in the sink," Mr. Gordon told Mr. Wells angrily. "When I told him to stop, he just looked at me and then started throwing water at me. If he was my child, I would've—"

Mr. Wells coughed and shook his head. "The game started." He spoke calmly and clearly. "Why don't you take my seat and I'll go talk to him."

"Good luck," muttered Mr. Gordon. "He tried running from me already."

As Mr. Gordon sat on the bucket, he tried sending in pitching signs to Jimmy.

"Sorry, Jerry," Mr. Roseburg said, using Mr. Gordon's first name, "but I have this inning." He knelt next to Mr. Gordon, but didn't look at him.

Making a sound in his throat, Mr. Gordon started to scowl, but thought better of it. Chewing on his bottom lip, he instead glared back in the dugout where Mr. Wells sat with Dominic.

Mr. Wells didn't say anything at first. He took a seat a foot from Dominic and spread his arms out so they rested across the back of the bench.

Dominic bent forward in his seat and picked at his hands.

After a while, Mr. Wells sighed and crossed a leg. "Watching the game?" he asked pleasantly.

Dominic merely grunted in response.

Mr. Wells nodded as if he understood. "You have to watch to learn," he said. "How else can you get better? There's one out and one base runner is on second."

The runner came when the second batter had hit a grounder to third and Shawn had rushed his throw. The ball had sailed over Tom's glove at first before crashing into the fence by the dugout. By the time Tom had gotten the ball back into play, the runner had advanced an extra base.

"The play will be at first, still," Mr. Wells told Dominic conversationally. Dominic slowly lifted his eyes to watch the field. "That's better," said his coach. "Now tell me, Dominic. What happened in the bathroom? Why did you throw water at Mr. Gordon?" Dominic shrugged. "What was that?" asked Mr. Wells. "I can't hear you. I'm a little old, you might've noticed."

"I don't know," Dominic said, still looking towards the field. "I just did."

"Well, you can't 'just do' here," Mr. Wells said. "You're supposed to be out there helping the team. Instead you're stuck listening to me. Dominic, I wanted you on this team and still do. But you have trust me and the other coaches. We can help you play baseball if you let us."

Just then Grayson fired a pitch that the batter knocked weakly toward first base. Phil came off the bag and charged forward. He settled to a quick stop just in front of the ball, putting down his glove in its path. His throwing hand poised just above his glove.

Meanwhile, Grayson sprinted from the mound to cover first. Jimmy ran toward the play to back up the throw if needed. At the same time, he kept close to home just in case an overthrow allowed the runner from second advance to home.

It all happened at once and ended in seconds. Phil gobbled up the ball and turned easily to pitch it to Grayson's waiting glove. The pitcher tagged the base for the easy out and instantly pivoted his body to face third. The runner on second had hesitated. He should've taken third easily, but held up to see the play. When he saw Phil go to first, he put his head down and broke late to the next base.

Grayson didn't rush. He stepped calmly forward and put all his might into the throw to third. It bounced once on the grass, but kept on target. Shawn crouched next to the bag and went to his knees to snag the ball.

"Get down!" roared the Yankee's third base coach. "Slide!"

The surprised runner tried to drop into a slide, but not before Shawn swiped his shoes with a sweeping tag.

"Out!" yelled the umpire from home. He'd run up the third baseline to make the call. It was a double play and sent the Dodgers to the dugout with spirits soaring.

Mr. Wells sighed with pleasure in the dugout as the crowd roared with approval.

"See?" he said. "We taught those boys that. They trust us and trust each other. Decide if you want to be like them, or to be like whoever taught you to throw water on adults." He patted Dominic on the shoulder and then slapped his knee. "The choice is yours. In any case, you're batting twelfth and will be in the field next inning. So be ready." Then he got up and stretched. "You know," he said to Dominic, "I kind of like being in here. Usually I spend all game sitting on the bucket. Maybe I'll visit more often. Now come with me and let's join the rest of the team."

The rest of the team already huddled around Mr. Roseburg in front of the dugout for a quick pep talk. Nothing fired up a team like great defense.

"Awesome play, boys," Mr. Roseburg said calmly. "If anybody wants to see it again, watch Sportscenter tonight. Now let's back it up with some hitting. Grayson, Jimmy, Shawn, you're up this inning. Chase, you're after Shawn."

Mr. Wells greeted the players as they entered the dugout with high fives. Dominic remained on his spot on the bench.

He looked to his right where the stands were for the Dodgers' fans. He saw Mrs. Roseburg sitting near the front, but didn't see Sara.

"Hiya, Dom," said a loud voice to his left. Dominic jumped as if slapped. Of course it wasn't Mack. The voice sounded too high and Mack was lying on the couch in the trailer. But for a split second, Dominic thought it was. Turning, he saw Chase staring at him with wide eyes.

"Uh," said Chase, "are you okay?"

"Yeah," Dominic said, shifting nervously in his seat. "I'm fine."

Chase sat down and stared at the dugout floor. He idly toed a pile of old sunflower seeds that were scattered throughout the dugout. "So, uh, you having fun?" Dominic grunted and looked away. Chase sighed and shook his head. "It's like talking to a pile of number two," he said under his breath. Then he got up to find his batting helmet.

12

The Dodgers wasted little time backing up their sparkling defense. Grayson led off with a sharp liner into centerfield that dropped for a single. Jimmy followed with a grounder that made it through the second baseman, putting him on first and moving Grayson to third. While on first, his dad gave the light two taps on his shoulder and patted the seat of his pants. Shawn took the first pitch for a ball low and Jimmy broke for second.

"He's stealing!" yelled one of the Yankees coaches. "Gun him down!"

"Eat it!" yelled another. Eating the ball meant not throwing it, but letting the runner have the base. The poor catcher was caught between following both orders. He ended up with a throw straight into the ground. It rolled toward the mound and both catcher and pitcher went for it.

Grayson immediately sprinted for home.

"He's going home!" roared the first Yankees coach. "Get the ball!"

Now totally out of sorts, the Yankee catcher dove on top of the ball, knocking his pitcher out of the way. He rolled to his knees to make the throw, but only saw the umpire covering home. Grayson crossed the plate easily. In the confusion, Jimmy raced to third and made it without a throw.

It was the season opener and teams still hadn't gotten everything figured out. At least most teams hadn't. The irate Yankees coach, who'd first yelled to throw to second, slammed down his hat. He glared at the Dodgers' dugout.

"Come on, guys!" he yelled. "We're facing all-stars here! We have to play like it!" He sounded angrier at Mr. Wells than his players.

Shawn didn't help the man's blood pressure when he nailed the next pitch deep into the left field. It landed just in front of the fence and rolled to a stop next to an advertisement for tires. Jimmy trotted home as Shawn turned for two and ended up with a standup double. Chase went up next and walked in four pitches.

After calling time, the Yankees coach stalked out to the mound and called in his infield for a quick meeting. Talking tersely for a few moments, he sent them back with a sharp clap of the hands. "We can get these guys still!" he said. "They don't all have the last name of Ruth!"

Phil went to the plate next. Tall like his father, he just wasn't as loud. His face was deceptively pudgy in appearance. Phil liked to talk up his game, but had more than just talk. After taking two balls and a strike, he turned on the next pitch and sent a scorching liner down the third baseline. The kid playing third actually ducked when the ball screamed past his head. It finally bounced in the grass before rolling to the fence. Another double and another run.

Two batters and two hits later, it was 5-0 Dodgers and the Yankees coach asked for the mercy rule. After a short discussion, the umpires granted it. The teams finally switched.

"What?" Mr. Gordon demanded when hearing the announcement. "This is spring ball, not baby fall ball!"

Parents groaned from the Dodger stands, but the fans of the Yankees cheered.

The home plate umpire shrugged. "New rules, this year, coach. For twelve and under, the mercy rule is in effect at the umpire's discretion. For this game it applies."

Mr. Wells nodded as moved to stand next to Mr. Gordon. "I heard about this," he said with a slight smile. "Parents were worried about our team running up the score."

Mr. Gordon's face started to turn red, but then it relaxed. "Guess it's an honor, then," he muttered. "I hope we win big."

Mr. Wells shrugged. "As long as the boys learn and have fun. That's what counts for now." He shifted toward the dugout and clapped his hands loudly. "Let's go, Dodgers! On the field!"

Dominic went to play in right and Chase grudgingly moved to centerfield. At first Dominic didn't seem like he was going to move from the dugout, but then Mr. Wells turned his cool green eyes on him and waited.

"Fine," Dominic had said huffily. He grabbed his glove and trudged onto the field. He probably could've stayed put the way Grayson pitched that inning. After striking out the first batter, he walked the next, and then struck out the third. The fourth batter only managed a weak popup to Will, who played at second that inning.

The Yankees coach sent his now filthy hat into the dirt again as his team filed dejectedly onto the field. However, he did make a pitching change. A kid by the name Chris Chosworth took the mound. He'd played catcher the inning before and had some scores to settle.

"He's good," Grayson said in the dugout as Will took up his batting helmet.

Will laughed. "We're better," he said confidently as he walked to the on-deck area.

Will, Mike, and Xavier were scheduled to hit that inning. If any got on base, Liam would be next. After him would be Dominic.

Jimmy smirked as he watched Chris warm up and knew Will would be in trouble. Chris was by far the best pitcher on the Yankees. The Yankees coach had hoped to save him for the later innings, but couldn't afford to wait any longer.

Sure enough, Will went down in four quick pitches. Tall Mike, who always hit well in practice, also went down swinging. His long arms were handcuffed by Chris's tight inside pitching. Xavier had better luck. Working the count to full, he managed to lay off on a low throw that was called ball four.

"Really?" hollered the head Yankees coach. "Can't we get a break too?" The umpire glared toward him. Immediately the coach raised his hand in apology.

As Xavier tossed his bat to the side and headed to first, Chase banged the bench area between him and Dominic. "Hey, Dom," he said. "You're on deck. Grab a helmet."

Dominic whirled on him with a snarl. "Don't call me that!" he snapped.

Chase jerked back, startled. "Whoa, okay, man. But you're hitting after Liam."

Mr. Wells turned from where he sat on the bucket just outside the dugout. "Let's go, Dominic. Grab a bat," he called.

Dominic stood without looking at Chase. "Which bat?" he asked.

"Over here," Jimmy called from the front of the dugout. "We can find you one."

Grayson had started putting on his batting helmet since he would be due up after Dominic. "Here, Dominic, you can use mine," he said. He pulled out a light black bat and held it up.

Jimmy nodded in approval. A light bat would be easier for Dominic to handle. It wasn't likely he would hit anything anyway.

Dominic snatched the bat from Grayson with a grunt and took the helmet offered from Jimmy.

"Now what do I do?" he asked Jimmy, not looking him in the eye. He didn't have any batting gloves, but would probably not need them.

"Oh, you stand just there outside the dugout," Jimmy replied with a shrug. "You just practice swinging, you know. Um, try to watch the pitcher and get his timing."

Dominic pulled up short just before exiting the dugout. As usual, parents and kids lined the fence around the on-deck area. No amount of talking would budge him. He was saved when Liam sent a slow roller to the mound and Chris threw him out at first. Just like that, it was back to the field.

Phil took over on the mound for the Dodgers next inning and Xavier went behind the plate to do the catching. The quiet boy, as Jimmy suspected, proved very capable as catcher and seemed to get better every time.

Jimmy moved to the shortstop position while Chase remained in center and Dominic in right. With Shawn still playing at third, Grayson positioned at second, and long-armed Mike guarding first, the Dodger infield was like a wall no ground ball could hope to pass.

The outfield, though, was another story. While the pitcher warmed up, Chase just tossed the ball to Liam in left while Dominic stood awkwardly in right field, pretending to adjust his glove.

Jimmy ignored them. After infield practice where he showed off slick fielding and throwing, he settled back in his position.

A big kid batted first. After fouling off an inside fastball, he took the next pitch high into left. Liam played deep and lost the ball in the sun. It dropped a few feet from where he'd stood searching for it. Growling in frustration, he threw the ball to Jimmy.

The parents and fans of the Yankees started cheering loudly. Finally, something had gone their way.

"You stopped them cold last inning! Now heat them up with some hits!" yelled a father. "Come on, Yankees!"

This set off the Yankees dugout and the voices of boys started chanting.

Jimmy grinned as he walked the ball in. "It was just a lucky hit," he told Phil as he tossed the ball to the pitcher. "We got this."

Phil nodded and wiped his brow. "As long as they keep the ball out of right field," he said ruefully.

Shawn trotted in from third. "Just worry about the batter," he said. "One out at a time. We got your back."

Nodding his appreciation for the support, Phil went back to mound.

"No outs! Play's at second or first!" Xavier shouted to his teammates.

The next batter was a small kid who looked to belong in the first grade. By crouching low, his strike zone was about the size of a marshmallow. His bat never left his shoulder and Phil walked him in five pitches. This prompted more cheering from the Yankees' supporters.

Chris Chosworth batted next. He'd struck out back in the first as the leadoff hitter. Crouching low and waving his bat dangerously, he didn't look like another strike-out victim.

Phil wiped sweat from his face again. He waited for the sign from Xavier, who'd first got it from Mr. Gordon. Mr. Roseburg had called all the pitching signs for Grayson, but had wordlessly moved back when Phil took the mound.

"Just fire it in there clean," Mr. Gordon yelled. "Let's get a strikeout!"

Phil tried his best to listen to his dad, but perhaps tried too hard. His first pitch got away from him and landed in the dirt. Squirting by Xavier, it ended up at the backstop.

"Eat it!" yelled Mr. Gordon. "No throw!"

Both runners advanced and Xavier fired the ball back to Phil.

"Play's at first," he called with disgust.

Another bad pitch like that and the Yankees would have a run. Runners were on second and third with no outs. The crowds for both teams grew louder.

Phil's next pitch was a fastball outside for ball two. Then he went too high and Chris had a 3-0 count in his favor.

The third-base coach put both hands up and motioned Chris to relax. "Let him throw you a strike," he said. "Hold off the next one."

Breathing deeply, Phil placed the next pitch carefully over the plate.

Chris didn't hold off. He swung away and lifted a low liner toward right field.

Grayson ran back and dove for the ball, but came up just short. It cleared his glove by inches and bounced into the grass before rolling toward the wall.

Chase had shifted toward left field since Chris batted right. Now he ran to the right in hopeless frustration. Dominic was caught looking into the stands and hadn't seen the ball until it'd landed. Then he just stared.

"Get the ball!" yelled Mike from first.

Grayson, still stretched out on the dirt, pounded his fist in anger.

Then Dominic started moving. One run had scored and the second runner had rounded third. Chris already thought about second as he reached first.

Dominic reached the ball and hesitated on what do next.

"Dom!" screamed Chase. "Get the ball and throw it in!"

Dominic jerked up his head. An ugly look crossed his face. Suddenly the ball was in his hand and cocked back to throw. "I told you not to call me that!" he said in a snarl.

Chase, charging from center, jerked to a stop so fast he slid to his backside. His eyes held fear.

Dominic glared straight at him. For a short moment it looked as if Dominic meant to nail his centerfielder with the ball.

Then Mr. Wells's voice rang out. "Dominic!" he cried. "Throw the ball to Grayson!" It was the loudest any of his players heard him speak. Thankfully it had the desired effect.

Blinking, Dominic shook his head as if trying to clear it and turned from Chase. He threw the ball clumsily to the second baseman. Grayson had to run forward and take it on the bounce. By that time Chris was already halfway home. No throw came and the Yankees suddenly had three runs.

"What in the world," Chase said, getting to his feet. "What were you doing, man?" he asked Dominic, still sounding shaken.

Dominic turned his back to him. "I told you not to call me that."

"Yeah," said Chase bitterly. "I'll call you something else. Like crazy."

Dominic just stalked away from him.

The inning ended soon after. Phil got three straight grounders that were each turned into quick outs. But the damage was done.

As the Yankees ran onto the field, they had an extra hop in their steps. On the other side, the Dodgers entered the dugout in a daze. There was no pep talk this time. Mr. Wells waved the players into the dugout while motioning Dominic to come to him.

"Did you see that?" whispered Liam to Will as they entered. "Dominic was going nail Chase in the head!"

"All right," Mr. Roseburg said, "Get your heads back in the game. That was good defense in the end. Who's hitting next?"

Mr. Gordon snorted as he headed out to coach third. "You don't want to know," he muttered.

Mr. Roseburg pushed back his cap and shrugged. "This should be interesting," he said. He turned and watched where Mr. Wells walked with Dominic away from the dugout.

The coach stopped the player behind first base. He knelt down and peered carefully at Dominic's face. "Son," he said, "I hope you weren't going to throw that ball at Chase. Were you?"

Dominic shrugged.

Sighing, Mr. Wells shook his head. "That will never happen again. You got me? Do something like that and you can't be on this field." Dominic went rigid. "Calm down,"

Mr. Wells said, softening his voice. "Just promise you won't even think about hitting another player with the ball."

Dominic dropped his eyes. "Okay," he said. "I won't. But he better not call me Dom again."

Mr. Wells's voice grew hard. "Not good enough. Look at me when you say it."

Dominic looked up quickly. "I won't!" Then he pulled away from the coach and dashed to the dugout. Mr. Roseburg tried to intercept him, but Dominic ran right by him.

"Where're you going?" demanded Jimmy's father.

"I have to bat!" Dominic said. "It's my turn!"

Still kneeling down, Mr. Wells suddenly looked his age. He waved a hand at Mr. Roseburg. "Let him go," he said tiredly. "Just keep an eye on him. If he starts swinging the bat at somebody, we may need to tackle him."

Jimmy silently handed Dominic his batting helmet and Grayson's bat. None of the other players looked their way. Many had angry looks on their faces. The Yankees had three runs they didn't deserve. All because of one player.

Dominic managed to hold himself together. When the umpire motioned him to the plate, he walked stiffly to the plate and stood awkwardly in the box. The barrel of the bat rested on his shoulder and he squeezed his hands tightly around the handle keeping them close to his chest.

The Yankees coaches must have known about him, because they shushed their team. The spectators also remained silent. They didn't quite know what had happened, but they knew this was not a time to yell.

Mr. Gordon and Mr. Roseburg stared intently from their base coach positions and looked ready to rush in at any sign of trouble.

Chris, still on the mound, coolly ignored the drama. Staring only at the catcher, he delivered three easy pitches that Dominic swung at each time.

"Strike three!" announced the umpire on the last one. Dominic missed by several feet on each pitch. Instead of getting angry, he just made a face before trudging back to the dugout. He only paused to give the bat back to Grayson, who headed to the plate.

"I don't like it," Dominic said. "It's too light."

Grayson took it with a surprised look.

In the dugout, Jimmy and Shawn exchanged glances. Dominic acted as if nothing had happened. He even offered some hitting advice as he made his way to the end of the bench. "That pitcher throws too slow," he said. "You guys could hit him easily."

"What a weirdo," Chase mouthed at Jimmy.

Jimmy shrugged and stepped into the on-deck area. He was due up next and needed to focus. Hitting, like pitching, required blocking everything out. Chris was a good pitcher and the Dodgers only led by two. They needed more runs.

If they were to come, it would have to be up to Jimmy. Grayson got called out on strikes on a low pitch just below his knees. He bit his lip as he turned back to the dugout. His eyes were watering as he took a seat just inside.

"Next time, bud," Mr. Wells said absently. "Next time you'll get it."

As Jimmy stepped to the plate, the fans started being heard again. The Yankees' supporters especially grew loud.

"One more out, Chris!" shouted a parent. "We got these all-star showboats!"

Jimmy calmly called for time and stepped out of the box. Taking one more swing, he crouched back in.

"Heavy hitter!" shouted the Yankees head coach. "Back up in the outfield!"

Wanting to back up the man's words, Jimmy swung hard on the first pitch. It was a fastball down by his knees. He barely clipped the top of it and sent a slow roller back to the mound.

Dropping his bat in frustration, Jimmy left the box for first just as Chris picked up the ball. He was out by a mile.

In the top of the fourth, the only change in the Dodgers' positions was switching Grayson and Chase. Will had been scheduled to play right that inning, but Dominic had taken his glove and immediately headed that way without being told otherwise. Mr. Wells kept his mouth shut and shrugged. Finally, he said, "We'll sit Dominic the last two innings. Will, Tom, you guys mind sitting once more?"

Mr. Roseburg shot Mr. Wells a look, but kept his mouth shut.

"If that boy was mine," Mr. Gordon growled softly as he moved to where he could deliver the pitching signs. "He wouldn't sit for a week."

"Maybe that's his problem," Mr. Wells said evenly. "All he knows is anger and violence when things go wrong. Don't worry," he added. "I'll deal with him next inning."

The Yankees smelled blood and tried to pounce early.

The first batter swung hard on the first pitch from Phil and managed a foul. Then, on the second pitch, he suddenly dropped his bat and delivered a perfect bunt down toward third. Shawn was caught playing deep and had no play. By the time Phil grabbed the slow roller, the batter stood safely at first.

The next batter tried the same thing. After bunting the first pitch foul, he sent a slow roller toward first. This time the Dodgers were ready. Xavier jumped from his catching position, throwing off the mask. He barehanded the ball and threw the runner out at first by a step.

Finally, the Dodgers' fans had something to cheer about. However, a base runner remained on second. The next batter, a short stocky kid, batted lefty.

"Lefty!" cried Jimmy. "Watch out in right field!" He looked over at Grayson. "He's a pull hitter, Gray!"

On his first at bat, the lefty had grounded out to first. There was no doubt he wanted something a little higher, but in the same direction.

Grayson shifted closer to Dominic. "Get ready, Dominic," he said. "It might come your way."

Dominic grunted. "If it comes near me, it's mine," he stated firmly. He'd started watching baseball with Mack and was getting a better understanding of the game. He knew players were covering for him and he was tired of it. He just had to keep in control…

The next pitch ended with a solid clink as the lefty lifted the ball over Chase, positioned between second and first. It was a shallow fly that started to drop in shallow right.

"I got it!" yelled Grayson, charging in from his center position. He never saw Dominic.

The larger boy wanted to make amends for his past actions. He knew he'd messed up with Chase. He also knew he could help the team. He just needed to show them. As the ball headed in his direction, Dominic raced after it with one intention. Get the ball.

Dominic wasn't stupid. The night before Mack had asked what position Dominic played. He'd laughed when Dominic told him right field. "That's where you belong— that's where the daisy pickers go," he'd told Dominic.

Dominic had never played baseball before being on the Dodgers. At first he felt like a newborn learning to swim. But, like Mr. Wells said, by watching he was learning. He'd show Mr. Wells and Mack that he wasn't out there just to pick flowers.

Eyes on the ball, he held his glove out. Then at the last moment, he saw the ball getting bigger and dropping fast. He also saw a blur of blue and white cross into his path.

Dominic closed his eyes just before impact.

13

Grayson had the ball lined up and was just about to dive for it when something big smashed into his side. He went flying headfirst before crashing hard into the grass. His chin bounced and his stomach landed on his glove. Suddenly he lost his wind and saw nothing but spots.

Jimmy watched in disbelief from his shortstop position. Dominic had run right into the smaller Grayson with his elbow extended. The ball ended up striking Dominic in the thigh and shooting forward. Dominic kept his feet and looked wildly for it. He totally ignored the prone player he'd just run over.

Chase ran into the field from second base. "What are you doing, you crazy?" he shouted. Snatching up the ball, he nearly faked a throw at Dominic's head, but knew better. Already one run scored. Turning, he threw to Jimmy, who covered second. It came late and the lefty batter ended up with a bizarre standup double.

Dominic stood blinking in confusion. "I had it. It was my ball," he said. "I had it."

Chase shook his head. "The whole team heard Gray call it, man," he said.

Grayson slowly got to his feet. Tears of shock and hurt filled his eyes. Wiping them away, he gestured to the umpire and coaches that he was fine. He didn't even look at Dominic. The umpire at second still called time and went over to check to make sure Grayson hadn't banged his head. A green smear marked his chin, but otherwise he appeared healthy.

Dominic stared blankly at him. Then he kicked the grass angrily.

"Time!" Mr. Wells yelled. "I want to make a switch in right field."

Dominic actually looked grateful as he trotted off the field to be replaced by Will. He still threw down his glove and kicked it as he headed for his seat. Tom shrank back from him as he passed.

"Hey!" snapped Mr. Gordon. "Treat your glove with respect!"

Dominic ignored him and Mr. Wells put a hand on the assistant coach's shoulder. "I got this," he said. "You take over."

Once again Mr. Wells sat next to Dominic. "Okay, Dominic," the old coach said, "what's wrong?"

Dominic shrugged his shoulders and kicked his leg at the floor.

Mr. Wells sighed and said, "Two innings in a row you messed up. How come?"

"Because I'm stupid," Dominic said. "I don't know what I'm doing."

Mr. Wells frowned and shifted his body to face Dominic. "Now you listen here, Dominic. You're not stupid. I've spoken to your mom on the phone. You're actually the opposite." Suddenly Mr. Wells peered at Dominic as if seeing him for the first time. "Hey, you've taken your medicine today, haven't you? Your mom mentioned that you take pills every morning."

Dominic shook his head. "I left too early," he mumbled.

"Okay, Dominic," said Mr. Wells, patting his shoulder. "I understand. Tell you what. You said you don't know what to do out there, right? That I can agree with. But you're not stupid. Why don't you and I spend the rest of the game here and I'll give you pointers. Okay?"

Dominic shrugged. "Fine," he said.

So for the rest of the game Mr. Wells sat with Dominic and tried his best to explain the game of baseball to a confused, angry boy who hadn't had his medicine.

The game ended two innings later. Riding high with momentum, the Yankees scored three more in the fourth and never looked back. The game ended when Grayson grounded out with Jimmy on deck. The Yankees won 7-5. All of a sudden, the Dodgers were beatable.

On the next field, the Cardinals took care of the Blue Jays 12-2.

"Stupid mercy rule," Mr. Gordon muttered, biting down curse words as he remembered the first inning. "If we didn't have that…"

Nobody disagreed, but more than one set of eyes looked to where Dominic continued to sit in the dugout. It resembled a doghouse in a lot of ways.

Somehow Dominic still made it to Jimmy's pool party. It turned out Sara and Rick spent most of the game walking on the nature paths in Northeast Sports Park and missed all the excitement. They hadn't, though, missed being invited to the party by Mrs. Roseburg. After the game finished and the players were dismissed with snacks and drinks, they appeared as if by magic and asked Mrs. Roseburg for directions. Not knowing what else to say, she told them they could follow their van.

The pool party did not begin like a party at all. It started more like a funeral.

Jimmy lounged with Chase and Shawn on the wooden deck by the pool. The boys lay on pool chairs in their bathing suits and sunglasses soaking up the rays. Even in the hot afternoon sun, nobody felt like swimming. Grayson had been torn up after the game—he left the field in tears after grounding out. He would be coming later since, so his father explained, he'd forgotten his swimsuit. Perhaps with Dominic there, he wouldn't show up.

Jimmy's parents were inside with Dominic's sister and stupid boyfriend. It turned out that the boyfriend was studying to be a psychologist and claimed to know all about Dominic's condition. On the way inside the house Jimmy heard him launch into an explanation to his father of how Dominic was a walking time bomb and couldn't control his actions. All of this while Dominic followed with his sister.

Not surprisingly, Dominic had refused to join the boys. At the first mention of swimming in the pool he'd retreated from the conversation and ended up in the living room watching television…with Brittany.

Chase shot a look in that direction. "What do you think they're doing in there?" he asked. They'd been lounging for nearly ten minutes.

Shawn made a kissing noise and immediately Jimmy rolled from his chair and gave him a hard slap on his bare back.

"Ouch!" Shawn yelped. "That hurt!"

"Good," Jimmy said, shoving Shawn's chair, nearly toppling his friend. "Because there's more where that came from. Don't you dare insult Dominic like that again."

Chase raised his head and gave Jimmy a hard look. "Why do you keep defending him? Look, your friendship plan is a complete failure. Grayson tried it and look what happened to him."

Jimmy shook his head. "That was just an accident," he said unconvincingly. "Dominic didn't know what he was doing."

"Right," said Chase caustically. "What about with me? I tried being nice and he just about took my head off with a beanball."

Jimmy sat on the side of his chair and scratched his stomach. "Well, you probably deserved it."

"Yeah, all I did was call him Dom," Chase protested.

"Who cares?" Jimmy said. "He just doesn't know baseball. It's not really his fault. Besides, we still did pretty good."

Shawn rolled to his side and raised his eyebrows. "Really?" he said in mock surprise. "We did 'good'? We lost the game, remember?"

Jimmy stood and stretched his arms over his head. "Well, you can't win them all. I seem to remember having a pretty good hit."

Chase frowned. "All you care about is your stupid batting average," he said sourly.

"Not true," Jimmy said. "I also care about my amazing abs." He sucked in his breath, throwing out his skinny chest while flexing both arms on either side of him.

Chase and Shawn both raised their eyebrows and exchanged looks. They seemed to read each other's mind.

"Should we?" Chase asked.

"Let's," Shawn replied.

Together, they suddenly lunged from their chairs and grabbed Jimmy. Chase got him around the chest and Shawn lifted him by the legs.

"Hey!" cried Jimmy, trying to squirm free. "Ow! Let go!"

"Oh, no," Shawn said. "You're too hot, showboat. We need to cool you off."

With that, Jimmy was carried bodily to the edge of the pool, his kicking and screaming having no affect.

"One," counted Chase, "two, three!"

He and Shawn swung Jimmy back and forth and then sent him flying into the pool. He landed with a loud splash and came up spitting.

"You guys are so dead," he spluttered.

"Maybe you should go get your friend to help," Chase said, standing on the side of the pool. "I mean, we can paper-rock-scissors all you want, but I think it's your turn to be nice to him."

"Maybe I should," Jimmy said. He paddled to the where his friends stood. "Here, somebody help me up."

Shawn bent down and offered a hand. Immediately Jimmy grabbed it with both of his and lunged backwards.

With a yell of alarm, Shawn went headfirst into the water.

Chase started to laugh but suddenly was shoved from the back. His arms windmilled wildly as he too fell in the water. Grayson had arrived from around the front and had managed to sneak up behind him.

"Nice shot, Gray!" Jimmy shouted.

Shawn and Chase both came up coughing. At seeing Grayson, Chase let out a deep breath. "Man," he said. "I was afraid you were Dominic trying to kill me at first."

Grayson kicked off a pair of flip-flops and sat on the edge putting his legs in the water. He'd changed into a Marlins T-shirt and bright red bathing suit, but his chin still bore a green stain over a purple bruise. "Is he still here?" he asked.

"Oh, yeah," Shawn said, eyeing Jimmy beside him. "He's in the house with Jimmy's sister. They're…just watching TV."

"Good save," Jimmy said, still looking ready to pounce.

"I hope it's something like Barney," Chase muttered. "That guy can use some love."

Grayson kicked water at him. "Or maybe he watches it too much at home and it drives him crazy."

"Oh, you mean like this?" Chase dove toward the wall and grabbed Grayson's feet.

"Hey, wait!" Grayson cried. "At least let me take my shirt off!"

"We'll help you," Shawn assured him. "Pull him under, Chase. His dry humor needs to get soaked."

With a yelp, the boy went under and his shirt floated to the surface.

As Grayson surfaced, sputtering and coughing, the mood lightened considerably. All four boys were in and all their troubles seemed to float away. After water wrestling, they'd started a game of Marco Polo when Chase suddenly yelled for everyone to stop.

"What's wrong?" Shawn asked. "Did you lose your suit?"

"Shut it!" snapped Chase, flushing. "Look who's here!"

The boys in the water all turned to the porch. Shawn gulped loudly. "What I said was just a joke," he said quickly.

Brittany peered down from the porch with her arms crossed. Looking lost and hopeful at the same time, Dominic stood next to her. He wore an undershirt over a pair of baggy swim trunks that Jimmy recognized as his dad's old ones. A mixture of fear and longing covered the awkward boy's face.

Brittany had on her pink bathing suit and carried a towel. She looked down at the boys in the pool and shook her head sadly.

"We came out here to find intelligent life," she said. "Apparently none of you have evolved far enough to qualify."

Jimmy flung a handful of water towards her. "Why are you really out here?" he asked scornfully.

"To swim, moron," Brittany replied. "But first I want you all to come here and have a talk. Dominic and I have some things to say to you."

Jimmy looked toward the sky as he sighed heavily. "Don't tell me you were talking to that psycho psychologist in there. Dominic, whatever you do, don't listen to her."

Brittany's cheeks glowed a deep crimson. "For your information, that's why I'm out here with Dominic. That guy is a complete fruitcake. He's trying to say he can hypnotize Dominic into behaving normally. Dominic, no offense, but there's no such thing as normal and you're not crazy. Now, Jimmy, bring your stupid little behind over here with your friends." Her voice grew hard and sweet at the same time.

Jimmy didn't try to argue anymore. The two siblings teased each other without mercy, especially at home with friends. Despite this, they had a fierce bond that nobody could break. Secretly they supported each other in their separate sports pursuits. Brittany had watched the entire game against the Yankees from the stands. She always cheered Jimmy's successes and mourned his failures. He did the same with her in softball.

"Come on, guys, and let's get this over with," he said to others. He swam to the edge of the pool and pulled himself from the water. The others quickly followed and soon the kids formed a circle on the deck to have their talk.

Brittany began by clearing her throat. "This is about Dominic," she said.

"No kidding, but he's right here," interrupted Jimmy. "He can speak too."

Immediately Brittany smacked the back of her brother's dripping back. "And you can shut your mouth and not speak," she said sharply.

"Ouch!" Jimmy cried, squeezing his eyes shut and arching his back in pain. He'd made the mistake of sitting next to his sister.

"See, I told you it hurts," Shawn muttered next to him.

Dominic squirmed from the other side of Brittany. "I know I can speak," he started to say, but Brittany quickly interrupted him.

"Remember what I said," she said hastily. "Let me talk first. Then you can talk. Promise."

"Great," muttered Jimmy. "We could be here for days." He flinched when Brittany made to raise her hand for another smack.

"That's better," Brittany said sweetly. "Listen, guys. I usually don't care about your stupid games, but I've been talking to Dominic. There're some things you should know about him."

She proceeded to tell them about how Dominic's dad died when he was three and how he lived in a trailer with a boyfriend of his mom's who didn't like him. All the good attention went to his little sister. He did nothing for fun but play video games, but mostly stayed in his room by himself. He didn't know why he did so many bad things. Sometimes, Brittany told them, he just got too angry to think properly.

"That's what happened today on the field, Chase," she said, looking at the boy across from her. Chase gulped and ducked his head. "You see," Brittany continued, "his mom's boyfriend calls him Dom." Then she went on to tell how nobody ever bothered to understand Dominic and how he always wanted to be part of a team.

The whole time the other boys sat as if wrapped in a spell. Jimmy eyed his sister with new respect. She should work for the police, he decided. She would be able to get even the most hardened criminals to confess their crimes.

When finished, Brittany turned to Dominic. "Now he wants to ask you something."

Dominic spent the time Brittany spoke with his head down, extremely embarrassed. Now he looked up and wet his lips. "Uh, I, uh, just wanted to know if I could go swimming too."

Shawn threw back his head and laughed. "Why didn't you say so, man?" he cried. "All you had to do was ask."

"Yeah," Jimmy said with a grin. "We would've dragged you in or thrown you in."

Brittany shook her head and rolled her eyes. "You're welcome," she said.

"For what?" Jimmy asked. "Getting us out of the water? Look, let the boys handle this one, sis." At the same time, he patted the back of her head in real gratitude. Then with a whoop, ran off the porch and leapt into the water.

Brittany couldn't help but smile. Sometimes it felt good to have a younger brother. Chase didn't join the other boys as they raced after Jimmy. He sat in stunned silence and watched them go.

Dominic went in last, his shirt covering any markings he wanted to hide. Brittany guessed about the markings. She only knew Dominic had refused to even consider swimming until she'd mentioned that he could wear a shirt. She hoped the boy just felt embarrassed about his round belly. She feared the worst.

Then she turned to Chase and smiled. "Okay, so what do you want to say?" she asked.

"Oh, uh, uh, I mean, thanks, I guess." Chase scratched his knee and couldn't meet Brittany's gaze. "I kind of acted like a jerk to Dominic. I didn't know about him and all…that stuff."

"It's not your fault," Brittany said reasonably. "He's on medicine, you know. He didn't take it today. Anyway, forget about all that. Where'd you learn to hit like you do?"

Chase couldn't help but perk up. "Well, I—"

Brittany interrupted. "Because you're good, but there're some serious flaws in your swing."

"What?!"

"You back away from the plate too much and leave too much of a strike zone. And—"

"Jimmy, help!" Chase burst out, backing away. "Your sister is ambushing me!"

"Welcome to the family!" Jimmy called out. "Jump in before it gets worse!"

Brittany only sighed as Chase hastily got up and sprinted down the porch before diving into the pool. "Boys…they'll learn some day," she said mostly to herself.

14

The afternoon passed quickly after that. Driven out by Rick's incessant chatter about his qualifications, Mr. Roseburg started the grill early and soon the wonderful smell of cooking steak filled the air. Brittany and Chase resumed their conversation on the porch while the other boys invented new water sports, such as body baseball.

Body baseball, an invention of Jimmy and Shawn, became, well, a hit. It involved somebody throwing a large inflated beach ball toward the edge of the long side of the pool where the "batter" stood. The "batter" would then launch his body at the ball and try to knock it past the outfielders set up behind the pitcher. A hit resulted if the batter managed to swim to the opposite side before being tagged by the ball. A run scored if he made it safely back to the side where he started from. Any ball smacked clear to the other side of pool without touching water qualified as an automatic home run.

Nobody was very good at it, but it resulted in spectacular dives, tremendous fails, and lots of laughter. Grayson and Shawn teamed up against Jimmy and Dominic.

The boy who loved it the most, amazingly, was Dominic. None of the other boys had seen him smile before, or heard him laughing so much. Spurred by his joy, the game ramped up into a rambunctious free-for-all.

With the score tied at three, Jimmy got set to pitch as Grayson readied to "hit"…or to be hit. This was when the other adults finally exited the house to join the party.

As Mrs. Roseburg took Sara to see the flowers growing on the side of the porch, Rick moved closer to the pool to "observe" Dominic closely. What he saw was a very happy boy standing chest deep in water telling Jimmy to throw the ball as hard as he could. What he didn't see was Grayson standing several feet behind him to get a running start. Perhaps if he understood the game, things would have ended differently.

Jimmy reared back and threw the ball toward the pool's edge. Rick thought the ball was meant for him and went to go catch it. By this time Grayson had already started his run. He began his jump just when Rick moved into his view. He let off a strangled yell before his knees plowed into Rick's back. He then went flying wildly. Boy and future psychologist plunged into the water with terrific splashes.

The adults turned at hearing the noise. Sara screamed. Mr. Roseburg, who'd set up the grill near the back of the porch, far from the pool, dropped his tongs and raced to where the accident occurred.

Rick's head burst from the water and he shouted an inappropriate word. "Who did that?" he yelled next, his eyes flashing.

Grayson surfaced next to him in time to hear the question. "I-I'm sorry," he sputtered. "I didn't see you." His voice quavered and he looked ready to cry.

Rick, his ruined suit and tie plastered to his skin, gave a murderous look at the boy and slammed a fist into the water.

Mr. Roseburg quickly bent down and scooped up Grayson by the shoulders. He pulled the boy from the water and sat him firmly on the cement next to him. Then he turned to Rick. "I'm sorry this happened," he said coolly, "but we don't allow language like that at my house."

Rick wiped water from his face and snarled. "That little mon—"

"It was an accident," Mr. Roseburg said firmly. "Now let me help you out and you can maybe go home and get new clothes."

"I won't be coming back," Rick said, extending his hand.

Mr. Roseburg didn't seem too upset by this as he pulled the young man from the pool.

"I understand," he said evenly. "I'm sure the boys will be sorry to see you go."

On dry land, Rick glared once more at Grayson and then over at Sara. "Come, Sara," he said stiffly. "We're leaving."

"What about Dominic?" Sara said, frowning. "Come on, Rick. He's having the time of his life!"

"Oh, he can stay," Mrs. Roseburg said immediately. Then she flinched. "Right?"

"Yeah!" Jimmy called from the pool. "We can give him a ride home, right, Dad? We need him to be on my team."

Mr. Roseburg frowned but it turned into a surprised open mouth when both Chase and Shawn echoed Jimmy's thoughts. Grayson still looked to be about to cry, but also managed a nod. Mr. Roseburg couldn't understand it. He didn't think the boys would ever get along with Dominic after the Yankees game, or would even want to make the effort.

"Sure we can," he said simply. Then an evil look entered his eyes. "Why not invite him for a sleepover?"

Rick had mentioned over three times he'd never trust Dominic sleeping under the same roof as him.

His face growing red, Rick stomped from the backyard heading to his car. "I'll be waiting there," he said gruffly to Sara. He never said goodbye.

As Sara raced inside with Mrs. Roseburg to make plans for the hastily arranged sleepover, Mr. Roseburg knelt in front of Grayson.

"You've had a whale of a day, son," he said gravely. "First you get steamrolled by a teammate, and now you steamroll an opponent." Then he smiled and tousled

Grayson's wet hair. "And let me tell you. That was the greatest play I've ever seen. Don't feel bad at all. If anybody deserved a soaked head, it was that guy."

Grayson blinked away his tears and managed a small smile.

Things fell quickly into place. The next day was Sunday and Grayson needed to be home for church. But Chase and Shawn were given permission to join the sleepover with Jimmy and Dominic.

Mrs. Roseburg had more trouble reaching Dominic's mom. Her first couple of attempts only reached voice mail. Shocked by the turn of events, Dominic had mentioned how they'd found the cell phone charger under the couch, so his mom should have a phone. Looking slightly worried, Jimmy's mom made the call one last time.

When Dominic's mom did finally answer and heard it was about Dominic, she'd immediately started apologizing. After hearing about the overnight invitation, she sounded stunned. Shortly after, she started thanking Mrs. Roseburg profusely. Before heading off to work that night she promised to stop by and drop off Dominic's overnight things. She had no problem with the Roseburgs taking Dominic to church with them the next morning. Any church, she assured Mrs. Roseburg, that preached peace and love was just fine with her.

Before Sara left with Rick, who sat stewing in the car in his soaked suit, she pulled Dominic aside.

Kneeling in the grass by the pool, she took her wet brother's arm and stared into his eyes.

"Listen, little brother," she said, "I'm really happy you're having a good time." She bit her lip. "And I'm also sorry about Rick. I thought he would be different than Mack, but he's just a different type." Then she looked serious. "Has he been hitting you again? Has Mack hurt you?"

Dominic shrugged and looked away. His shirt stuck to his skin and hid all the bruises. "When will I see you again?" he said, avoiding the question.

"Oh," said Sara, smiling sadly, "soon. I didn't tell you, but I had to leave my apartment. Nursing school is getting too expensive. I'm moving back into the trailer. Sorry, but you're going to have to move back with Rose for a little while. I'll have to take your room. Is that okay?"

Dominic nodded. "Yeah. Will you still bring me some books?"

"Of course, silly! I still have my job. Now go back and have a good time." She patted his shoulder. "I'll go back with Rick, but promise to borrow Mom's car and come straight back with your overnight clothes and toothbrush. Okay?"

Both siblings knew their mom often made promises she didn't keep. Dominic gave his sister a hug and said it would be okay. Sara did her best not to mind his soaked body and grinned.

That night after a full meal of steaks, chips, grilled vegetables, baked beans, and coleslaw, with cookies and ice cream for dessert, the boys were stuffed. Dominic had three helpings of everything and literally licked his plate clean. The other boys politely ignored it as Mrs. Roseburg happily kept the food coming.

Finished eating, they'd gone back out and played tag in the backyard around the pool until the sun fully set and Mrs. Roseburg called them in. Grayson had left during the game of tag—so exhausted that his dad nearly had to carry him to the car. The four boys slumped back into the house, also feeling ready to collapse. They needed no urging to get ready for bed.

"First shower is mine!" Shawn yelled, stumbling up the stairs to the deck.

"No way!" protested Chase. "Come on, I sweated way more than you!"

"Is that sweat or drool?" Shawn asked him, smiling wickedly.

Jimmy gave them both a hard look. "Whatever, idiots. Dominic hits the shower first. My mom's orders."

"Okay," Dominic said with a shrug. "I'll try to go fast."

None of the boys argued. They knew Dominic probably hadn't had a shower in days.

"Take your time," Shawn told him. "There's a baseball game I wanted to watch anyway." He glanced at Chase. "And I think Brittany's already watching it."

"With my dad," Jimmy said sharply. "And you two stinkheads better sit on the floor. You're both filthy."

He left them to guide Dominic to the second-floor shower. During dessert Sara had stopped by and dropped off a change of clothes for Dominic, including pajama pants and a T-shirt. She didn't bring Rick with her.

Dominic waited for Jimmy to leave before easing off his shirt. It had dried from the swimming, but now once again dripped, this time with sweat. He eyed the greenish bruises mixed with the darker purple ones. Then he quickly shook his head. He didn't want to think about Mack right now.

Looking around the bathroom, easily the size of his old bedroom, that now would be Sara's room, he couldn't keep his mouth from dropping. The gleaming counter, glistening toilet, and extra-large tub were nothing like he was used to.

"This is amazing," he mumbled, not believing his good fortune as he started undressing.

He didn't mean to, but he spent a long time under the hot water…washing away dirt, sweat, and a lot of bad memories.

Later, the boys settled to sleep in sleeping bags on the floor of Jimmy's room. Dominic had been given Mr. Roseburg's bag to use. After everyone showered, changed into pajamas, and had brushed teeth, the last overseen by Mrs. Roseburg, the boys settled into their bags and tried to start up a conversation.

Usually sleepovers meant no sleep and lots of video games, but the day had been so full that none of the boys could find the energy to turn a game on. In fact, not one protested when Mrs. Roseburg put her head in and turned out the lights.

Then Dominic started talking.

"I should warn you guys," he said, "sometimes I wake up screaming at night."

Chase, who'd been just drifting off, sat up. "What?" he asked. "You wake up screaming?"

"Yeah, really loud," Dominic said seriously. "I mean real loud. One time I woke up the neighbors. Oh, and I also sleepwalk sometimes."

Shawn couldn't help it. Dominic sounded so casual about it, like he was explaining his rock collection. He started laughing and Chase soon joined him.

"What?" Dominic said. "I'm serious. I do."

"Sorry, man, really," Chase said finally. "Just don't step on me. Then I'll wake up screaming."

"Shut up," Jimmy murmured from his bag. "As long as nobody rips one, we'll be fine."

A loud nasty noise sounded seconds later. "That was me," Shawn apologized. "Sorry."

"I hate you all," Jimmy muttered. All four were out like lights shortly after. Nobody woke up screaming—or if they did, they were too tired to remember.

The sleepover proved to be a huge success. All four boys ended up attending church with the Roseburg family and then they went out for a big brunch at a pancake house. Once again Dominic ate as if he'd never seen food before and managed to spill syrup on his pants, but nobody seemed to notice. The boys laughed and carried on like teammates. Brittany and her parents watched it all with a mixture of amazement and amusement. Everyone had a good time.

After dropping Dominic off after pancakes, Jimmy really thought they'd seen the last of Dominic's tantrums. The whole time when at his house and at church, Dominic had acted like a different person. He was polite, followed directions, and seemed like a happy kid. This way of thinking lasted until Tuesday when the Dodgers next met for practice. That was when everything fell apart.

The practice began normally—first were the usual warm-up drills consisting of catching, running, and stretching. Then Mr. Wells had the boys stand in a line near home to go over hitting drills and bunting. All obeyed, except one.

Dominic walked to the mound and stood firmly in the center. Mr. Roseburg and Mr. Gordon had arrived earlier that day to bring out the artificial mound so they could simulate game situations like defending a bunt.

"Dominic," Mr. Wells said patiently, "I asked everyone to stand over here."

Dominic pursed his lips and banged his glove against his thigh. "I want to pitch," he said. "You said I could pitch last practice. I'm ready now."

"Look, Dominic," Mr. Gordon said sharply, "now is not the time. Move with the rest of the team."

The boy on the mound shook his head and banged his thigh again.

Jimmy started to speak, but his dad looked at him sharply and shook his head. Dominic would have to learn to obey even when he didn't want to. None of the other boys dared to speak. They couldn't believe anyone would challenge Mr. Wells like this.

For a moment Mr. Wells looked confused, but then he sighed. He turned his back on Dominic and started talking to the team as if Dominic wasn't there. As he did so, he walked backwards toward the mound.

When reaching the mound's edge, he nodded at Mr. Gordon. "Go ahead and continue. I'm going to talk with Dominic for a minute."

As Mr. Gordon droned on about timing the pitcher and the proper bunting techniques, Mr. Wells turned to Dominic and stared at him. The boy stared back. Standing elevated on the mound with the coach off, they were almost even in height. After a long moment, Mr. Wells licked his lips. "Dominic," he said softly, "a pitcher needs discipline. You know what that is, right?"

Dominic bit his lower lip and dropped his gaze. "I just want to pitch," he muttered. "I'm tired of doing nothing for the team."

Mr. Wells nodded as if understanding. "That may be so, but you need to listen and follow directions. Otherwise you'll only hurt the team and yourself." He sighed. "More importantly, I can't have you pitch to batters until you know and I know you won't throw the ball at them on purpose, or on accident. Pitching with no batter is very different than when there's a live human being standing there. I'm being honest with you. Now you need to come join the team. You'll get your chance when you're ready. Now is not the time."

Dominic scrunched his nose. "I won't throw at anybody," he said again, "I just want to pitch."

"Dominic," said the old coach, sounding tired, "if you listen—"

"No!" Dominic suddenly screamed. "Why won't you let me pitch?" Then he flung his glove in Mr. Wells's face and raced from the mound. He left the field and disappeared around the school.

Mr. Roseburg move to give chase, but Mr. Wells told him to stop. "He's just going home," he said tiredly. "There's a path in the trees behind the fence he's going to. Let's go ahead and start the drills."

Mr. Roseburg nodded, but then called Jimmy to him. Tapping two fingers on his son's shoulder, he told him to go fetch an extra bucket of balls from the shed. "Just in case," he added.

Jimmy nodded in understanding. Just in case Dominic was hiding in the shed, or worse, messing it up, Jimmy was sent to check.

He trotted from the field with his mind a jumble of thoughts. Why did Dominic act the way he did? Why couldn't he just go along with everyone else? At the same time, he remembered what Brittany said on Saturday at the pool. Dominic lived a hard life. A life that Jimmy couldn't ever imagine living himself. He just had to try to understand.

He reached the shed and saw nobody around. The basketball courts were empty behind it. The shed's door did hang open slightly.

"Dominic?" he called out tentatively. He was sure he heard movement from inside—a faint bump like somebody ran into something. "You in there?" he walked to the door and pulled it open. It squeaked loudly and Jimmy nearly jumped at the sudden noise.

The outside had a fresh coat of green paint that gave it a friendly appearance. But the inside walls were stark and bare, except for cobwebs. Immediately the odor of old wood, linseed oil, and something else, a funny smell, socked him in the face, causing his eyes to water. The funny smell wasn't something he'd smelled before and it carried a sharp sting that burned his nose.

Frowning, Jimmy wiped his nose and hesitantly entered the shed. "Dominic?" he called.

There was no light to turn on and it looked and felt like walking into a giant mouth that ate junk.

Garden tools, batting helmets, bats, buckets of baseballs and softballs, and cans of paint were just some of the things found in the assortment of odds and ends gathered over the years. Most of it was hidden by shadow. Jimmy couldn't shake the creepy feeling of walking into a dangerous cave.

"Dominic, are you in here?" Jimmy said louder. Not a noise answered. Suddenly it became too quiet.

Long shelves hung from the ceiling on either side where the old wooden and metal bats were stored.

Then from the back of the shed, he heard a faint sneeze. At the same time, he smelled smoke beneath the strange sharp smell.

"Hey, Dominic," Jimmy said, "what are you do—"

He never got a chance to finish.

A noise above caused him to stop and look up—which he did just in time to see a bag of bats fall straight at him. He didn't even have time to cry out before it smashed into his head, just above his right eye. Immediately the impact sent him crashing to the ground.

As his body collapsed, he saw stars and heard the clatter of metal bats banging together. Then darkness clouded his vision. Dimly aware that he lay on his side with his cheek pressed on the hard wooden floor, he thought he heard voices above him.

He tried to call out, but only managed a tiny cough. Pain quickly took over.

Everything throbbed and he couldn't open his eyes. Strong hands grabbed around his ankles and dragged his body across the shed. Dirt and old dust filled his mouth and nose as his cheek scraped hard wood. He'd managed to close his mouth and cough louder.

Spitting, he called out weakly, "D-Dom…" At once his ankles were dropped and footsteps scurried away. He thought he heard a muffled curse, but couldn't be sure. Everything started to swim… Darkness came soon after, carrying away the pain, and his body went still.

15

Jimmy's absence didn't raise concern until several minutes later. Mr. Wells wanted to divide the team into groups and go over more intense bunting drills while the other coaches worked on pop flies in the outfield. The only problem, there was only a single bucket of balls out for practice.

"Didn't you send Jimmy for more baseballs?" Mr. Wells asked Mr. Roseburg, almost sounding annoyed. "Isn't he back, yet?"

Mr. Roseburg creased his forehead. "I'll go check on him."

Jimmy woke up to intense pain covering the entire top of his head. His throat felt as dry as sandpaper and his whole body ached. All he could see was darkness. At first he had no idea what happened or where he could be.

Then he heard a familiar voice.

"Good grief, Jimmy," said Dominic somewhere above him. "What happened to you? You're bleeding!"

Jimmy thought this was a funny question and tried laughing, but it hurt too much. He settled for closing his eyes. Suddenly his eyes flashed back open. The bats—somebody had dumped a pile of bats on top of him. All at once, he wanted to get up.

A hand pressed down on his back. "Lie still," Dominic said. "Don't move. You'll be okay."

"G-get away from me," sputtered Jimmy, twisting his back.

Then he heard his dad's voice from a distance calling his name. Shaking his head, he lifted it from the ground. "D-dad?" he croaked weakly.

Dominic's hand vanished and he heard the sound of movement leaving him.

It would be okay. His dad would find him... Laying his head back down, Jimmy drifted off again.

When Mr. Roseburg reached the shed, he saw Dominic step out. The boy looked like a frightened rabbit, clearly shaken by something. Then Mr. Roseburg's eyes went wide. Dominic's hands were stained with red. It resembled paint, but too bright...and Mr. Roseburg got a very bad feeling.

"Where's my son?" Mr. Roseburg barked, breaking into a run. "Where's Jimmy?"

Dominic jerked when hearing him. He took one step back and all at once turned and fled. He raced across the basketball courts, leapt a drainage ditch and disappeared into the trees.

Mr. Roseburg let him go as he headed for the shed. Finding his son lying motionless with blood on his head, he cried out in alarm and fell to his knees.

Jimmy woke up when his dad checked his breathing. Immediately the boy raised himself up on an elbow and threw an arm around his dad's waist.

Seeing his son conscious, Mr. Roseburg had him lie back down. He pulled out his cell phone and called Mr. Gordon's number.

Practice ended shortly after. The boys were sent home with little explanation. Those without rides had to wait with Mr. Gordon in the parking lot. Once finished giving the quick directions to the shocked team, Mr. Wells hurried to the shed. Both men determined Jimmy had no broken bones and decided to skip the ambulance. Using a soothing tone and keeping his son talking, mostly about baseball, Mr. Roseburg lifted his son in his arms and carried him around the school to his car. He would take him straight to the hospital.

Mr. Wells, meanwhile, had another place to visit. After stopping to ask Mr. Gordon to pick up the equipment from practice before leaving, he got in his car and drove to the trailers in Queen's Gardens. Dominic had a lot of explaining to do.

In the end, no charges were filed. The police weren't called and Mr. and Mrs. Roseburg decided to just be happy their son would be okay. Jimmy had a concussion and would spend the night in the hospital for observation. A full recovery was expected.

At the hospital, talking with his dad, he couldn't remember ever seeing Dominic before being knocked out. He'd thought he'd heard a voice just before, but he couldn't be sure.

Later, using a powerful flashlight, Mr. Roseburg investigated the shed and found multiple footprints and a pile of used cigarettes. The cigarettes were old and none of the footprints matched Dominic's shoes except the few found near the entrance. The old bag of bats had fallen from a high shelf. He had a friend from the police force come by to help him and together they searched and failed to find proof of Dominic's guilt. They did find an old cigarette on the shelf, but it wasn't fresh.

For Dominic, the boy swore he had nothing to do with hurting Jimmy. He claimed to have run from the ball field to go home. Then, when halfway there, he decided to go back. He saw the shed door open and went to investigate. That's when he found Jimmy. He didn't see anybody else and had only run from Mr. Roseburg because he got scared. That was something he promised over and over.

Mr. Wells stood on the dingy porch of the trailer listening to him with a tired face. They both stood outside, but the front door was open.

From inside the trailer, Mack coughed harshly from the couch. "If that boy is getting arrested, then it's about time. Just don't send him back here! His mom don't need that. I told you he was a loser. You should've listened, Coach!"

Hearing him, Dominic stiffened and dropped his gaze from Mr. Wells. "I didn't do nothing," he said quietly.

"I want to believe you Dominic," Mr. Wells said sadly, reaching back to scratch the back of his head. "I really do."

"He did it!" Mack yelled. "You should see what he does around this place! How he steps on bugs and breaks things."

Dominic's face twisted in anger. "Shut up!" he screamed.

Mr. Wells tried to soothe him, raising a hand to calm him. Instead, Dominic flinched and tore away from his baseball coach.

"Leave me alone!" he cried. "Just leave me alone!"

Ripping open the screen door, he disappeared into the trailer, running past Mack and straight to his room. The door slammed behind him, louder than a bat slamming a ball over the fence. It actually sounded more like a strikeout.

"Told you, Coach," Mack said calmly. "That boy is out of control."

Coughing slightly, Mr. Wells stared into the trailer. "Keep an eye on him," he finally said. "I'll get back to you about baseball."

In the end, the official report labeled it an accident. Gravity had caused the high shelf, old and warped, to shift and cause the bag of bats to tumble down. Jimmy had just happened to be in the wrong place at the wrong time.

Unofficially, everyone on the Dodgers knew Dominic did it. At least they suspected he could have done it, and that was just as bad. He wasn't welcome back to the Roseburgs' house anytime soon. Mr. Wells thought it best he took a few days off from the baseball team before any formal decision was to be made. Word spread fast. It was doubtful Dominic would be welcome anywhere for a long time.

Sara stood by her brother the whole time, but Mack only shook his head in contempt.

"I knew something like this would happen one day," he told Mr. Wells when the coach stopped back a few hours later to check on Dominic and deliver the baseball suspension in person. "The boy is crazier than a loon and dangerous as a rattlesnake."

Mr. Wells left the trailer sad and shaken. When he'd left, Dominic had locked himself in the bathroom and refused to come out.

As he drove away, for the first time in his life, Mr. Wells felt too old to coach baseball.

Dominic didn't show up the next day in school. Neither did Jimmy. Everyone in the fifth grade had heard what had happened and all agreed Dominic did it. Otherwise, why would he be too scared to show up at school? Jimmy was well liked by teachers and classmates and nobody stood up for Dominic. Chase sat by himself at lunch and angrily smashed the food in his tray.

Later that afternoon, Jimmy learned he would have to miss over two full weeks of baseball before being allowed to play again. At least he would be allowed to go home...where he was immediately sent to bed in a darkened room. The headaches still bothered him, but even worse was the feeling of being wrong about Dominic. It felt like somebody had stabbed him in the back and twisted the knife.

Brittany came to visit him before bed that night and said it best.

"The worst part," she said glumly, "is knowing that Rick the moron was right." She then apologized sincerely for trying to help Dominic. She vowed to protect her brother from all other creeps like him. Her dreams of teaching crashed and burned. Now she wanted to be a nurse.

Meanwhile, the baseball season moved on. The Dodgers played the Marlins on the next Saturday morning, right after the official little league ceremonies that Jimmy had to miss. Even without Jimmy the Dodgers won easily with the score of 8-3. Chase and Shawn led the way with three hits apiece. Grayson had struck out twice and grounded out once. He also gave up all three runs when pitching.

The Dodgers won again on Tuesday, beating the Blue Jays 9-7. Chase and Shawn once again provided most of the fire power with Phil and Xavier lending their support. Chase had two doubles and Shawn hit a scorcher that ended up at the fence and got him around for an inside the park home run. Grayson got a hit, but also struck out two other times.

Dominic had returned to school that Monday, but only for brief periods, so it seemed. He got in so much trouble in class that he'd ended his first day back in the principal's office and received in-school suspension for the next three days.

Jimmy returned to school the day after the Blue Jays win. The teachers and students treated him like a celebrity and he managed to get out of doing homework until his "headaches" completely cleared. The dark bruise over his right eye drew all sorts of attention, especially from girls.

He didn't bump into Dominic until the following Monday.

The two passed each other in the hall and Jimmy coolly made sure to look the other way. Dominic made a noise as if trying to speak, but Jimmy kept going. The bruise had started to turn yellowish green around the edges, but the pain of betrayal had never faded. Not even a little.

Later at lunch, Dominic walked by Jimmy's table and dropped a handwritten note near Jimmy's tray.

Without looking at it, Jimmy grabbed it and tore it in half. Ripping it into tiny pieces, he dumped the remains on his steamed broccoli.

Dominic stood there for a full two seconds, frozen and wordless. His face tilted to the floor and his entire body slumped down.

Jimmy didn't look at him, but he could feel the despair radiating from the former Dodger as he angrily stabbed his Styrofoam tray with a plastic Spork.

Seeing his note ripped up, the one he'd spent an entire hour writing and rewriting the night before seemed to tear Dominic apart. Making a faint squawk, he slumped off, leaving Jimmy alone. It would be for good.

His friends at the table around him at first were silent, but then started laughing.

"What a complete spaz," Chase said, sitting across from Jimmy.

Jimmy just frowned. "Shut up," he said, putting down his Spork. He felt his face grow hot. "Just leave him alone."

His friends instantly shut down their laughter and quickly changed subjects to the major league standings. Jimmy barely heard them.

Ripping the note had felt like a real bush-league move. But he had to do it. Dominic deserved it. He pressed his lips tight and took up his Spork again. For the rest of lunch, he stabbed into the broccoli, mixing in the green mess with Dominic's ripped note.

He'd been burned by Dominic. Never again. Baseball was his life—besides his family, it was the one thing he loved more than anything else. And Dominic had robbed him of two weeks of it—two weeks he would never have back as a ten-year-old playing with his friends. If it were up to him, he would never speak to Dominic again and be very happy about it. The only problem was, then why did he feel so miserable when Dominic had run off?

16

Jimmy's mood only darkened as the week rolled on. Rain cancelled a Tuesday game, which actually made him happy, but then it all went downhill. The Dodgers had practice on Thursday and then a big game against the Cardinals on Saturday. Jimmy was all set to attend, just to watch from the bench if he couldn't play. Two weeks had passed since the injury, but his parents were still cautious. Then he woke up with a splitting headache and his parents decided it best to keep him home. He spent the morning in bed.

The Cardinals easily won 6-2. Suddenly the Dodgers were playing .500 baseball and were no longer feared. Instead, the Cardinals, undefeated at 4-0, became the talk of the league. Nate Dyson and Joey Carter proved to be a lethal duo, both on the mound and at the plate.

Just like that, Jimmy's spot on the all-star team looked less than certain. How could he prove himself if he couldn't play?

Later that afternoon, all of these questions whirled in his mind when his sister asked if he wanted to play catch.

Jimmy lay on his stomach, stretched out across his bed and staring listlessly at the wall when Brittany barged into his room. He'd gone straight to his room after coming back from the phone and hearing Chase's description of the game, and had slumped to this position. His headache, which had left, was quickly coming back.

"Go away," he said without turning to her.

"Why?" demanded his sister, stepping boldly into his room. She crossed her arms, pinning her softball glove against her chest. "So you can wallow in self-pity and misery?"

"Why not?" Jimmy replied, flicking a glance at her. "I can't help it with you being my sister."

His sister huffed. "I'll have you know, since your injury, I've been quite popular. Your bruise actually makes you more attractive, Jimmy. I know a couple of girls in my class who want your phone number. They keep begging me for it."

"Tell them to get in line," Jimmy grumbled. "I got three birthday invitations this week from girls that I hardly even know."

"Poor girls," Brittany with a flick of her hair. "You know, of course, they just want to meet me. Dating the little brother of the most popular girl in middle school must be every girl's dream."

"Only in your dreams," Jimmy retorted. "Now go away... Leave me alone."

Brittany grunted and took her glove in her right hand while placing her left hand on her hip. Then she smiled evilly.

All around, Jimmy's walls were covered in baseball posters of big stars and smaller photos of him with various little league teams. He had two bookcases, both holding more baseball trophies than actual books. She knew her brother just needed to get out there and feel the ball again. He'd come around.

"You know," she said sweetly, "dearest brother, this is for your own good."

"What? You're finally leaving?"

"Something like that. I'm definitely leaving my mark."

Smiling like a lunatic, she strode to the bed and slapped her glove down hard, right on Jimmy's rump. It smacked with a solid thump.

Jimmy wore thin gym shorts and a T-shirt. Yelping, he lashed out with his foot and spun to his side. "Hey!" he shouted. "What was that for?"

"To get you up and outside!" Brittany said, gleefully jumping back. "You need to get out in the sunshine."

"I already got nailed in the head!" Jimmy protested. "Remember?"

"Oh, yeah…" Brittany had retreated to the door, but now stopped and put on a sympathetic face. "And I just smacked where you keep your brains. Sorry, Jimmy." Then her eyes glinted with mischief. "But the last one to the backyard is a lard burger!"

Laughing, she raced from his room to the stairs. "And if I win we have to start with softball!"

Mumbling about wishing that he had a dog instead of a sister, Jimmy swung himself from his bed and hurried to find his glove. Still, he wore a grin as he dashed for the stairs.

During the long winter months, Jimmy and Brittany would play catch on a regular basis, but with spring's arrival they had to stop and focus on their seasons. Still, standing in the grassy area just beyond the pool, the two quickly fell into a smooth rhythm of catching, throwing, and repeating.

After a few minutes, Brittany caught a low throw and delivered an imaginary tag to a ghost runner sliding for home.

"Nice," Jimmy said.

His sister jumped up and grinned. She wore her short dark blue softball shorts and a pristine white shirt with sky blue sleeves to her elbows. Flipping back her hair, she licked the corner of her lips.

"Say, where're Shawn and Chase these days?" she asked nonchalantly. "I mean, Chase lives right across the street."

Jimmy frowned slightly. "Both their moms won't let them come over until my head is healed." Inwardly he sighed. Yet one more casualty from Dominic…none of his friends had visited him since the incident. Dominic sure had a lot to pay for.

Brittany's face fell, but her eyes brightened as she cocked back her arm. "Oh, so you mean they're never coming over, huh?"

"Not if you're around," Jimmy retorted, grabbing her return throw. "They're also afraid of rabies."

Brittany grinned. "At least you're feeling better now." She snapped her glove over the hard throw back from Jimmy. Trading insults with the ball…it was just like old times.

"Hey, want to see my pitching?" she suddenly asked, gripping the ball tight in her glove.

"Sure, but you'd better not," Jimmy cautioned her. "I don't have my catching gear on, and if Dad finds out you nailed me in the head…"

Brittany widened her eyes and pressed her lips tightly. "Oh, yeah… Sorry."

"Just do one," Jimmy said instantly, hating hurting his sister. He knew Brittany meant well and he also knew he needed to get back to baseball. The Dodgers needed him just as much as he needed them. That meant taking chances. He pounded his mom's oversized softball glove. "Come on, put it here."

His baseball glove rested at his feet. He would switch once they grew bored of the softball and started tossing the baseball. Jimmy knew this would come soon. Brittany loved softball, but nothing beat the feeling of throwing the smaller, harder baseball. Nothing. He couldn't wait to get back in the game.

His sister smiled. "Okay…but just stand still and hold your glove steady…"

Jimmy crouched and widened his stance. "Just hit my glove, just like always." Even he had to admit, Brittany was easily the best pitcher on her softball team. All the hours she practiced with him catching had paid off.

Nodding, Brittany stared across their backyard at her brother.

Then, taking a breath, she leaned her body forward before extending both her arms toward Jimmy. All at once, she swung her pitching arm up over her head and right into a back swing, shifting her weight forward at the same time. Stepping toward Jimmy, she released the ball just as it passed her waist.

People thought softball was easy, but pitching fast in softball was anything but easy. It was more like an art, and Jimmy couldn't help admiring his sister's form. He got caught watching her motion and suddenly noticed the blur shooting straight at him.

Handcuffed, his glove totally out of positon, he nearly panicked. Eyes shooting wide, he jumped up and managed to block the ball just as it blasted right for the front of his shorts, right where it would hurt the most. He caught the ball with a thundering smack that stung his hand. The glove, much too large for his small hand, shot free and went skittering between his legs before rolling to a stop with the ball. It could've been worse. Jimmy stood frozen in place with his eyes as big as softballs.

"Jimmy!" Brittany screeched.

"Brittany!" Jimmy screeched back, his body finally moving again. He slowly stood before sighing in relief. "Were you trying to kill me?"

"Sorry, I was aiming low to avoid your head…"

"Next time aim lower…" Still shaken, Jimmy bent down to grab his baseball glove with a baseball nestled inside. "Let's switch to baseball. I don't need any real soft—"

"Okay, Jimmy," Brittany said hastily. "I got it. I'm really sorry. I mean, I just… well, usually you're more focused."

"Yeah, well, usually my sister isn't trying to nail me."

After standing with his glove, he wiped sweat from his forehead using the back of his throwing arm. As he did so, he winced when getting too close to the bruise.

"Still hurts, doesn't it?" Brittany asked, suddenly sounding like the worried older sister.

Grunting, Jimmy answered by delivering a sharp throw that she easily swallowed in her bigger softball glove.

"I just want to play on the team again," he said ruefully.

Brittany nodded. "I know. I still don't get it… I really thought Dominic was good. I mean, I can't believe he did that to you…and after all we did for him."

Jimmy said nothing as he caught her return throw. But his next throw went even harder.

"Guess we won't have to worry about him now," he said through gritted teeth. "He'll never be back here."

Brittany nodded grimly. "Not on my watch. Nobody hurts my little brother, except for me."

Jimmy finally grinned, but it was forced. Even gone, Dominic continued to bother him. The two played catch until it became too dark to see and their mom called them in for dinner.

After dinner and a shower, he spent Saturday night lying in bed tossing a ball up in the air and catching it with one eye open. On the third toss, he missed completely and the ball nailed him in the open eye, thankfully the one farthest away from his bruise.

He winced as he shut both eyes. How could he have been so blind about Dominic? The kid was a cancer like Chase had said from the beginning. And he didn't even play on the team anymore.

Dominic also lay on his bed Saturday night. Only instead of quiet, all he heard was shouting.

"I'm sick of that sack of nothing messing up his life and your life!" Mack shouted at his mom. "Do you know how many calls from school I got this week? They quit suspending him because they know he's hopeless!"

"He's going through a rough time," his mom said, her voice more tired than angry. "He misses his father."

"His father is dead! And so is his future! I've had it with that boy!"

"Mack!" His mom's voice raised to a shout. It was one of her rare days off, but instead of peace and quiet, she got into it with Mack…almost all day.

It all started when he tried to get her to go out to lunch. Sara had left with some friends and wouldn't return until late that night—she rarely stayed around the house with Mack there. His mom said she couldn't leave her youngest children, but Mack refused to bring Dominic. Rose was fine, but Dominic had to stay grounded in his old room…that led to the yelling…

Dominic spent most of the day on the floor with his cars. Only this time, instead of racing, they became ball players. He had Bud pitching while Mack stood on the plate.

At first he started by striking out Mack—using his imagination to turn the red car into a Dodger pitcher, rearing up and throwing nothing but speed. Mack went down time after time in three pitches. But as the voices grew louder outside his door, he started beaming Mack with all his might. Right in the head.

All of a sudden he heard a loud bang and saw Mack's beat-up car bouncing from the wall before landing on the bed. A huge dent remained. He stood frozen in place from where he'd pitched the car.

"Is that you in there, Dom?" screamed Mack. "You stupid son of a—"

"Stop it!" his mom yelled. "Just leave him alone! Come to the kitchen and I'll cook you a burger, Mack. Come on, baby."

"You stay in there!" Mack hollered, but his voice calmed. "Stupid kid."

That had soothed the yelling…until nightfall. Now it was back on, full force.

Dominic lay on his old mattress and stared at the wall. He'd refused to leave Sara's room to sleep in Rose's room, so Sara would have to take his bed for the night…when she returned. The lights were out, but he could still see the large dent where Mack's car had struck. Alone in the darkness, he started to feel his body quiver and tears well up in his eyes.

Then a soft knocking at his door caused his body to tense. He'd feared Mack, but quickly relaxed.

"Dommy?" Rose's tentative voice asked. "Dommy, can I come in?"

Sighing, Dominic got up to a seated position and wiped his eyes. His little sister, annoyingly cute, never failed to bring him to his senses.

"Yeah, sure, Rose," he said. He got up stiffly and went to open the door. He'd last seen her at breakfast when he'd eaten his only meal of the day. Earlier, his mom had stopped by with packages of cold pop tarts and a bottle of fruit juice for his supper.

Rose darted into the room and sat down immediately by Dominic's feet. "Why is Mack so mad at you?" she asked.

"Because he's an idiot," Dominic responded, closing the door and locking it. He reached down and scooped Rose up, sitting her on his hip. "Come and lie on the bed. I'll tell you a story until they stop yelling."

"Isn't this Sara's bed?" Rose asked. With Sara back, Dominic had to share Rose's room, which he didn't mind too much. Still, it felt good to be back in his old room.

"Not tonight," Dominic mumbled. "Tonight we're switching rooms."

"Okay. Tell me about baseball again!" Rose said, letting her little body sink into her brother.

Since he stopped playing with the Dodgers, Dominic had started making up baseball stories for his sister at night. Darkness scared her and Mack wouldn't be bothered with comforting her at bedtime, so Dominic took up the task. In a few short weeks, his little sister grew very close to her older brother. It at least gave him something to do and look forward to…now that he had lost the Dodgers, he had little else in his life to enjoy.

"Sure, Rose," he said, settling her on his bed and laying her on the mattress. "Once there was this kid named Jimmy."

"And he had a sister, Rose, right?"

"Right…uh, Jimmy had a sister Rose and a best friend Dominic."

"Did he have a sister Rose, too?"

"Uh, just let me tell the story…"

Rose drifted off to sleep with her head resting on Sara's pillow. Dominic sat beside her still form and continued the story in his mind. As he did so, the tears started to well again. And the screaming voices only grew louder.

"I'm done being a babysitter for your fat brat!" Mack yelled.

"Oh, let's just drop it," his mom finally said wearily. "Don't let him ruin our weekend…what's left of it."

Dominic quietly cried. The resulting silence seemed a lot worse than the yelling.

In another household, that same night, Grayson changed into his pajamas and had just climbed into bed when his father knocked on his door.

"Anybody awake in here?" Mr. Daniels asked, entering. "I saw the light and hoped you were still up."

Grayson flopped back on his pillow and breathed out heavily. His batting slump continued—he hadn't reached base once against the Cardinals. Worse, his pitching had fallen off and Mr. Wells was considering putting Tom on the mound. It seemed the harder he tried, the worse he played.

To make matters even worse, his dad kept coming home late from school and still hadn't solved the Kelvin and Richie problem. Those two were obviously cheating, but Mr. Daniels couldn't find any proof of it. All their assignments were typed and even contained a few obvious errors—like they were put there on purpose. Grayson only heard about this late at night, when his parents didn't think he was listening. Mr. Daniels tried to act like everything was going great with him. It made everything feel even more miserable.

"So, guy, what are you thinking?" Mr. Daniels asked, walking over to sit on the edge of Grayson's bed. He smacked Grayson's stomach lightly. "Everything good at school?" Grayson grunted a yes. "What about baseball? Still bothering you?"

Grayson sighed and sat up. He scooted across the bed to sit next to his dad. Both their feet dangled over the edge, Mr. Daniels's reaching the floor. "I just keep striking out," he said. "I don't get it."

"Hey, son," Mr. Daniels said, putting arm around Grayson's shoulder, "your mom and I keep telling you. As long as you try your best we're happy for you."

Grayson frowned. "Oh, so you're happy I strikeout?" he asked in sarcasm.

"Well, no, but we're definitely not upset with you." Mr. Daniels looked at his son curiously. "What's really bothering you? Is it about Jimmy? I know he's your catcher."

Grayson shrugged. "Maybe," he muttered. "I just don't get Dominic. Why would he do something like that?"

Mr. Daniels moved his hand up to the back of his son's head and ruffled his slight curls. "You know, son, nobody ever proved he did anything to Jimmy. I can't tell you in this world how many people have had their lives ruined just because somebody says they did something. That's why we have courts—to prove somebody guilty, or innocent."

"So you think he could be innocent?"

"I don't know," admitted Mr. Daniels. "I just don't think anybody has proved him guilty." He suddenly dropped his hands in his lap and breathed out heavily. "You remember asking me about my students Kelvin and Richie?"

Grayson leaned against his dad's shoulder and nodded. "I know, Dad. I hear you and Mom talk about them all the time now."

"No kidding?" Mr. Daniels asked in surprised. Then he chuckled. "I guess we can't be surprised with a sharp kid like you around. I wonder if I have any secrets."

Grayson grinned. "I know about your stash of chocolate behind the radio."

"Oh, er, don't tell your mother and you can take some. Well, er, about Kelvin and Richie, you know about my situation. I think and feel they're doing something wrong, but without proof I would be doing something even worse by accusing them. The situation with Dominic is sort of the same way. If you accuse him without proof you could be hurting him just as much, if not worse, than Jimmy was hurt. Even if he does get in trouble a lot, it doesn't mean Dominic is wrong all the time."

Grayson thought about this for a while. Then he sighed. "Maybe. Yeah, I guess you're right."

Mr. Daniels snorted. "You calling your dad right is proof you're not a teenager yet. That means it's past your bedtime." He smacked Grayson's knee and told him to get some sleep.

Grayson had a hard time following his father's last advice. Lying in the dark he could only think of what it must feel like to be Dominic. He lived a miserable life and nobody liked him…or ever believed him. There were things in the world worse than striking out, he decided. Then his eyes slid shut and sleep finally came.

17

The month of April slipped into May and baseball continued to heat up with the days. The Cardinals finished the first half of the season undefeated and started the second half by thrashing the Blue Jays for the second time—this time 15-0 in a four-inning game ended by the mercy rule. The Yankees were just behind them. Their only loss came at the hands of the Cardinals. Meanwhile, the Dodgers continued to stumble. Just after the halfway point they were 4-4.

Even with Jimmy's returning to the lineup, they lacked something in their game. Grayson managed to improve his hitting, and his pitching righted itself with Jimmy behind the plate, but overall the team lacked a spark. There were too many fielding errors—misplayed grounders, wild throws, or just poor decisions. Then at the plate they failed to hit with runners in scoring position and swung at too many bad pitches. Mr. Wells tried everything from scheduling grueling practices to outright canceling them. Nothing worked.

In the rematch against the Yankees, their ninth game of a fourteen-game season, they lost 6-4. Once again, Grayson had ended the game—this time by striking out. For the first time that season they were a below .500 team.

Grayson couldn't stop the tears from flowing during the postgame team meeting. It was a Tuesday night and the game had started at 7:30 at night. It was now nearing 9:30 and his father hadn't shown up yet.

"Come on, guys," Mr. Wells said, clasping his hands together in front of him. "I know it's been a long night and we have had a trying season so far. But don't get down. Good teams rise when they fall, and I promise you, we're a good team. Now go get your gear and get some rest. We play the Marlins on Thursday and we can right the ship then."

The coach sounded more tired than confident. He left soon after dismissing the players. Mr. Roseburg stayed behind to organize the cleanup and to make sure everyone got their gear and found their parents.

Still wiping his tears, Grayson gathered his bat and glove, stuffing them in his bag.

"Gray, is your dad here yet?" asked Mr. Roseburg.

Swallowing hard, Grayson zipped up his bag before answering. "I'll go check."

"All right," said the Dodger assistant as he pulled down a clipboard holding the lineup sheet. "If not, go find my van and sit with Jimmy. We'll wait with you." Turning, he tapped Grayson's head with the clipboard. "You still played good defense today, Gray. And don't forget your pitching. Hang in there and you'll get another chance."

The boy nodded and rushed out with his bag before a fresh wave of tears struck. Kids and parents were quickly exiting the parking lot, but he couldn't spot his dad's pickup in the mess.

The Dodgers and Yankees had played on the field closest to the woods where the nature trails ran. Just in front of the tree line sat a giant pile of clay used to repair and upkeep the infields. Roughly the size of minivan, the pile of clay had been placed on the edge of the trees to keep it away from little kids looking to climb or slide down its red, clinging banks.

As Grayson moved toward the parking lot, he saw a face peering at him from behind the clay pile. It quickly ducked out of sight. Startled, he stopped in his tracks.

"Dominic?" Grayson said dubiously. "Is that you?"

"No," spoke Dominic's sullen voice behind the clay.

Grayson dropped his heavy baseball bag in the grass and walked tentatively toward the clay. "What are you doing here?" he asked, still surprised.

He hadn't seen Dominic since the fateful day Jimmy had been hurt. And he hadn't spoken to him since the pool party on the first day of the season.

Dominic slowly stood from his hiding spot and blinked down at Grayson. He looked leaner and a bit shaggier. His hair hung just in his eyes, but his deep scowl remained. Only now it looked more embarrassed than angry. Caught in the lights from the field, his face appeared dirty and streaked with tears, probably very much like Grayson's own face.

Grayson swallowed. He never thought somebody like Dominic would cry… Blinking, he eyed the forlorn boy again. Dominic wore stained baggy blue jeans that hadn't been washed in a long time with a dark T-shirt that hung on his slouched frame. Busted sneakers covered his feet, making him look like anything but a baseball player.

"I just came to watch you guys play baseball," Dominic mumbled. "I'm going home now." But he didn't move.

Grayson quickly wiped his eyes with the back of his hand and made a decision. Looking at the parking lot once more, he failed to spot his dad's pickup. He started climbing the clay pile until he reached the top where Dominic stood.

"Is it okay if I join you?" Grayson asked, almost shyly. "My dad still hasn't come yet."

"I walked here. I don't care," Dominic replied, though clearly pleased. He stepped back and sat on a small shelf in the clay.

Grayson moved and squatted down across from him, resting on his haunches. For a moment neither boy spoke. Then suddenly a loud click snapped through the night and the lights of the sports park went out. The boys were plunged in blackness. Only faint light from the parking lot mixing with the moonlight allowed them to see each other.

"Are you sure your dad isn't here?" Dominic asked, frowning across the abandoned field, now bathed in darkness.

Grayson shrugged. He stood and again searched the parking lot. The last of the cars were just pulling out. "He'll be here," he said confidently. "He's late a lot."

Dominic grunted. "I wish I had my dad," he said glumly. "Even if he did come late."

Grayson swallowed. Squatting back down, he made a decision and sat. Hugging his knees, he rested his chin on top. "You didn't hurt Jimmy, did you," he said.

"No. I keep telling everybody that! I wasn't even there until after it happened!" Dominic huffed. "Nobody ever believes me."

Grayson glanced at him. "I believe you."

Dominic nearly gasped. "Really?" Relaxing, the larger boy sat down and put his hands in his lap glumly. "Nobody else does, that's for sure."

"Ever since you left we really stink," Grayson then said. "I mean, we lost before, but we were getting better. Now we're getting worse."

Dominic grunted. "You know, every day I can I practice throwing an old tennis ball I found. I throw it for hours at the back of an old abandoned trailer…" His voice fell, suddenly embarrassed.

Grayson coughed ruefully. "We could've used your arm today. I stunk at pitching."

"No way," Dominic said. "You did all right… From what I saw." He couldn't hide the wistfulness in his voice, though. Clearly he'd wanted to be out there.

Grayson relaxed his chin on his knees and bit his lip.

The two boys fell into a calming silence beneath the stars. With the merest of breezes, the sky seemed to relax with them. Soft moonlight continued to shine down as for a moment the boys just sat. Then Dominic shifted awkwardly.

"Thanks," he said, "for, uh, talking to me." Then he frowned in the shadows. "Hey, uh, shouldn't we get down and get closer to the parking lot? If your dad comes he might not see you here."

Relieved not to be left alone, Grayson quickly agreed. Standing, he brushed the back of his pants and then coughed. "Um, the hard part is getting down in the dark."

"That's easy," Dominic told him. "The hard part is doing it without falling. Just follow me."

Led by Dominic, the two boys half climbed, half slid down and found Grayson's bag, a giant shadow on the grass. Lugging it between them, they were headed to the parking lot when lights appeared from an approaching vehicle.

"That's probably my dad," Grayson said, relieved. "Do you want a ride home?"

"Uh, no," Dominic said, shaking his head. "I come here a lot at night. It's quiet and…sometimes I run the bases." The boy had already retreated into the shadows. "Just do me a favor and don't tell your dad you saw me here. I don't want to get in trouble."

Grayson frowned and never made the promise. "I'll tell Jimmy you didn't do it," he suddenly blurted.

He wasn't sure if Dominic heard him and didn't have time to find out. Tires squealed in the parking lot as the lights swung his way and bathed him in bright light.

Grayson squinted and shielded his eyes. He wondered why his dad had his brights on. Even without the field lights on, the parking lot remained well lit with streetlamps. Then the doors swung open from the vehicle. It was a pickup, but larger than the one his father drove. All at once Grayson grew scared.

"There he is!" crowed a young voice. "I told you I saw him here alone!"

A boy a little older than him walked in front of the blinding light. Two large figures followed.

Squinting from the headlights, Grayson still recognized the boy. His blood ran cold.

Rufus grinned evilly at Grayson. "Scared yet?" he asked. "You should be."

The lights suddenly went out and Grayson stood as if his feet froze. He blinked rapidly as he momentarily lost his vision, but couldn't think at what to do. This couldn't be happening…where was his dad?

"Get him!" shouted a rough voice. The two large figures suddenly charged from the truck behind Rufus and went straight for Grayson.

Caught by surprise at the sudden turn of events, Grayson barely had time to register that the figures were none other than Kelvin and Richie. Then they were nearly on him.

Dropping his heavy bag, Grayson finally made to run, but had no chance.

After only a few steps Kelvin reached him. Grabbing Grayson by the back of the shoulders, he slammed the boy down onto the grass. Richie whooped from behind.

"Take him out, Kelv," he cried.

Crying out, Grayson tried to twist free, but the much larger teen sat on the back of his legs and grabbed his hair. His baseball cap had gone flying during the initial attack.

"Get off!" Grayson shouted.

Grunting, the teen slammed Grayson's head into the ground, shoving his face hard into the grass. That was when Grayson started screaming.

"Shut him up!" Richie said worriedly. "Somebody's going to hear us!"

"Not just yet they won't," hissed Kelvin. He wrapped a hand tightly around Grayson's mouth and leaned close to his ear. "Scream again and I'll choke you out. I want you to know what's happening. Why this is happening to you."

"It's your daddy's fault," Richie said meanly. He moved forward and crouched down by Grayson's face, speaking softly in his ear. "Yeah, kid," he said gruffly. "Nothing personal, but your daddy really messed us over."

Grayson went still as his eyes grew wide with fright.

Kelvin snarled. He planted a knee on the back of Grayson's pants, pressing down hard. "I'd say he did. Did you know, kid, that your nosy father accused us of cheating to the school board? He did today. That son of a—that piece of—that stupid moron actually failed us in his stupid class! I bet you didn't know that. Just like I bet your stupid dad doesn't know where you are right now. Does he?"

Richie snorted and said. "But we know where he is right now."

Grayson struggled against Kelvin's hand, but couldn't open his mouth. The teen removed his knee and sat back down, trapping the boy's thighs with his knees. The bully used his free hand to grab Grayson's right wrist. This he cruelly pulled back on, forcing Grayson's arm behind his back causing intense pain in his right shoulder.

Kelvin laughed at the boy's muffled cries of pain. "It's sort of ironic. Your dad is with my dad right now tattling on us for cheating. Well, my dad's kid, me, is with your dad's kid, you, and about to beat the living snot out of him!"

Rufus's voice spoke nervously from the truck. "What're you going to do to him?" he asked.

"Not your concern, Rufus boy," Kelvin said with a grunt. "Thanks for the phone message, though." Kelvin hissed in Grayson's ear. "Yeah, kid. Rufus sold you out. He texted me ten minutes ago saying he saw you out here all alone."

Rufus laughed nervously. "You said you would just scare him a bit."

"That's just what we plan to do," Kelvin said. He relaxed his hand over the mouth slightly. "Scream—" Kelvin's words were cut off by his own screaming.

As soon as Grayson felt his mouth free up, he started squirming and biting. His teeth managed to catch the fold of skin just under Kelvin's thumb. Instantly, the teenager pulled his hand free and grabbed his injured hand with his other. As he did so, he drew back from the boy.

Crawling on his elbows and twisting his hips, Grayson managed to slide and wiggle his body from underneath Kelvin. He rolled to his back to deliver sharp kicks into the bully's midsection. He still wore his baseball cleats.

Kelvin gasped in pain, but then leapt on top of the smaller boy, more angry than hurt.

"Yo, man!" cried Richie. "What are you doing?"

"Choking the little punk out!" shouted Kelvin. "I've had it with him!" He rammed his forearm down on Grayson's chest, sitting his full weight on the boy's thighs. His other hand slapped hard into Grayson's hip. "Then we'll have our fun. The twerp nearly killed me!"

Grayson fought back in desperate silence, but was quickly overmatched.

"Get off me!" he pleaded.

Kelvin only snickered. "Shut up, shrimp." He knelt above the much smaller boy and, pinching his hip hard, used his brute strength to roll him to his stomach.

"Help!" Grayson screamed, twisting his body to no avail.

"Uh, I don't know about this," Richie said with uncertainty.

"Just wait a second," Kelvin said with a grunt. "This kid has it coming…him and his dad are the same."

The former football player and wrestler wrapped an arm around the front of Grayson's throat and jerked the boy up, instantly cutting off the boy's shouts. Now in a sleeper hold, Grayson had no chance. Forced up onto his knees with Kelvin's arms around his neck and head, he desperately tried to pry loose and fight for a breath. His hands gripped and tore at Kelvin's arm, but to no avail. In seconds, his struggles weakened and then the boy's body suddenly went limp. He sank into the bully's arms.

Kelvin breathed out heavily and relaxed, letting the boy flop to the ground where he didn't move.

"Dude," Richie said in awe. "Did you, did you kill him?"

"He's just sleeping," wheezed Kelvin. He got to his feet and grinned. "Out like a light." He nudged the unconscious body with his toe. "We did this all the time to each other at football camp."

"Huh," muttered Richie. "That explains a lot." He swallowed nervously. "You sure he's not dead, right?"

Kelvin snorted. Using his foot, he dug under Grayson's stomach and rolled his body over. "Look, see his chest? It's still moving. Now stop being such a wimp, Rich. We're in this together. You and me, man."

Richie nodded and wiped his brow. "Yeah, yeah," he said. "Of course, man."

Rufus walked stiffly from the front of the truck. "So now what?" he asked. He eyed Grayson's still form with a mixture of fear and excitement.

"First things first," Kelvin said with fury. "I get rid of his shoes. They nearly ripped a hole in me."

Bending down, he ripped the cleats from Grayson's feet and flung them into the darkness toward the trees. Then he turned to Richie. His eyes gleamed and a malevolent grin twisted across his face.

"Hey, doesn't Mr. Daniels love putting his son's baseball pictures in his stupid lessons?" he asked, his voice laced with malice.

"Yeah. So?"

"Well, let's teach him a lesson he'll never forget. Here, help me pull off his shirt. We'll dump it on Mr. Daniels's lawn and let him know what happens when he messes with us."

"What about the kid?" Richie asked dubiously. He and Kelvin had been drinking earlier…he doubted Kelvin had quite sobered. This did not seem to be a good idea. Still, he always followed Kelvin's lead…

"We leave him here," Kelvin said with a chuckle. "We'll hide him in the woods. Daddy's boy will wake up wondering what happened while his daddy will also be wondering what happened to his precious little boy."

"Come on, Kelvin," Richie protested. "We're going to get in trouble, man."

"Yeah, I know," Kelvin spat with hatred. "All because Mr. Daniels flunked us. This is payback, man."

Richie squeezed his eyes shut for a moment and then relaxed, letting out his breath. He'd started hanging out with

Kelvin sophomore year for no other reason than they both shared the same taste for skipping class and doing drugs. They'd yet to do something really bad. Until now.

"Mr. Daniels, you deserve this," he mumbled. Then he smiled. "Hey, I got an idea. Let's put some of our stuff in the kid's pocket. That way if he tells he can get in just as much trouble! Everyone will think the kid was doing drugs!"

Kelvin chuckled. "Great idea," he said. "Ruf, go to the truck and grab the bag under my seat." He grabbed Grayson by the arms and easily hefted him up to a standing position before dragging him backwards over to the clay pile. The boy's head flopped forward and his arms dangled limply at his sides. "The kid is lighter than paper, man," Kelvin said.

Richie sniffed the air as he followed. Suddenly he laughed. "Hey, the little stinker wet his pants!"

Kelvin grunted. "Serves him right. He nearly bit my thumb off."

Richie snorted. "The baby was just trying to suck his own thumb, but missed." He cackled at his joke, suddenly feeling good.

Having drugs stashed with the kid would save them. It would look like a drug deal had gone wrong, with the kid caught right in the middle of it. Maybe they could even force the kid to take some and completely fry his mind! Then he wouldn't be able remember anything! Just like that, Richie allowed himself to breathe easy. They would get away with it. His dad would take care of Mr. Daniels, just like he took care of everything else whenever he got in trouble. Everything would work out just fine.

At the clay pile, Kelvin dropped the boy and moved to stand over him.

"This is your old man's fault," he said thickly, looking down without remorse. "He should've listened."

Crouching down, he grabbed the front of the boy's shirt and then yanked him up, leaning him back against the clay in a sitting position. He'd barely started tugging the shirt over the kid's shoulders when a loud angry yell from just above him caused him to stumble backwards.

With a startled yelp, he raised both hands over his face. He'd never believed in monsters, but this sounded like one and he couldn't help but panic.

Sharp, stinging missiles then fired down from the dark and started pelting him in the head and shoulders. It felt like something was spitting bullets at him.

"What the—" he screamed, before something hard slammed into his mouth, causing him to squawk and duck down.

The horrible screaming continued. It seriously sounded like the waking of the dead.

Letting curses fly, Kelvin kept his face covered as he stumbled to his feet. Turning, he left the unconscious boy and ran for the truck.

Richie started to follow right after him, yelling in terror. Unlike Kelvin, he did believe in monsters.

But then Rufus, still in the truck, beeped the horn. "It's just a kid!" he yelled. "Turn around and look! It's some dumb kid from my school! It's that weirdo Dominic kid! I recognize his yelling anywhere!"

He flicked on the headlights in the truck. They lit up the pile of clay and clearly identified the source of the screaming.

Dominic stood in the center of the pile with his arms full of clay pellets and chest heaving in anger. Seeing that he'd been spotted, he stopped his screaming. His face twisted into a sneer and lips curled back in a snarl.

"Leave my friend alone!" he yelled. "I'll rip you apart if you don't!"

"Shut up and get out of here before you join him!" Kelvin yelled back. "Scram, you spaz!" He dabbed at his face in disgust. "You nearly broke my tooth!"

This only caused Dominic to widen his stance and lift his arms from his side. The remaining pellets clattered from his hands. Standing on the clay pile over the unconscious Grayson, he looked poised to attack with nothing but pure anger. In the bright lights, his eyes were lost in the shadows and gave him a murderous look.

He wasn't going to back down.

18

"Come and get me!" Dominic cried.

"He's stupid," Rufus said from the truck. "He's just a loser. Don't even worry about him."

Hearing Rufus and the seeing the two teenagers eyeing him angrily, Dominic crouched low and reached behind him to pick something up. He didn't care what the bullies thought of him. When he heard Grayson's screams, all his personal feelings flew straight up to the sky. He'd let his instincts take over, led by his cold, pure anger.

Kelvin's fear quickly turned into anger of his own when watching him. Uttering a curse word, he wiped his cheek where a clay missile had left a welt. His lower lip had started to swell and he tasted blood.

"You stupid trash!" he cried. "You're trailer trash and we're going to rip you to shreds with your little friend, you punk! Let's get him, Rich!"

Richie breathed a sigh of relief and nodded. His first step came awkwardly and he rubbed a wet stain in front of his pants. He'd wet himself, too.

"I'm right behind you," he wheezed, stumbling after the charging Kelvin.

As Kelvin reached the clay pile, Dominic didn't wait for him. He ran down like a charging bull, unleashing another primal scream just before leaping over Grayson's form, right onto the larger teen's chest.

Totally surprised, Kelvin had just enough time to raise his hand before Dominic's full weight crushed him to the ground. He ended up on his back and still had no time to react. The points of Dominic's knees landed right on Kelvin's stomach, driving the teenager's breath straight from his lungs.

"You piece of garbage!" Dominic yelled. He gripped an old glass bottle in his hands. Raising it high, he smashed it down on the teen's face. Glass shattered and Kelvin let off a choking scream. Blood started to cloud his vision.

Taken back by the ferocious and unexpected attack, Richie cautiously approached from the side. Eyeing the smashed glass, he tried to grab Dominic from behind and drag him off, but Dominic set his full weight on Kelvin's middle and refused to budge. He started screaming and flailing his arms, ripping at the teen's face.

Under Dominic, Kelvin started screeching for help, saying he was bleeding to death.

Grayson woke up coughing and sat up with a start. The last thing he remembered was being choked by Kelvin. Now he found himself slumped against the clay pile with screaming all around him. As his vision and mind cleared, he quickly took stock of his surroundings. Just beyond his feet, he saw Dominic struggling with Richie while straddling Kelvin's middle. Everyone was screaming and Grayson's head hurt.

Getting unsteadily to his feet, he stumbled forward and almost immediately gasped with pain as something sharp stabbed into his foot. The pain served to wake him fully. Somehow he'd lost his shoes...but that wasn't important right now.

Richie, being unable to physically move Dominic, had resorted to hair pulling and raking his fingers across the boy's face, aiming for his eyes while pulling hair. Dominic responded by trying to bite his fingers while still pummeling Kelvin's face below him with both fists.

Kelvin's pitiful wails rose to full-blown cries for mercy. Blood splattered from his face as Dominic continued to pound away.

"Leave him, man! I'm going to rip your eyes out!" Richie cried. Then he yelled out in alarm.

Grayson had leapt on his back and started beating at his head.

This unexpected attack from the rear sent Richie into hysterics. In a sudden show of strength, induced by blind panic, he staggered to his feet and shook Grayson loose. The boy flew off and bounced into the clay pile.

Richie didn't bother to see this. Finding himself free, he sprinted immediately for the truck as if death itself pursued him.

"Start the engine!" he cried. "We have to get out of here! Those aren't kids, they're little demons!"

Seeing him go, Kelvin all at once remembered his own strength. Roaring, he rolled to his right and sent Dominic reeling away. Clawing at the ground, he too got to his feet and stumbled for the truck. He had to wipe his eyes free of blood as he went.

"I'm dying!" he howled as he reached the parking lot. "Get me out of here! He ripped my face off!"

Inside the truck, Rufus, seeing the terror in the eyes of the teens, frowned in surprise. Then he saw the blood on Kelvin and drew in a sharp breath. He too wanted to leave. Hastily he climbed from the truck's cab and leapt into the back.

In moments, the older teens were both inside and the tires squealed as the truck reversed quickly. Spinning wildly, it fled from the crime scene, zooming over the grass and back down the road before accelerating into the night.

Dominic rose to his feet and went to where Grayson lay in front of the clay pile.

"Are we safe?" the smaller boy asked, sounding dazed as he looked up. "Oh, man, I see stars."

Dominic grunted. "It's not over yet," he said, almost no emotion in his voice. "I heard everything. I didn't come out until I found the glass bottle. I used it to bash the big guy in the head."

Grayson grimaced and then whimpered slightly. "I think I stepped on a piece... I lost my shoes."

Dominic moved to inspect Grayson's feet. His left sock had a dark stain on the bottom.

"Uh, yeah," Dominic said, sounding mildly alarmed. It was as if he woke from a bad dream. "You're bleeding."

Grayson closed his eyes and sucked in his breath. "I just want to go home. Where's my dad?"

Tears ran down his cheeks. His foot burned like crazy and his wet pants clung to his thighs. He was too exhausted and scared to feel shame.

"We'll have to go to my place," Dominic told him firmly. "Those guys might come back. First we need to find your bag."

Grayson sat up slowly. His face appeared ghostly white in the moonlight. "Why do we need that?"

"Because," answered Dominic, "if those guys do come back we'll have baseball bats and baseballs to use as weapons. Trust me. I know how to handle trouble."

Grayson's body shuddered as he watched Dominic walk toward the parking lot to retrieve the bag. Before now Grayson's biggest pain had been about losing in baseball. Now life took on a whole new meeting. He felt glad to have Dominic on his side.

Dominic returned with the bag set on his back like an oversized backpack.

"Hey," he asked Grayson. "Can you walk?"

Gritting his teeth, Grayson got gingerly to his feet and limped a few steps. His face contorted in pain and he sat down abruptly. "It hurts too much," he gasped.

Dropping the heavy bag, Dominic bent low and inspected the injured foot. He found a shard of glass the size of a thumb nail poking out of his sock.

"This might hurt," he said, reaching for the glass.

Putting a hand on Dominic's back to steady himself, Grayson just squeezed his eyes shut. He gasped when Dominic all at once pulled the glass shard free.

"Hold on," Dominic said, in complete control. "You probably want to stay down for now. This may take a minute."

Grayson grimaced in pain. "Where's my dad?" he asked again.

"Don't know," Dominic grunted. "We can call at my place…if I can find a phone. Hold your foot still."

Dominic reached up Grayson's injured leg and pulled down the long baseball sock, ripping it free from the smaller boy's calf.

"I've seen this done in movies a lot," he explained. "And my mom is pretty good when I get hurt. And I get hurt a lot."

Taking the sock, partially saturated in blood, Dominic deftly turned it sideways and wrapped it over and around the injured area of Grayson's foot before tying it in a tight knot.

As he did so, he noticed a stream of blood running down his own arms. He was surprised to find that both his arms and hands were nicked with multiple cuts. He'd forgotten all about bashing Kelvin with broken glass. He wiped his arms on his shirt.

"All done," he said. Standing up, he reached under Grayson's arms and pulled him upright.

"Let's go," he said gruffly, reaching to pick up the heavy baseball bag. "We have a long walk. You can lean on me if you have to."

They'd left just in time. As they reached the trees behind the clay pile, fast moving lights appeared and headed in their direction.

"Come on!" cried Dominic. "They're coming back!"

He broke into a stumbling run with the heavy bag on his back weighing him down.

Limping behind, gasping in pain, Grayson struggled to catch up. He never once thought about stopping. He would never forget the smell of sweat, fear, and urine as Kelvin's arms choked him out. He'd thought he was being murdered.

His soaked pants clung to his legs to remind him of his fear. He also remembered seeing Dominic pounding Kelvin's face like a ferocious animal. He made sure to keep close to Dominic's side.

Moments later, Mr. Daniels jerked his pickup to a halt in the empty parking lot. There was nobody in sight and he banged his dashboard in frustration.

Earlier that day he'd found a thumb drive on the floor in his classroom. When he plugged it in, he found it to be from a student in a different English class…but it contained a lot of files with Kelvin Michelle's and Richie Jollster's names. Further research showed that the student had been using his own assignments and just changing them to suit Kelvin's and Richie's needs.

Furious, Mr. Daniels had hunted down this student and received an immediate confession. He'd turned in the evidence to the principal that afternoon.

What should've been a clear case of cheating turned into a huge ordeal of arguing and accusations. Mr. Daniels was accused of manufacturing the evidence and after school he'd ended up at the school board office with Kelvin's father.

Hours later, Mr. Daniels was called to an emergency school board meeting that dragged on for even more hours. He'd completely forgotten his son's baseball game until making it home, exhausted and worn.

His wife had greeted him at the door and had looked at him. "Where's Grayson?" she'd asked.

Now he needed to ask that same question.

19

Once in the woods, the two boys moved slowly. The trees blocked most of the moonlight and Dominic had to rely almost entirely on his senses and memory to lead the way. He told Grayson it would be about a thirty-minute walk. They needed to make it back to Knox Elementary and then through another short path to reach Dominic's home.

"But don't worry," Dominic said confidently. "I do this a lot."

Grayson's heart beat wildly and he wiped sweat from his forehead. He kept quiet and looked to be going into shock. Only the pain from his foot with each step kept him going. That and Dominic's leading the way.

Dominic gently took him by the arm and pulled him through the dark forested path. The trail had been cleared for runners so thankfully had very little obstacles. Still, every step proved painful for Grayson and every noise nearly spooked him. As they traveled, Dominic talked nonstop. His voice kept them from thinking about what might be behind them…and ahead.

At first he talked about watching the Dodgers that night and how he'd wished he'd been playing. Then he spoke confidently about what must've happened to Jimmy.

"I've seen those guys lots of times in my trailer park," he told Grayson. "Oh, duck your head, there's a low branch. I think they're some of the guys buying drugs from Bobby Wayne and Dill Coose. I overheard them all once, talking about a new place to, you know, buy drugs. I bet they used the baseball shed. Man, those guys were probably in there when Jimmy went in. I bet they're the ones who hurt him." It came out jumbled, but the more Dominic thought about it, the more it made sense.

He didn't even think Grayson had been listening until the exhausted boy suddenly asked, "What about Rufus? Is he part of it?"

"Oh, yeah, Rufus." Suddenly Dominic felt light and free. He'd found a way to prove his innocence. "Rufus was the one who asked me about the shed. He's the one who set it all up! Come on," he said excitedly. "Let's hurry."

Grayson gasped with pain as his injured foot stepped on a root. Oblivious, Dominic yanked him forward.

A half hour later, the exhausted, sweaty boys reached the edge of the trailer park. Dominic dropped the baseball bag down and sat next to it, breathing hard.

Grayson kept his feet and stared worriedly at the jumble of trailers. Most still had lights blazing.

"Those guys who attacked us," he asked nervously, "they're not here, right?"

"I don't think so," Dominic said with little reassurance. "But we need to stop and make a plan. Uh, Mack, my mom's boyfriend, isn't going to like you being here. I'll have to sneak you in."

Grayson swallowed and looked ready to faint. He was hungry, exhausted, and scared out of his wits. His foot stung and felt wet and squishy with every step. "What do we do?" he whispered fearfully.

Dominic thought for a moment. "Leave it to me," he said. "I'll see my sister. She can help. She's in nursing school." He got up and grabbed Grayson's arm. He led the way into the trailer park. Forgotten, the baseball bag was left behind.

Just in case the teens were at the park, he kept them in the shadows whenever possible. Reaching his trailer, Dominic had Grayson crouch down under his old bedroom's window. The boy obediently sat and stared apprehensively at Dominic. In the light, his hair hung limp with sweat and his eyes were wide with fear as he stared at Dominic.

Dominic swallowed and puffed out his chest. All his fear had dissipated when he realized Grayson had his complete trust. He wouldn't let down his teammate.

"I'll be back," he promised. "Real soon."

Sara stayed in his room now, but her light was dark. Dominic hoped she hadn't gone out. Assured that Grayson wasn't going anywhere, Dominic hurried to the front of the trailer and entered as quietly as he could.

Closing the door softly behind him, he tiptoed into the main room and let out a sigh of relief. Sara stood at the counter drying dishes, wearing old gray sweatpants and a ragged white T-shirt with a credit card logo on the back. That definitely meant she didn't have plans on leaving anytime soon.

Mack lay sprawled across the couch in front of the television, snoring.

"Dominic!" hissed his sister when seeing him. "Where have you been? You need to stop running out at night! Don't you know sickos are out there?" Then she saw his scratched face and bloody arms and clothes. She covered her mouth to stifle a scream.

Dominic motioned her to be quiet and pointed at her room. Nodding, Sara put down the plate she'd held and followed her brother to the bedroom. Her face was ashen. Both walked on their tiptoes to keep from waking Mack. He'd been drinking a lot that night. Waking him up in that condition was never a good thing.

Once inside the room, Dominic rushed to explain everything that had happened. At first his sister couldn't make any sense of it, especially when Dominic went into his theory about the shed. Then she suddenly held up her hands.

"Wait," she said. "You mean there's a boy under the window bleeding worse than you?"

"Yeah," said her brother, staring at her. "I already told you that."

"Why didn't you say that at first?"

"I did, but you didn't listen."

"Never mind," Sara snapped, immediately going into nurse mode. "We have to get him in here so I can check him out. He could be infected."

Dominic sighed. "I know that, but Mack can't know about it. That's why he's lying under your window. We can lift him up and pull him through."

Sara looked at her brother in a new light. "Dominic," she said. "You're either a genius, or a complete fool. Let's do it."

It took some teamwork, but brother and sister managed to make it happen. Sara opened her window and removed the screen. Poking her head out, she saw the small huddled form of the frightened boy. He looked barely conscious. When seeing her, his eyes went wide, though.

"Don't worry," Sara whispered. "My brother is coming to lift you up. Just hang on."

Dominic hurried around from the front of the trailer and helped Grayson to his feet. Sara reached down her arms, but was a few feet short of reaching the injured boy.

Grayson swallowed a whimper. "Now what?" he asked, looking and sounding like a frightened puppy.

Dominic squatted low with a grunt. "This," he said to Grayson. "Good thing you're not heavy."

Wrapping his arms around the injured boy's waist, Dominic stood slowly, lifting Grayson up to his waiting sister. He adjusted his grip to Grayson's thighs to lift him higher until Sara got hold of Grayson's arms. Deftly she pulled him up so she could wrap an arm around his middle. The she tugged him up and into the trailer before sitting him on the windowsill in front of her.

"Hi, I'm Sara, remember?" she said in a way of greeting. "I usually don't invite cute boys into my room like this, but for you I'll make an exception."

Grayson merely blinked at her with his owlish eyes. He looked ready to pass out, or scream, but managed to just stare.

Lifting him gently, Sara carried him to her bed and had him sit still.

She went to one of her bags, lying on the floor near the bed, and returned with a pouch of bandages and disinfectant. Removing Dominic's makeshift bandage of smelly sock, Sara winced more from the smell than anything else. The foot was covered in dirt, blood, and dried urine.

"I'll clean it now to look at how bad it is," she told Grayson, "but you're going to have to wash before I bandage anything." Grayson only swallowed in response. "Oh," added Sara, "and this is going to sting."

She poured the solution over the foot and started wiping it down with gauze. Grayson winced, but kept from crying out. He felt more embarrassed by the strong odor and still damp spot staining his pants.

Dominic returned and quietly closed the door as his sister finished the initial cleaning. "How is he?" he asked.

"Not too bad," Sara said cheerfully. "I don't think it needs stitches, but I'll check later. First, Dominic, we need to get our patient to the bathtub." She patted the top of Grayson's foot and smiled up at him. "He needs a real good soak."

Grayson stared at his reflection in the mirror of Dominic's bathroom. Blinking at what he saw, he was surprised he could still stand. He'd lost his hat in the struggle with the teenagers and his hair was a tangled mess. Stains of dirt and blood splattered over his shirt and pants. A dark bruise marked his left cheek from the fight. There would be plenty more, he felt sure, under his clothes.

Sara knocked on the door gently. "I'll leave some of Dominic's old clothes for you to wear and here's a towel," she whispered. Opening the door a crack, she pushed the items through. "Sorry the door doesn't have a lock, but it broke years ago," she said as Grayson took them. "Don't worry, I'll distract Mack if he wakes, and Dominic is going to hide in my room and pretend to be taking a bath. Once you're finished, meet him there."

Grayson mumbled his thanks. As soon as Sara left, he sank to the cracked floor of the bathroom and leaned against the door that couldn't lock. His mind had been numb since the attack from Kelvin. Now the floodgates opened and the tears flowed. He'd never understood how hard it was for Dominic until now.

Sure, Grayson could struggle during a baseball game. But when it ended, win or lose, he went home to parents who loved him and a safe comfortable bed. Dominic had only this place. No wonder he acted the way he did…

Dominic, he decided, had to be a lot stronger than him when it came to living life. When the tears finally ran out, he took a deep breath and got to his feet.

As soon as possible he meant to get back home and tell the truth about Dominic. First to his dad and then to Jimmy. Dominic belonged on the team. He was a true Dodger.

He quickly pulled off his filthy shirt and stripped off his soaked pants, careful not to hit the wound on his foot. It had stopped bleeding and Sara promised to bandage it once he'd bathed. Once out of his clothes, he limped over and stepped into the bath.

Dominic had filled it earlier while Sara had gone to get something for Grayson to eat. She'd returned with a breakfast bar that Grayson had gulped down in a few bites.

Now he sat and stretched out in the warm water, shuddering with relief. The water felt good and took away most of the pain…for a moment he started drifting off to sleep. Then he jerked awake remembering where he sat. He reached for the bar of soap, managing to bang his hand on the tub, knocking the soap into the water and causing a splash. Immediately, a loud angry voice erupted from outside the bathroom.

"Hey!" it shouted. "Who's taking a bath now?"

Mack had woken up. All the bustling back and forth proved too much. Sitting groggily on the couch, he stared about wildly with bleary, bloodshot eyes.

"Nobody is supposed to use the bath at night—you take all my hot water!" he barked drunkenly.

Sara darted in from Rose's room and put on a false smile.

"It's just Dominic," she said soothingly. "He came back filthy. And, uh, he cut himself a few times."

Mack blinked at her. "Your brother is a stupid sack of bricks. I hope he cuts his own throat one day. Tell him to get out of the tub. I want to talk to him."

Sara's face flushed. "You leave my brother alone," she said evenly. "He's not going anywhere. Here, I'll get you a beer."

She walked hurriedly to the fridge, but as she went by the couch, Mack suddenly lunged from his seat and grabbed her arm, gripping it painfully.

"I'll get my own beer when I want, girl," the man said with a snarl. "I told you to get your brother. Now do it before I take you over my knee and give what's coming to you."

"Let go!" screeched Sara, fighting to free herself. "Why do you want him anyway?"

"Because he took my phone, you stupid nitwit!"

Sara's face went white. She'd lost her cell phone when she'd lost her apartment. The bills had been too high. When Grayson had gone in for his bath, after she'd bandaged the worst of the cuts on her brother's arms, she'd told him to swipe Mack's phone—he'd left it lying on the floor next to his beer cans—and call somebody to let them know about Grayson.

Mack yanked on her arm harder, snapping her back to the moment. "I'm on to you!" he hissed, blasting foul breath in her face. Sara could only scream again.

Dominic had followed his sister's instructions, forgetting his own bruises for the moment. Sneaking into the room with the snoring Mack, he'd quietly crept to the couch and had grabbed the phone before racing back to Sara's room. Once inside, door shut, he only knew one number to call. Flopping down on his sister's bed, he took a deep breath before dialing. He'd memorized the number the day after Jimmy had been hurt. Many times he'd dialed it on his mom's phone but he'd never let it ring until now.

Just as somebody answered it, Sara started screaming.

Jimmy held the phone to his ear. "Hello?" he said in a shaky voice. "Is this Grayson?"

His dad had gotten the call from Mr. Daniels about Grayson missing nearly forty-five minutes earlier. Mr. Roseburg had immediately rushed up the stairs and banged on the bathroom door where Jimmy had just started to shower.

"Grayson is missing!" he'd shouted. "I'm going out to look for him. Get out of the shower and man the phone. Call my cell at the first hint of news." He'd sounded strained with worry. "This is serious, Jimmy."

Shortly after, Jimmy had rushed from the bathroom wearing his smelly baseball pants and dirty jersey over his soaked skin. Brittany already manned the phone by the time he reached the first floor. Mrs. Roseburg had headed straight to the Daniels's house when hearing the news.

Brother and sister had watched the phone intently for several minutes. When the doorbell had rung, they'd both jumped as if zapped with electricity. Jimmy had reached the door first and found Chase blinking at him when he'd opened it.

So the three kids had found chairs around the kitchen table and stared intently at the portable phone lying in front of Jimmy, willing it to ring. Chase had also failed to change from his Dodger uniform. Nobody spoke. The air was thick with worry and the stench of unwashed boys when the phone had started ringing.

"Hello?" repeated Jimmy. Brittany and Chase watched him with strained faces. They saw Jimmy's eyes go wide and hands start shaking. "Dominic?" he said. "What?"

Neither Chase nor Brittany could catch what the other person said, but they did hear the muffled screaming from the phone. Then it suddenly went dead.

Jimmy slammed down the phone and stared at his sister. "That was Dominic. He said Grayson is there, but got hurt. And they're in big trouble."

"What do we do?" Brittany asked.

Jimmy was already on his feet. He tossed the phone to his sister. "You call Dad," he said. "Chase and I will ride our bikes. I remember where he lives."

Brittany didn't argue. "Fine," she said, pressing speed dial for her dad's phone, "but then I'm calling the police."

As Chase met Jimmy on the road, both on their bikes, they were hailed by a third Dodger.

"Hey!" yelled Shawn from up the street. "Where're you guys going?" He coasted toward them on his own bike, also wearing his Dodger uniform. "I just heard about Grayson. I had to sneak away from my sisters to get over here so fast."

Jimmy exchanged looks with Chase. Only Shawn would immediately hop on his bike in the middle of the night and ride off by himself when hearing about a friend being possibly kidnapped.

Still, Jimmy was glad to have his company. As they rode, he hurriedly explained about Dominic's frightening phone call. All he'd heard was Dominic's voice telling him to come as fast as possible. Grayson was trapped in his trailer and in trouble. Then a high-pitched scream had erupted in the background. The call ended abruptly after.

None of them knew what to expect as they pedaled furiously down the road. All they knew was a friend was in trouble.

Shawn started to voice the thought shared by all. "You don't think Dominic took him—"

"No!" Jimmy yelled. He leaned forward on the bike and pedaled even faster.

The remainder of their terrifying journey went by in a blur as the boys fell into a grim silence.

20

As soon as Dominic hung up on Jimmy, he'd dropped the phone and rushed from his sister's room. He found Sara's face being shoved against the wall by Mack. Mack's eyes blazed red with a drunken craziness. He gripped the girl's wrists tightly behind her and laughed at her struggles.

He looked just like the goon who'd attacked Grayson. Just like that, Dominic lost all his fear as his anger spiked again.

"Where do you think you're going to go, girl?" Mack said with a sneer. "You should like this."

"Get off me, you pig!" Sara said through gritted teeth.

"Make me," Mack said, grinning.

"I'll make you!" Dominic screamed. "Leave my sister alone!" For the second time that night he lost control. Charging with his head lowered, Dominic rammed into the back of Mack's legs.

Giving off a startled grunt, Mack flung Sara to the side and spun away to face Dominic. "You stupid brat!" he yelled. "I'll pound you to pulp for that! You have it coming!"

"Dominic!" yelled Sara. "Watch out!"

Dominic didn't flinch. Backing from Mack, he curled his lip into a snarl. "I'm not afraid of you," he growled. "You don't hurt my sister!"

Mack snorted. "You should be afraid, fatso," he said. Then he slapped a hand in Dominic's face, sending the boy reeling back. Mack stepped forward and delivered a second stinging slap and another.

Suddenly, Dominic found himself lying on the floor with his ears ringing and the taste of blood filling his mouth. Through it all, he heard his sister's screams. Mack had abandoned him and now chased her around the sofa.

A loud wail erupted from Rose's room. That settled it. Dominic had had enough. Getting to his feet, he ran from the trailer.

Grayson trembled like a leaf as the screams intensified. He sat in the tub hugging his knees. The water, cloudy with dirt and blood, rippled around them. Then he heard the sharp sounds of flesh on flesh and Dominic's cries of pain. Earlier that night Dominic had saved him. Now it was his turn to repay the favor. Grayson forced himself to stand and climb from the tub. In the process, he banged his injured foot and reopened the cut.

Once out, he didn't bother drying off. He tugged on the old faded shorts left by Sara—they had to have been around for years because they actually fit his narrow waist—and a T-shirt much too large for him. He ignored the socks and underwear. Leaving a trail of blood behind him, he pulled opened the bathroom door and hobbled into a horror scene of chaos.

In the main room, a large grizzled man stood over the huddled form of Sara. The girl had curled herself into a ball and lay just beyond an overturned couch. Beer cans were scattered across the floor. Chairs were knocked on their side.

Since moving back, Sara had cleaned a lot of the mess, but old pizza boxes, clothes, and books were still scattered about. Many greasy pizza boxes were now on the floor among the beer cans.

Grayson lost his breath when seeing the man holding a lit lighter in his hand. For several seconds, he froze and could do nothing but stare.

"You get up, before I start burning your pretty hair," the man said nastily. "I see you combing it every morning. How'd you like to have it torched?"

From somewhere in the trailer, a small child wailed in the background. Nobody paid any attention to the cries.

"Just leave us," Sara begged. "Just go away!"

"Not until you and your fat brother show me some respect!" the man said. He knelt beside Sara and picked up an empty pizza box. Holding it to the lighter, he grinned as the flames started licking the cardboard greedily. "I'm going to drop this on your back in three seconds."

Seeing the box start to flame propelled Grayson to action. In baseball you couldn't panic, no matter the situation. You had to know the options and pick the best one to make a good play before it was too late. All he knew was, doing nothing was not the best option. Taking a deep breath, he felt his body settle.

"Leave her alone," he heard his voice say. He was surprised to hear how calm it sounded.

The man turned to him in confusion. The burning pizza box remained in his hand.

"Who are you?" he asked in genuine puzzlement. "What are you doing in here and where'd you come from?"

Grayson licked his lips. "I'm the kid who's going to ruin you if you don't leave her alone," he said levelly. This time his voice came out squeaky, like a mouse on helium.

"Is that right?" the man asked, sounding suddenly amused. "I think I've been drinking too much. I'm seeing things. All right, kid. Have a nice hot pizza. It's on you."

Grayson saw the man's intent and instinctively ducked. The flaming cardboard sailed over his head and flopped to the ground behind him. Sparks exploded in all directions as it landed. Grayson was already moving.

All the rage and unfairness of the evening welled up inside of him. Screaming, he ran at the man. Just steps away, his bloody foot slipped and he ended up falling head first into the man's middle.

Perhaps slowed by alcohol, the man just stood watching stupidly until Grayson's head smacked into his stomach. The boy crashed down to the floor on impact. The man stumbled back, bawling in pained surprise. Then his foot slipped on an old paper plate and he fell backwards with a loud crash.

For a moment, Grayson saw stars as he lay stunned on his stomach.

Sara remained curled up just beside him. She opened her eyes and blinked at him when hearing the crash.

"Wh-where's Dominic?" she asked dully. Then her eyes widened as she stared past him. "Fire!" she cried. "The couch is catching on fire!"

The grease from the pizza box had fed the fire. Now it spread to not just the couch, but also older magazines and other food boxes lying nearby. The flames were small, but growing by the second. The rancid smell of smoke grew thick.

The wails of the child grew louder and more frantic.

"Rose!" screamed Sara. "Rose is going to be trapped!" Her face panicked, she lunged to her feet, stepping over Grayson's form. "Get out of here!" she yelled down at him. "I'm getting Rose, you just get out!" She hurried toward the little girl's screams from across the trailer, dodging the flames as she went.

"Hey!" shouted the man as he struggled to his feet. He blinked his eyes blearily. "Who lit the fire in here? Are you crazy? What's going on? Get back here! Where's Dom?"

He swayed drunkenly for a moment. His unfocused eyes fell over Grayson. "Dom?" he asked. "Is that you?"

Grayson found his breath. He painfully got his knees and looked fearfully up at the man. "No, I—"

The man's features twisted in sudden fury. "You did this, Dom!" he cried. "You stupid, fat moron!"

Grayson tried to protest that he wasn't Dominic, but the man's hands grabbed the front of his shirt and yanked up.

"Didn't I tell you never to play with matches?" the man roared.

His stinking breath of stale beer, old smoke, and unwashed tongue blasted into the boy's face. Scared out of his mind, Grayson only stared back with wide eyes as his feet lifted off the floor.

The man snarled as he tossed Grayson toward the back wall and looked surprised at how easily the boy flew. Grayson yelled out just before slamming against the wall, banging his right side and head before bouncing off. His body crashed down and went still.

"Dom, what happened to you?" the man asked, blinking. "You're as light as a feather. I barely touched you. I never meant to do that…" He looked dumbly around the room and frowned when seeing flames lick his favorite couch. Small fires burned in front of the TV. "Dom, you'd better get up and turn off the oven in here. Dom?"

Grayson opened his eyes and fought hard to keep from blacking out. His entire right side felt numb and his head rang. He groaned and managed to roll to his back. Seeing the man shuffle toward him, all he could do was let out a weak moan.

Then the man's face grew wide with shock. He went to his knees and stared at Grayson in terror.

"You're not Dom," he said, his voice trembling. "Where's, where's Dom? What happened?"

That's when the front door burst open and Dominic lunged through with a wild look. He carried Grayson's slim black metal bat in his hands.

"Mack!" he yelled. "I'm going to kill you!"

Grayson squeezed his eyes shut and escaped into darkness.

Dominic remembered Mr. Wells telling him once in the dugout that bats were for hitting baseballs only. He'd made

Dominic promise that day to only use them for hitting baseballs and nothing else. Well, suddenly Mack's round head looked exactly like a giant baseball waiting to be smashed.

Mack turned to face him and blinked stupidly. On his knees, he resembled a human t-ball set. Dominic advanced with his face a mask of fury. The bat went to his shoulder and readied to swing away.

He never even noticed the still form of Grayson lying in a heap just behind Mack. All his focus and all his anger went straight at Mack the Monster Jerk. Without even realizing it, he growled through bared teeth.

"Put that down!" Mack barked at him. "Drop it, now!"

Dominic just shook his head. "You're done hitting me and my sisters," he said grimly as he kept advancing. "I'm going to knock you into the next world." He swung the bat viciously in front of him.

Mack's eyes grew wide with fear. Still on his knees, his arms started to tremble. "D-Dom," he sputtered. "Don't be crazy."

"I am crazy, remember?" shouted Dominic. "I'm fat and stupid too! You told me that a million times!"

"It was to make you stronger, really," Mack said, shaking his head, as if trying to clear it. "I did it all to make you stronger."

"Let's see how strong you made me, then," Dominic said, moving the bat up to his shoulder as he stepped in to swing.

Grayson groaned from where he lay on the floor. "Dominic," he cried groggily. "Don't do it!" His eyes fluttered open. Seeing Dominic about to swing, he rolled to a sitting position and nearly passed out again in the effort. "Come on, Dominic!" he gasped. "He's not worth it! Think what Coach Wells would say!"

Hearing Mr. Wells's name, Dominic checked his swing at the last moment. He blinked and looked down at Grayson in confusion. "Hey," he asked. "What are you still doing here?"

"Just leave the guy alone, Dominic," Grayson pleaded, putting his head between his knees. He felt too sick to stand.

Dominic looked at him and then at Mack. The man trembled before him and had covered his face with his hands. Dominic swallowed. He'd dreamed of this moment for a long time. Mack would beg for mercy and he would smash him to bits. But now that it became reality, he suddenly felt sick. He wasn't a monster…he wasn't like Mack.

Then he noticed the fire. It was spreading rapidly and coming his way. Terrible heat baked the air. When he'd entered the trailer, he brought in a gust of wind that had fanned the flames. They now engulfed the couch and the front door. Like a true living monster, the flames roared and licked hungrily toward him.

Suddenly, he realized the danger. He, Mack, and Grayson were trapped in what pretty much amounted to a large tinder box. In moments, the entire trailer would be a giant fireball. Stepping abruptly away from Mack, he flung the bat back out the fiery doorway and hurried to Grayson.

"Can't you ever take care of yourself?" he said when reaching him.

Grayson blinked away tears and he grinned faintly. "Only with you not around," he managed to say. "Wh-what do we do?"

"We get out of here!" Dominic cried. He grabbed Grayson by the arm and tried to yank him up. Grayson cried out in pain and nearly collapsed. "My side," he gasped. "It hurts too bad."

"Here," said Dominic. "Get on my back!" He turned and bent low.

Grayson, totally petrified, quickly complied, wincing in pain as he did so. Grabbing Dominic's shoulders, the smaller boy managed to haul himself up before throwing his arms around Dominic's neck. He hissed from the pain, but hung on.

Dominic bent forward to keep his new burden from slipping off. He felt his friend's body tremble with fear and he needed to duck his head down to keep his neck from being choked. Using his hands to hold Grayson up by his legs, he staggered forward. Together, the teammates stumbled toward safety.

Dominic took the only clear path left—toward his old room, now Sara's room. Mack begged for him to come back, but Dominic kept going.

"I didn't mean it!" Mack yelled. His eyes darted wildly around. He no longer sounded like a monster…just a scared man not knowing what to do. "I didn't mean anything, Dom! Don't leave me!"

Dominic never looked back. Upon reaching his sister's room, he walked straight to the open window where Grayson had first entered.

"You're going to thank me for this later," he said, but Grayson's body had gone slack. The boy had passed out from exhaustion and fear.

Grunting, Dominic, turned and backed to the wall before going to his knees. He let the boy slide easily off into a seated position against the wall under the window.

Mack screamed for help behind him, but Dominic still ignored him. Standing, he turned to Grayson. "I'm glad you're small," he muttered. Bending down, he hauled the unconscious body up by the arms and threw it over his right shoulder.

"On second thought," he mumbled, "you're not going to thank me for this. This might hurt."

Dominic lifted the unconscious load to the open window and leaned against the sill, dangling out Grayson's legs.

From below he heard Rose crying and his eyes blinked away tears. He'd forgotten about his sisters.

"Sara?" he asked hoarsely.

"Dominic!" screamed Sara's voice. "Get out of there! I already got Rose out!" She ran from the shadows and stopped under the window.

"Just take Grayson," Dominic said. "I need to go back and get Mack."

"No!" his sister cried. "Just leave him! He's big enough. He can get out by himself!"

Dominic stubbornly shook his head. "I have to get him," he said. Then he shoved Grayson out to his sister, who caught him by the legs and then his waist, hauling him down into her arms.

Once seeing Grayson safe, Dominic waved to his sister and turned and ran back toward the flames.

His sister's wails followed him. He never listened.

21

Jimmy, Chase, and Shawn arrived at the trailer park to a scene of horror. Dominic's trailer was entirely engulfed in fire. Only the back remained untouched by the flames, but sparks shot out from the roof and started landing on neighboring trailers.

"What happened?" Shawn asked in hushed dismay.

Not answering, Jimmy jumped off his bike and ran toward the fire. Chase and Shawn followed an instant later. As the three boys drew near, they heard voices around the back.

Running in that direction, they found Sara wringing her hands in frustration. A little girl, barefoot and only wearing an oversized T-shirt, sat at her feet bawling softly. She clung to Sara's legs and never opened her eyes. Grayson, looking dazed and spent, lay on his back next to them. He, like Sara, stared bleakly up at the burning trailer.

Jimmy demanded, "What's going on? Who's in there?"

Sara stepped away from the little girl and collapsed to her knees. She covered her face with both hands when seeing him. Sobbing, she just shook her head.

"Gray!" yelled Chase. "What happened?"

Grayson's tanned face looked deathly pale. He'd lost his baseball uniform and now wore tight shorts that ended above his knees and a white shirt so large the collar had slipped below one of his boney shoulders. Barefoot like the little girl, only his right foot was stained by dark blood. He stared at his friends with desperate, groggy eyes.

"Dominic is in there," he shakily. "He pulled me out and went to get somebody else. He saved me."

"Ah, man," Shawn said solemnly. "Ah, man."

Jimmy swallowed hard. Then he kicked the ground savagely. "How long has he been in there?"

"I don't know," Grayson bleakly. "I just woke up…" He sat up stiffly and painfully got to a seated position. "Guys," he said. "We have to save him."

"How?" Chase asked doubtfully.

Sara, still wracked with sobs, provided no help. The little girl beside her started wailing louder and collapsed against her older sister's side.

"That's it," Jimmy said, wiping sweat from his upper lip. "I'm going in there."

Chase grabbed his arm. "Are you crazy?" he said. "Wait for the fire department."

"It'll be too late then," Jimmy said hotly, shaking him off. He wiped his palms on his pants. "Just give me a boost to the window and I'll look around. If I don't see anything then I'll come right back down."

Shawn breathed out loudly. "If you go in there, man, I'm following. You know what Mr. Wells says, always back the play up."

Chase sighed heavily. "Fine, but let's hurry. Remember, if you don't see anything, you get down. Fast."

Moments later Jimmy scrambled up Chase's back to sit on his shoulders. They leaned against the side of the trailer below the open window to keep their balance. Placing a sneaker on Chase's right shoulder, Jimmy slowly stood. Shawn stood beside them, acting as a spotter if Jimmy fell. Jimmy's head just cleared the opening. Heat gushed out, burning his face.

"Dominic?" he called loudly. "Are you in there?" He turned his face away and winced. Sparks from the interior were shooting into the bedroom and lighting the bed on fire.

"Dominic!" he called loudly. "Do you hear me?"

At first there was nothing but the sound of flames. Then a faint voice answered.

"Jimmy? Jimmy, is that you?"

In the end, it was the bathtub that saved Dominic. When Dominic returned to get Mack, he found the man had become like a giant blubbering baby. Mack sat against the wall staring at the approaching fire with tears streaming down his face. His hands were clasped in his lap and he rocked back and forth.

"Go away," he wailed when seeing Dominic crawling towards him. Standing was no longer an option due to thick smoke. "Leave me alone!" He flailed his arms wildly when Dominic reached him and tried to grab him.

Dominic yelled, "Stop being a baby and come with me!"

Shocked by Dominic's harsh tone, Mack stared at him. "Dom," he said, suddenly coherent. "Why'd you come back?"

Dominic grunted and said, "I don't know why. My mom likes you. And I don't want barbecued Mack stinking up my trailer. Now just follow me and we can get out of here."

"We'll never make it," Mack said, shaking his head. "I think I sprained my ankle and the fire is spreading too quickly."

"Just keep low and crawl," Dominic said to him harshly. "Don't be a wimp about it. We can make it to the bathroom at least."

Again, surprised by Dominic's tone, Mack didn't argue. Sniveling, he got on his hands and knees and obeyed. The two crawled through smoke and under the worst of the hot flames. Once they'd reached the bathroom, Dominic kicked the door shut behind them. Smoke started seeping in from under, but not enough to choke them. Dominic rose to his feet and stumbled to the tub still full of water.

"Get in," he snapped at Mack. The large man meekly complied.

Once Mack had climbed over the side, curling into a ball, Dominic turned on the water to full blast and also crawled in the tub, squeezing next to the monster. The two lay huddled in the lukewarm water with cold water blasting around them. They waited to see what killed them first—fire, smoke, or drowning. At least it wouldn't be each other.

But then Dominic heard Jimmy's voice…

"Jimmy?" he yelled out tentatively, in disbelief. "Jimmy, is that you?"

What he heard next sounded like boys cheering.

"He's alive!" yelled Jimmy excitedly.

"Boys!" yelled a voice. "What's going on?"

Chase turned with a start and nearly sent Jimmy tumbling down.

"Mr. Wells?" Shawn asked stupidly. "What are you doing here?"

Their baseball coach ignored the question. He'd rushed from the front of the trailer and took charge immediately. In reality, he found himself passing the trailer park often at night, always wondering about Dominic. On this night, he'd seen the flames and had immediately pulled over.

"Dominic's in there?" he demanded.

"Yessir," Jimmy said, still perched on Chase's shoulders. "I heard him, but I think he's trapped."

"Get down from there," Mr. Wells told him. "Shawn, Chase, run and find all the garden hoses you can. Jimmy, knock on all the doors and warn people about the fire. Get some help." Keeping his voice calm, but firm, he turned to Sara and told her to snap out of it. "You have a hose nearby, get it," he said to her. "Gray, you look after the little girl. Come on, let's move!"

Nobody questioned the old baseball coach and all practically jumped to obey.

Minutes later, just as the faint sound of sirens blared in the distance, three garden hoses sprayed thin streams of water into the back window of the trailer. Several more were being used to hose down the surrounding trailers. Nearly the entire population of the trailer park had risen to the task.

Several bucket chains had been formed—starting in nearby trailers, pots, buckets, cups, and just about anything that could hold water were being filled in sinks and passed down the line. The men and women at the end of the lines threw the water into the burning trailer.

It looked impressive, but did little to slow the flames.

Mr. Wells stood at the back window, directing the garden hoses. Jimmy had climbed back up to Chase's shoulders and served as his eyes into the trailer, peering through the window that Sara had come through. He desperately searched for any sign of Dominic, but only saw smoke and glowing flames.

Tears streaking down her sooty face, Sara stood clutching Rose close to her in the midst of neighbors—the ones too old to help. Many of the neighbors were also openly crying.

Shawn and two men from the park held the hoses and kept steady streams of water directed into the room, desperately trying to keep it clear of fire.

Grayson lay watching it all on his side from where he'd awakened. His pain had vanished as he cried silent tears for the boy still inside the trailer.

They had lost contact with Dominic, but had not given up hope. Not just yet.

Then, with the sirens drawing closer, but still far out, the entire trailer park shook as a massive explosion erupted from the burning trailer. The entire front part of the trailer bucked and shook as it turned into a giant fireball that soared two stories into the air. Huge flames shot up, engulfing the trailer. Sparks and embers started to rain on the onlookers. Only a single section remained standing.

"No!" screamed Jimmy, nearly tumbling from Chase's shoulders. Swinging his right leg free, he slid down and stared helplessly at the roaring flames.

"Get back!" yelled Mr. Wells. "Everyone get back and let the firemen do their jobs!"

The men with the hoses needed no urging. Dropping the hoses as if they'd just turned into snakes, they raced away with stricken faces. Only a single hose kept trained on the trailer.

"I'm not leaving!" Shawn screamed, refusing to go. "What about Dominic? It'll be too late by the time they get here!"

Mr. Wells licked his dry lips and eyed the burning trailer grimly, grief etched on his stricken face. "I don't know, son. I think it's too late already…" His voice choked off in a near sob.

The entire bathroom shook when the explosion occurred. It jolted Dominic from a smoke-induced stupor.

Mack's arms tightened around Dominic's chest. "We're going to die," the terrified man whimpered. "We're going to die."

Dominic blinked and stared over the edge of the tub. He saw a stream of water rapidly covering the floor—like a small river rushing in from under the door. That's when the lights blinked out and only the ghostly flames provided light. As they did, Dominic suddenly sat up in alarm.

The tub had just started to overflow, but the water coming in from the door ran towards him, not away.

"The water!" he cried. "It's coming from the outside! We can still be saved. Come on!"

Mack, still blubbering, followed Dominic like a dog with his tail between his legs. He crawled from the tub, snot trailing from his nose as he stifled sobs. On his hands and knees, he followed after the boy, his soaked clothes dripping.

Dominic paused at the door. The sound of roaring flames filled the air and smoke threatened to choke him.

Mack coughed hoarsely behind him, but kept silent. His eyes, bloodshot and frightened, just stared expectantly at Dominic.

Dominic felt the urge to yell and demand the grown-up do something, but instead he jutted out his lower lip. He knew the way out. He would save them. On his knees, he felt the bathroom door and proved his theory right. Water definitely flowed from the outside. Feeling the door warm, but not burning, he gingerly twisted the knob and opened…to a burning world of terror.

Immediately Dominic received a smack in the face of heat, smoke, and burning embers. But a path opened up before him…marked by the stream of water.

Putting the collar of his wet shirt over his nose, he got back down to his hands and knees and followed it. It had to lead to a way out. It had to lead to safety.

"Don't leave me!" Mack called out behind him, scrambling on his own hands and knees to keep up.

Dominic ignored him. He had seen more than enough TV shows about fire. He knew to keep low and to follow the water. As he crawled, he kept his breath even. The last thing he wanted, he decided, was to become the basis of the newest TV episode about fires—the show where the kid died before the firefighters could save him.

The water led to his old bedroom, Sara's room. Usually it would take him five seconds to make the journey. This time it felt like five hours…

The blue jeans chafed against his skin and his knees slopped in the soaked floor. Burning embers stung the back of his neck and the bare spot on his lower back from where his shirt rose up to cover his nose. Steam wafted from his clothes as the bathwater quickly started to evaporate in the heat. Sweat and soot covered his face. Ignoring the pain, he kept going.

Finally, after what seemed like a mile, he made it to the doorway of the room. Tiny flames licked greedily at the walls and ceiling, around and above him. Only a single path through it all remained. The trail of water had to come from the open window where Grayson had escaped.

Dominic ducked his head low to the soaked floor and tried to breathe in deeply. He knew they could make it, but it would have to be soon.

The water flow had stopped and by now the fire had burned most of the oxygen away. With smoke stinging his eyes and nostrils, breathing became real labor. Fortunately, the open window in Sara's room provided fresh air…that also served as fuel for the fire. He just had to get closer and get up…

Just as Dominic started to crawl into his old bedroom, Mack panicked from behind him. Seeing a way out, he lunged to his feet and stepped hard on Dominic's back. Dominic went down with a grunt of pain and surprise.

Choking, the man fled for the open window, his arms waving wildly in front of his face, warding off any flames. Sparks rained from the ceiling, setting his greasy hair ablaze.

In an inferno of fury, the fire chased after him, filling the doorway with a wall of flames.

Dominic, his back aching in pain, was forced to scoot backwards. "Help!" he shouted feebly. "Help!"

Only flames answered him. They blocked the entrance to his sister's room and seemed to laugh in his face. There was no escape.

22

Mr. Wells crouched and lifted Grayson into his arms to carry him to safety. His eyes tightened as he stood. The trailer looked to be turning into a giant fireball and it threatened to spread. The hoses were not enough. The bucket lines were already falling back as wailing fire trucks neared.

"We can't leave yet," Grayson pleaded through tears. He buried his head into his coach's shoulder. "Dominic's still in there."

"I-I'm sure the firefighters will find him," Mr. Wells said, blinking back his own tears, squeezing Grayson tightly and patting his back without realizing it. "It's all we can hope for now."

Just then a terrible yell came from the house and a man with flaming hair launched himself from the window above them. He belly-flopped hard on the ground and went still, groaning loudly.

Immediately Mr. Wells put Grayson down, plopping the injured boy to a sudden seated position, before running to the man. He beat out the flames and shook his shoulder.

"Where's Dominic?" he shouted. "What have you done to Dominic?"

Mack just shook his head and blinked through red, bloodshot eyes. "I…I didn't mean nothing…" he wheezed. "I, I need a drink," he mumbled. "I didn't do nothing…"

Mr. Wells's eyes blazed stronger than the fire. He gripped the back of the man's smoldering shirt and shook it. "I said, where's Dominic?"

Grayson then yelled out. "I can hear him! He's still inside!"

Dominic's faint voice carried through the roaring flames and thick smoke. "C-coach Wells?" he asked, sounding weak and surprised. It grew stronger. "I knew you'd be back."

"Where are you?" Mr. Wells shouted, abandoning Mack and turning back to the trailer. "Dominic, where are you?"

Inside the trailer, Dominic lay outside his sister's room against the wall, too tired to move. He wiped sweat, blood, and grime from his stinging eyes.

His heart raced with fear and his eyes darted wildly. Mack's wild escape had left flames rising in his wake and now Dominic lay stuck between the bathroom and his sister's bedroom. Wind from the open window had fanned the flames and they roared angrily at him, blocking all escape. Looking toward the tub, he saw the path fill in with fire falling from the ceiling.

"I…I'm stuck!" he managed to shout, before coughing from the smoke. His eyes stung and tears ran down his cheeks. "I really messed up this time…"

"You didn't mess up!" Mr. Wells yelled, sounding ragged. "We messed up, Dominic!" He stared wildly at the trailer, but had to duck back from the flaming window.

Mack crawled to him and grabbed his leg, desperately trying to pull the older man down. "It wasn't me," he blubbered. "It wasn't me…it was Dom… The kid is a psycho."

Mr. Wells struggled to get free as the fire raged.

Horrified onlookers just watched. A few had pulled their cell phones out to film.

Grayson ignored his hurts and the blood soaking his foot. Standing hesitantly, he limped toward the trailer.

"Get back!" Mr. Wells screamed at him. "It's too late!"

Jimmy and Shawn rushed to him from the crowd.

"What are you doing?" Jimmy shouted at him. "Are you crazy?"

"He's there," Grayson muttered grimly, wiping his eyes, blackened by soot. "I heard him. He's just behind that wall."

Shawn took him by the shoulder. "Coach is right. It's too late, man," he said sadly. "Too late."

"No," Grayson muttered. He winced as he took another step and seemed to collapse into Shawn's arms.

"Boys!" Mr. Wells shouted, trying to kick free of Mack. "Get back!"

Jimmy looked down at Grayson's grimy, tear-streaked face. "Save him," the injured boy mumbled just before his eyes slid shut.

Shawn staggered holding the suddenly limp weight and he started to drag Grayson back. "Help me, Jimmy!" he shouted.

Jimmy shook his head. "You've got him," he said calmly. "I have to help Dominic."

Shawn turned and hefted Grayson into the arms of Chase, who had gone after his friends. "Fine," he said. "I'm coming with you."

"What about me?" Chase asked, taking the unconscious body and moving Grayson up and over his shoulder.

"Take Gray to someplace safe," Jimmy said. "And stall Coach Wells. This is one time I'm not listening to him."

He could hear Dominic's faint cries loud and clear now. They were just a few feet from him…blocked by the peeling siding of a burning trailer.

"Get back!" Mr. Wells roared, still trying to free himself from Mack and intercept them.

Chase hurried toward him, gripping Grayson's knees tightly to his chest. "Trust us, Coach!" he shouted. "You taught us how to handle pressure!"

"Not this!" Mr. Wells snarled, finally pulling free of Mack. He raced after Jimmy and Shawn.

Mack blubbered, burying his face into the dirt. "It wasn't me," he wheezed. "It's not my fault…"

Inside the trailer, Dominic ducked his head and curled his body over his knees. Pulling his arms in tight to his sides, he squeezed his eyes shut and waited for the end… His voice had turned ragged and raspy and he could barely speak if he'd wanted to. Not that it would matter… Nobody really cared. His sisters were safe and he'd gotten Grayson out. Heck, even Mack had managed to escape. Everyone would be happy now and forget about him.

After all, this was his life…this putrid trailer that had now turned into a fiery inferno. In a way, he knew, the trailer was just like him—a dirty piece of trash that nobody really cared about…and would go down in fiery anger.

He felt no anger now. Just sadness. Jutting out his lower lip, he blinked away any tears and let the fire come to him. This is what anger did…it burned you and consumed you until there was nothing left. Nobody would miss him…just his mom and sisters who were probably better off without him…

As his eyes closed, he felt a faint breath of air on his cheek…fresh air.

Blinking his eyes open, he coughed. "D-dad?" he asked. "Is that you?"

Then, through the smoky haze, he heard the muffle shouts of high-pitched excited voices.

He lifted his head in puzzlement. "Jimmy?" he rasped. His voice barely spoke above a whisper. "You're still out there?"

Then sparks started to rain over him and he ducked his head down. His only big regret, he would never get to apologize to Jimmy's face for messing up his chance with the Dodgers. At least they had Grayson…

"What do we do now?" Shawn yelled in Jimmy's ear as the boys stood just outside the burning wall.

Dominic's faint calls for help could be heard just on the other side.

"You boys get back to safety, now!" Mr. Wells demanded, rushing up to them. His face carried a wild look that the boys had never seen. It also held a steely firmness that would not crack.

"Coach!" Jimmy yelled. "Look, there's a crack in the wall! We can maybe open it up and get Dominic through!" He pointed where the siding had a gash of several inches that exposed wisps of old, thin insulation sticking out.

Mr. Wells took a look at it and pulled the boys back. "Find something to pry open that crack. Be quick about it!" he snapped.

The boys needed no urging. In seconds they sprinted to the crowd yelling for a stick or an ax.

It was Shawn who found the baseball bat. He'd nearly tripped over it—a metal Louisville youth slugger. Not bothering to think where it came from, he snatched it up from the ground and raced back to his coach.

"I got this!" he shouted.

"Just toss it and keep back!" Mr. Wells yelled at him. Mr. Wells looked like a wild man, his white hair sticking up in different angles and his wiry frame lit by the crackling flames behind him. Reaching out a hand, he grabbed the bat in midair from Shawn's toss.

"Nice find," Jimmy said, coming up behind him and grabbing Shawn's shoulder. "We got this... Coach will get him out."

Shawn only drew in his breath in response. Neither boy heeded their coach's command to retreat. They watched grimly as Mr. Wells took the bat to the burning trailer.

Their coach swung like a man possessed. He wasn't chopping down trees, but hitting home run after home run. First he stuck the barrel of the bat into the small rent in the siding and pried it into a fist-sized hole. Then pulling the bat out, he started swinging with all his might into the siding. Every swing smashed into the thin wall, cracking like a ball being launched in the air.

Only, this time, nothing happened. The trailer wall stood firm. But after the seventh swing it started to buckle. Mr. Wells didn't swing wildly. Instead, he swung in a tight square pattern, peppering the trailer siding in one small area until a final mighty swing sent a large section of it tumbling free, falling into the flaming insides. It all happened in less than a minute, but it felt much longer.

"Dominic?" called Mr. Wells. "Are you there?"

No answer came.

Jimmy's hand dug into Shawn's shoulder, pinching hard. Neither boy dared to breathe.

Suddenly a face appeared at the hole and Dominic blinked out dully. Sweat, blood, and soot plastered his features, but couldn't hide his surprise.

"Coach?" he coughed weakly. "What are you doing?"

Dropping the bat, Mr. Wells immediately reached for his player. The hole was only roughly two feet in diameter and very ragged on the edges. "Getting you out, son," he said, breathing hard.

Shawn and Jimmy ran to help. Behind them they heard the first fire truck arriving and flashing red lights lit their backs.

Dominic ended up collapsing into the arms of Mr. Wells with his teammates assisting. With his eyes shut tight, he clung to his coach until going limp.

"I thought I'd lost you," Mr. Wells said hoarsely, cradling Dominic in his arms, not once sagging under the boy's weight. Relief flooded into his voice. "But I've got you now. You're safe now, son."

Dominic only coughed and relaxed against his baseball coach. "Didn't think anybody cared," he mumbled.

"We all cared, Dominic," Mr. Wells told him, rushing away from the trailer that now started to completely collapse inward. "We cared the entire time. Believe me."

Both sagging in relief, Jimmy and Shawn kept on either side of Mr. Wells and Dominic as a line of firemen came charging toward them carrying axes, oxygen masks, and powerful hoses.

The fire died soon after, but taking the trailer and everything inside with it. Thankfully, what truly mattered, the lives of the people, had all managed to escape.

When Mr. Roseburg and Mr. Daniels finally managed to arrive at the scene, they found their children tired, exhausted, but safe.

They'd have gotten there sooner, but had been searching the woods near the ball field when Brittany's call had reached her dad's cell phone. Earlier they'd found Grayson's hat and baseball cleats among the signs of a scuffle that included patches of blood. Brittany's call had filled them with a mixture of fear and hope all at once. Then they'd gotten lost in the woods on their way back to the parking lot. When they'd finally made it to their vehicles and neared the trailer park, they were met by flashing lights stopping all traffic.

A fleet of fire trucks, police cars, and ambulances had beaten them to it. Both men had immediately pulled off the road and ran the rest of the way. Finding everyone alive, Mr. Daniels started weeping while Mr. Roseburg just clutched Jimmy close to his chest and held on.

Though bruised and with a deep cut on his foot, Grayson suffered more from exhaustion than anything else. He woke up in his father's arms, grinning sleepily when hearing that Dominic had made it.

Mr. Wells had disappeared inside an ambulance with Dominic. The boy was breathing on his own, but had inhaled a lot of smoke and appeared injured. Besides bruises on his body, his hands and knees were scorched and rubbed raw from crawling.

Sara stood outside the ambulance holding Rose and talking on a cell phone to their mom. It had been a close call, but in the end, everyone was called safe.

23

The day after the fire, Jimmy woke up early to the sound of small rocks hitting his window. Rolling out of bed, he shuffled tiredly to the window and peered out to see Chase fully dressed and waving him down.

Sighing, Jimmy opened the window and pulled up the screen. "What?" he asked sourly, leaning his head out. "Don't you know we have school in two more hours?"

Chase frowned. "Are you going?"

"No."

"Me neither. Come on. Get dressed and let's ride our bikes to Gray's and find out what happened last night."

Jimmy started to say something sarcastic, but curiosity won out. Nodding, he closed the window and quickly threw on shorts and a shirt. After a quick stop to use the bathroom and splash water on his face, he ran down the stairs to meet Chase. The two quickly grabbed their bikes and were on their way.

They arrived at Grayson's house to find Mr. Daniels pacing the front yard angrily. Surprised to see the boys, he waved them over and put a finger to his lips.

"Grayson's sleeping," said in a hushed tone "He'll be fine, but the doctors want him to get a lot of rest today."

"We can't see him at all?" Chase asked.

After a moment of hesitation, Mr. Daniels turned and beckoned the boys to follow him. They went into the front room and Mr. Daniels silently pointed to a couch where Grayson lay on his side under blankets. The boy looked peaceful and in deep sleep.

"I gave him some medicine that will keep him out for a while," Mr. Daniels said. Then he choked back tears. "I thought I lost him… I-I wasn't there for him." He wiped his eyes and turned to Jimmy and Chase. "Thank goodness you boys were there… You keep sticking up for your friends, okay?"

Chase and Jimmy nodded and looked uncomfortably at each other.

"Um," Chase said, clearing his throat. "Mr. Daniels, do you know what happened? I mean, all the stuff before the fire?"

Both Jimmy and he had to know. Was Dominic a hero or a villain? Last night had ended in a jumble of confusion. Once the police and firefighters swarmed the scene, Jimmy and Chase had been pushed into the background. Dominic had been taken away on a stretcher to an ambulance, but only with Mr. Wells accompanying him. A police officer also had gone with them in the ambulance. The man who'd jumped from the trailer just before Dominic escaped had been taken away in a police car. Grayson, after being checked over in an ambulance and interviewed by police, had been released to his father and left almost immediately to go to the hospital for a further checkup.

Later, Shawn, Chase, and Jimmy were made to give statements to police officers, but they were given no information in return. It was near midnight by then and Mr. Roseburg drove them home after—their bikes were stored in the back of the van.

Now, hearing Chase's question, Grayson's father's eyes grew hard and he shooed the boys outside. At first Jimmy thought Mr. Daniels was angry at them. Once outside, the high school teacher blew out a deep breath. "That's a good question," he said sadly.

"Um, sorry if we disturbed you," Chase said quickly. "We can go now."

"What?" asked Mr. Daniels, sounding surprised. His eyes softened. "No, you boys aren't disturbing me. Believe me. I'm glad you showed up. I've been going crazy and trying my best not to go to school and get myself arrested. You boys just stopped me from doing that."

Jimmy raised his eyebrows. "Is everything okay?" he asked.

"Oh, I hope so," Mr. Daniels said with a sigh. "At least for me. Some of my students are going to be in for a big surprise when the police pull them out of class. Their fathers won't be very happy either, I imagine. Let's go for a walk and I'll tell you everything I know."

Mr. Daniels proved to be a good storyteller and didn't leave anything out. He'd had a long talk with Grayson and the police the night before. Starting with his battles with Kelvin and Richie, Mr. Daniels repeated to Chase and Jimmy everything his son told him—including about Dominic's theory with Jimmy and the shed.

When they returned to his house several minutes later, both Jimmy and Chase looked lost in thought.

"Thanks, Mr. Daniels," Jimmy said sincerely, meaning it. Mr. Daniels was one of the few grown-ups that treated kids as equals. "We have to go now."

"Yeah," Chase added. "We need to go see a friend."

Mr. Daniels smiled and nodded. "I'll tell Grayson you both stopped by when he wakes up," he said. "Take care of yourself… And when you see your friend, make sure you thank him for me."

It turned out that Kelvin and Richie were too afraid not to show up for school—they didn't want anybody to know something was wrong. Thankfully Kelvin turned out to be way more frightened than hurt from the night before. The gash on his head had needed stitches, but Dominic had never "ripped his face off." He'd told his dad he got the injury "messing around" with friends. They'd heard about the fire at the trailer park, but didn't know any details.

Then, just as the first bell rang, they could only stare in shock as two burly police officers strode through their homeroom door. They carried handcuffs and grim faces. The principal followed helplessly after, looking lost and befuddled.

The two teens, suddenly scared, stood and meekly offered no resistance.

Beating on little kids did not sit well, no matter who their fathers happened to be. Both teens were sullenly cuffed by the officers. Then they were led away in front of the shocked faces of their classmates.

"This mean the party is cancelled on Saturday?" called a boy, who immediately ducked low when one of the officers glared back at him.

Kelvin and Richie could only hang their heads. Their dads could not help them this time… One of them was too busy writing a letter of resignation from his school board position.

That afternoon, Chase, Shawn, and Jimmy went to Eastland Hospital to visit Dominic. They found him sleeping in bed and covered in bandages almost from head to toe. Mr. Wells sat in a chair next to him reading a book. He looked just as surprised to see the three boys as they were to see him.

"Uh, he's sleeping," Mr. Wells said unnecessarily. "Don't worry, he just has a lot of cuts, burns, and bruises…nothing serious. Mostly I think he's exhausted."

Dominic's eyes blinked open. "I'm not sleeping," he mumbled. "I'm bored." Then he saw the boys and struggled to sit up. "What are you guys doing here?" he demanded.

Jimmy dropped his eyes and held up a baseball. "We, uh, came to give you this," he stammered. "We, uh, well, most of the Dodgers signed it for you."

"Yeah," Chase added. "And we got you this." He held up a brand-new baseball glove. "We know your old one got burned up."

Dominic blinked rapidly. "They both did," he said dully. "My dad's glove too…"

"Don't forget this, too," Shawn said next, pushing his way past his two friends. He knew Dominic didn't want to show his friends any tears. He held a new baseball bat. "I had to stick it down my pants to hide it from the nurses," he said. "They thought I sprained my knee."

"Too much information, Shawn," Mr. Wells said gruffly. The coach pushed himself to his feet. "Well, since you boys are here, I'm going to stretch my legs and maybe find something to eat." He yawned and stretched out his hands. "I trust you all have some talking to do."

"Bring me back a soda!" Dominic called to him. Then he swallowed when Mr. Wells turned on him with raised eyebrows. "I mean, please," Dominic added.

The coach nodded as he left. He wore a faint smile.

Left alone, the boys fell into an awkward silence. Then Jimmy moved to the side of the bed and extended his hand. "Uh, and I came to say sorry. I know you didn't do anything in the shed. I, I was wrong to think you did. I was an idiot."

Dominic looked at the hand and then at Jimmy. "How'd you know?"

"I, er, we spoke to Grayson's dad this morning," Jimmy said. He ducked his head, but made sure to look at Dominic. "Besides that, you always were trying to help me. I know that now."

Chase came up from behind and smacked Jimmy's back hard. "And he needs the help." Brushing hair from his eyes, he grinned and his voice grew excited. "And Grayson's dad called Jimmy's dad a few hours ago. He gave us the update."

"Yeah, didn't Mr. Wells tell you?" Shawn said, putting down the bat and going to stand on the other side of Jimmy. "The police got all the guys who did it. Rufus confessed everything. Kelvin, Richie, and two guys from the trailer park were all arrested." His eyes carried respect and his smooth face broke into a smile. "I heard Kelvin had two black eyes and a three-inch cut on his forehead…"

Jimmy couldn't hide the awe in his voice when he added, "He said he got attacked by a grizzly bear."

Dominic grunted. "I got mad at him," he muttered. Then his mouth twisted into a frown. "Bobby Wayne and Dill Coose were the two guys from the park," he said. "I bet it was drugs. Everyone knew they were selling junk."

Chase nodded. "Yeah, you were right the whole time. Uh, I think your trailer park got raided… You lost some neighbors, dude."

Dominic grimaced. "I don't live there no more," he said. "My trailer is burnt to a crisp." He smiled slightly. "But it's a better place without those guys. Most people are nice there. It's good all the bad stuff is gone."

Chase nodded. "Still, dude, we should've listened to you."

"Yeah," Shawn added. "We were wrong. Seriously."

"So," Jimmy said, keeping his hand extended in front of Dominic. "Are we friends?"

Dominic looked at the hand with wide eyes and then up at Jimmy. In a single night, his whole life had flipped upside down. Sara had told the police everything about what had happened the night before. The doctors had also found many old bruises among his new injuries. Mack, once checked at the hospital, went straight to jail, charged with child abuse, arson, and attempted murder. It didn't really matter to Dominic… After what he'd gone through, Mack the Monster Jerk would no longer haunt him. Never again. It was time for Dominic to start a new life. A life where he didn't have to worry about turning into something he was not.

Dominic reached up and met Jimmy's hand with his own. Even though it was covered in white bandages, he squeezed hard and shook. "Friends," he said.

"And are you ready to play for the Dodgers?" Chase asked him eagerly, practically shoving Jimmy to the side, breaking the handshake and solemn mood.

"Yeah," Shawn added, "because I didn't smuggle that bat in for nothing. You got to practice your swing!"

Dominic's eyes dropped and he frowned. "I'll have to ask Mr. Wells about that," he said gravely. "He's letting my mom and my sisters stay at his place for a while. I get to go there tomorrow, but I don't know if he'll let me play baseball again."

Jimmy, Shawn, and Chase all shared glances.

"Want to bet?" Jimmy asked, his eyes gleaming.

When Mr. Wells walked in with five cans of soda cradled in his shirt, he was nearly tackled by three excited boys. The cans went crashing to the floor and rolled in all directions as Shawn and Chase each yanked an arm and Jimmy practically leapt on his chest. A fourth boy watched with pure pleasure on his face. Mr. Wells had no choice but to promise to let Dominic rejoin the Dodgers as soon as the doctors cleared him. Otherwise, he may've ended up in the hospital as another patient.

The visit ended with the three boys and Mr. Wells being kicked out for spraying the room with soda and making too much noise.

After all the excitement, it was tough returning to the baseball field, especially without Dominic. The Dodgers had a game the following day against the Marlins. They'd beaten them easily the first game, but that was ages ago…almost a lifetime had passed since then.

To make matters worse, Mr. Wells wouldn't be at the game. Dominic had been released from the hospital but was confined to bed rest. The coach didn't want to leave his side. Mr. Roseburg and Mr. Gordon would do all the coaching. Mr. Gordon looked and acted quiet and subdued. He never raised his voice the entire time.

Before the game, the Dodgers team got a standing ovation from the crowd. Their heroic actions from Tuesday night were widely known. Even the Marlins coaches and players came out to clap.

Grayson had managed to convince his dad and doctors that he could play and warmed up on the mound with Jimmy. He had bruising on his side and ribs and a heavily taped foot, but otherwise seemed recovered. He wouldn't pitch that day—the cut on his foot made it too hard to plant on his windup. Still, out of habit, the battery mates threw a short session.

"Foot okay?" Mr. Roseburg asked Grayson when they'd finished and returned to their dugout.

The boy nodded, stamping it to offer proof. His face carried a dark bruise on his cheek and more bruises were hidden by his new Dodger uniform. The old one had been ruined in the fire and he had to get new baseball pants and the last Dodger shirt left—a jersey so big that half his number fourteen got lost in the back of his pants when he tucked it in. Still, his face had the glow of pleasure as he returned to the game he loved.

Mr. Roseburg knocked the bill of his cap askew and good-naturedly rubbed the top of it before patting his back. "Atta boy, you'll be back on the mound in no time." Looking at Jimmy, who still stood on the field, he grunted. "You set for a ball game? Get back out there and lead this team to victory."

Jimmy grinned. "Yes, sir, Dad."

"Let's go, boys!" Chase yelled from behind Mr. Roseburg, shoving by Grayson. "Let's win this thing!"

While the Dodgers charged onto the field, fired up to begin with, things quickly settled down. Shawn started on the mound for the Dodgers and immediately gave up two straight hits on only three pitches. The third batter walked after five more pitches.

In a blink of an eye, the bases were loaded and there were no outs.

Jimmy, playing behind the plate, called time. He waved in the infield as he walked to the mound.

Phil at third, Chase playing shortstop, Grayson from second, and Mike from first all trotted to the mound.

"Listen," Jimmy began, keeping his mask on, "we're playing a game we love, right? Win or lose, we still love it, right? Well, we know what happened the other night. Dominic isn't here because of it. That is somebody who has never won before. So let's go out and win for him. Got that? From now on, we win for Dominic." Finished, he slapped the ball in Shawn's glove and turned back to the plate.

At first there was stunned silence behind him. Then Chase beat his hand against his glove. "That's right!" he said loudly. "Let's get this game, boys! Let's *really* go this time!"

Shawn nodded grimly and fingered the ball. All at once he had a game to play. Wiping off early sweat from his brow, he settled on the mound.

The Dodgers quickly returned to their positions with a new intensity.

"Play in!" yelled Mr. Roseburg. "Ground ball goes home!"

The next batter had no chance for a ground ball. Shawn, clearly fired up, blew in three straight heaters that smacked into Jimmy's glove for strikes. The batter swung on the last and went back to the dugout with disgust written all over his face.

After him came a long-legged kid named Ken Banks. A potential all-star, he was good player with a lot of pop. Jimmy looked to his dad, but Mr. Roseburg shook his head and snapped his fingers twice. It was their signal for good luck. Jimmy would call the pitches.

Calling for a fastball, Jimmy shifted to the inside part of the plate, hoping Shawn could jam Ken into hitting a ground ball.

Ken was too smart to let that happen. As Shawn threw for the inside of the plate, Ken brought in his hands and managed to get the fat part of the bat on the ball. It blasted straight up the middle back at the pitcher.

Shawn instinctively lifted his glove at the last instant and managed to deflect the ball into the ground near the mound. It bounced crazily toward first base.

Grayson, playing up near the infield grass, tracked the ball with his eyes and dove forward, snatching the bouncing ball from the air with his glove. He ignored the pain from landing on his bruised side. Swiftly rising to his knees, he smoothly transferred the ball from glove to throwing hand and fired back to home.

Jimmy had yanked off his mask at first contact. Stepping on the plate, he'd had his glove up in hopes of a throw. He got it just before the runner from third crossed the plate.

"Out!" yelled the umpire at home. Jimmy was already stepping forward and pulling the ball from his glove. With all his might, he fired to first.

Mike stretched out his long arms and with his foot barely on the bag made the catch just as Ken reached the base.

Briefly hesitating, the second umpire pumped his first emphatically. "Out!" he yelled.

The Dodger crowd, led by Brittany and Mrs. Roseburg, erupted in cheers. On the other side, the Marlins stared in disbelief as not a single run scored after loading the bases with no outs. Ken had both hands on his helmet and stared at the departing infield in disbelief. All he could do was get sympathy from his first-base coach.

Mr. Roseburg greeted the Dodgers with a smack on the backside for Jimmy and high fives for Shawn, Mike, and Grayson.

"Nice play, now go get some hits to back it up," he said.

Grayson tried, but after taking two strikes he swung and missed on a high fastball. At first he looked ready to cry when he returned to the dugout with a slight limp, but then blinked the tears away. Taking a seat on the bench, he calmly took a deep breath and clapped his hands.

"Get a hit, Jimmy!" he called.

Eyes on the pitcher, Jimmy didn't disappoint. After taking a ball low, he crushed the next pitch and sent it screaming into left field. The Marlins knew he had pop and had played him deep. However, the fielder ran up early and then misjudged its flight. Before he could recover, the ball went over his head before bouncing onto the grass. It rolled all the way to the fence and after a poor throw from the frustrated fielder, Jimmy made it to third. It was his first triple of the season. Standing up from an unneeded slide, he pulled off his batting glove and brushed dirt from his knee. He ignored the cheers of the crowd as he looked toward home. All that mattered was making it there.

Shawn followed with an RBI base hit to right that allowed Jimmy to jog to home. It was only the start. Shawn scored when Chase nailed a hard grounder just fair down the third baseline and ended up with a double. Just like that, the rout was on.

By the fourth inning the score was Dodgers 12 and the Marlins 0. After his strikeout, Grayson had two sharp singles and two steals. Everyone, in fact, had at least one hit on the team. Everyone but Dominic…

When the game ended as the Marlins coaches conceded with the mercy rule, the Dodgers did little celebrating. They still had a ways to go to save their season. But they were on their way.

Dominic returned to school the following Monday. By then the Dodgers were back over .500. They blew out the Giants, a team that had beaten them before, 10-3 on Saturday.

When Dominic walked into his school that morning, he found the halls strangely empty and quiet. Puzzled, he wrinkled up his nose in a frown. Sometimes he felt that he had to be dreaming. He and his sisters now lived with Mr. Wells in a spacious two-story house while his mom had found an apartment closer to her jobs. She visited on weekends. Mr. Wells had been shocked to learn Dominic had shared a room with Rose and now made sure each of the siblings had their own room… To Dominic it felt like living in a castle. At some point he expected to wake up and be trapped back in the trailer…

Thankfully, it had yet to happen. But now he seemed to be by himself in an empty school. It felt as if he'd just walked into an episode of the *Twilight Zone*, an old sci-fi show he used to watch. Could he be dreaming? Sara had taken Rose to school that morning, but Mr. Wells had dropped him off late—he'd lost his keys during breakfast and finally found them in the fridge.

Dominic swallowed. School had never been this quiet before. He felt the urge to run back outside to find Mr. Wells, but knew it was too late. His car had zipped away as soon as Dominic climbed out.

"Hello?" he called, walking stiffly through the hall. This was getting really weird. None of the classrooms down the hall on his right made any noise. These were the kindergarten rooms and were usually always bustling with young voices giggling and teachers trying to give directions. Now they were as silent as sleeping mice.

"Where is everybody?" he wondered aloud.

As he reached the fifth-grade hall he was surprised to see a sign on the wall with his name on it. An arrow under it pointed toward the Cafeteria. He still couldn't hear or see anybody in the classrooms, so, completely mystified, he followed the sign. Reaching the Cafeteria, he found another sign with another arrow. Even more bewildered, he followed this one too… More signs finally led him to the gym in the back of the school. Over the gym's double doors was a large sign with his name written in Dodger blue. Under it was the word *ENTER*.

As soon as Dominic opened the door, the clapping began. The entire school sat in the gym facing him. Everyone started to stand and cheer. Swallowing, Dominic quickly shut the door and turned to run. That's when he saw Mr. Wells standing behind him.

Letting out a surprised squeak, Dominic nearly jumped straight out of his shoes. "Where did you come from?" he demanded.

"I parked around back as soon as I dropped you off," the old coach said mildly. Then he grinned. "You don't like pep rallies for your honor, huh? I don't blame you." He shrugged his shoulders. "Sorry, but we went through a lot of trouble setting this up, bud. A lot of kids have sacrificed their class time for this, so you'd better go in there. Besides, there's cake."

Dominic wiped his eyes furiously and shook his head. "Why?" he asked, his voice barely above a whisper.

Mr. Wells walked to him and put an arm around his shoulder. "Because they now know what I know. You're a very amazing person, Dominic. You're not just smart, but you're loyal, brave, and as tough as nails. And you're a hero. Come, we'll go together. You know, I had to pull several strings to make this happen. I even got Grayson and Shawn out of their school to be here."

They stopped just in front of the gym door. Dominic squeezed his eyes shut and sniffed loudly, refusing to go another inch. "Don't you know I have an emotional disability here? They think I'm bad."

Mr. Wells shook his head sadly and then bent down, moving both his hands to Dominic's shoulders and turning him so they were eye level. "Son, the whole world has an emotional disability. It doesn't matter what you have, or what people think you have. All that matters is what you do with what you have. And you, Dominic, are not bad. You did a man's job. Understand? With a lot on your plate, you stepped up and crushed it. You protected Grayson, helped your sisters, and even saved Mack's life. That's no small stuff. Don't you ever forget that. You're not bad and you never were."

Nodding sharply, Mr. Wells straightened back up and dropped his hands to his sides. "You ready to go in, now?"

In response, Dominic flung his arms around his coach and held tight. They stayed this way several seconds before entering the party.

The rest of the month of May went by quickly. Rain played havoc with the schedule. Some teams had extra days off, while other teams had to cram multiple games in a single week. Dominic and Mr. Wells remained absent from the Dodgers, which proved as frustrating as motivating. The team wanted them there, but also fought hard to win for them. By the time June rolled around, and the final rain makeup games were played, the Dodgers finished with eight wins and six losses. They'd won four straight before dropping their finale to the Cardinals by a single run, a score of 6-5. Nate Dyson had quieted their hot bats and scored the winning run on a double in the sixth from Joey Carter. The loss only served to make the Dodgers even hungrier for the championship.

In the first playoff game, the quarterfinals, the Dodgers smashed the Marlins for the third time. In the semifinals they faced the Yankees. Down 2-0 early, the Dodgers roared back in the fourth with consecutive hits from Grayson, Jimmy, Shawn, Chase, and Phil. Chase had his first home run of the season. By the sixth inning the Yankees had nothing left and fell 11-4.

The Cardinals, unsurprisingly, would face the Dodgers in the championship. They'd easily won their game 12-0.

24

Jimmy's dad drove Jimmy, Chase, and Shawn to the field early for the big game. It was a cool Saturday morning on the first official day of summer vacation. With a gentle breeze and barely a wisp of clouds in the sky, it promised perfect weather for baseball. The championship game would start at ten that morning, but they arrived closer to nine. They wanted to be there first. Not only would this be a championship game, but it would also be the first game since the fire with Mr. Wells back on the bench. In his absence Mr. Daniels had helped out, but he was the first to admit he knew more about the English Renaissance than coaching bases. Not only would the coach be back, but Dominic would also be in the lineup. In fact, he was scheduled to pitch first. That was why Jimmy begged his dad to take them early. They wanted to be there to prepare Dominic for the big day.

Since the Cardinals had the better record, they were the home team. This meant the Dodgers had to bat before Dominic's first pitch. All the boys wanted to make sure Dominic took the mound with a lead.

"Want to throw?" Chase asked Jimmy and Shawn as they unloaded their gear from the back of the van. He sounded tight.

Strangely, Jimmy also found it hard to swallow and he had to nod his answer.

Shawn tried to chuckle, but it came out more like a choking noise. "Man, I can't believe how nervous I am," he said, shaking out his hand.

Mr. Roseburg slammed the driver's door and said, "You boys better get loose. You've all played in championship games before. This is nothing new."

Chase swallowed. "Yessir," he said, "but this is Dominic's first."

Jimmy nodded. "And it could be his last," he added. Ever.

Mr. Roseburg made to say something, but jammed his ball cap on and turned away.

Jimmy felt numb as they walked across the grass to the field. His dad was trying to hide it, but Jimmy knew he also felt the same nervous tension. What if Dominic couldn't throw a strike? Or worse, what if he had one of his tantrums? Or hit a batter?

The three boys soon fell into the familiar rhythm of throwing the baseball. They tried to block out all the negative thoughts.

Grayson joined them next. The boy had completely recovered from the fire and had completely recovered his hitting. He now led the team in batting average, just slightly ahead of Jimmy. Jimmy would've had a stronger average, but his dad did the team's official scoring. He didn't like giving free hits to his son for any bobbled ball, missed grounder, or bad throw that led to Jimmy getting on base. These were always put down as him reaching on an error.

Nobody made much conversation and it was turning into a somber affair. Finally, Shawn, not taking it any longer, let out a loud belch.

"Hey, let's play pickle," he said.

Jimmy looked up and grinned. "Good idea. I'm thrower first!"

"Me too!" Chase immediately chimed in.

Pickle was the game where two throwers stood at two bases while everyone else were the runners and stood at one base. The object of the game was for the runners to "steal" as many bases as possible without getting tagged out.

It was a fun, fast game that easily got out of control. Ordinarily Mr. Roseburg would never allow it before a game, especially a big game. But on this day, seeing the boys laughing and goofing off like normal, he didn't say anything.

When Mr. Gordon arrived moments later, he saw the pickle game and was about to bark at them to stop, but then thought better of it.

"Go join them, Phil," he said, grabbing his son's gear and giving his head a quick rub. Phil didn't need a second invitation.

Other Dodger players trickled in and all eagerly joined the wild game. The Cardinals also started arriving and their coach had them gather on the opposite side of the field from the Dodgers.

"You boys don't need silly games to get ready," the Cardinal head coach barked loudly to his team. He glared toward where Mr. Roseburg calmly sat in the dugout, writing out the lineup. "We win because we focus and take things like this seriously! Let's warm up like champions and show those boys how it's supposed to be done."

Mr. Gordon eyed him for a moment and then belched loudly before turning to watch his team become a disorganized mess. Grayson and Xavier were caught on the ground with Chase looming over them, whacking their pants with his glove yelling, "Out, out, out!" The other players were running wildly past toward Jimmy, who urged Chase to get him the ball. Mr. Gordon couldn't help but smile.

The Cardinals players fell into organized drills. All but one…

Nate Dyson strolled over to the pickle game and politely asked Jimmy if he could join.

"Sure," Jimmy told him. "Just watch out I don't accidently bean you."

Nate snorted and entered the fray. One red shirt among blue hardly stood out.

By the time it was time for infield practice and batting practice, Mr. Wells and Dominic had still not shown up. Mr. Gordon called for the pickle game to stop and for the players to gather around him.

Nate gave Jimmy an extra hard smack in the back and said he hoped he lost. Jimmy responded by kicking the Cardinals' player in the seat of the pants and promised to bring more of that on the field. Laughing, Nate ran to join his team.

Mr. Gordon waited for the players to sit and settle in front of him. He licked his lips nervously and scratched his chin. Finally, after looking at his watch, he told Grayson to warm up his pitching arm with Jimmy and for everyone else to split up into groups of outfielders and infielders for drills.

Jimmy had just gotten his gear on in the dugout when Grayson smacked his head with his glove.

"Ouch!" cried Jimmy. "I'm glad I'm wearing a helmet."

Grayson ignored him and bounced up and down like a human pogo stick. "They're here!" he cried. "Look! Dominic is here with Mr. Wells!"

Shawn ran over to join them and started beating Jimmy's head with his glove, jumping up and down like it was Christmas morning. "Isn't this awesome?" he shouted.

"Yeah, my teammates are idiots," Jimmy said, but breaking into a grin. "It's totally awesome." Still, he had to blink back a tear when he looked over at the parking lot.

Soon after, the entire Dodger team abandoned any drill they'd started and rushed to the fence. Mr. Wells walked stiffly and a bit nervously toward the field. At his side, Dominic wore a gleaming Dodger uniform and carried his glove and the bat presented to him in the hospital.

Chase stared clapping and soon everyone, even the fans in the stands, followed.

"Guys!" hissed Jimmy. "Stop that. You're going to make him nervous!"

"Okay, boys!" Mr. Gordon barked loudly. "Back to drills! If you don't pay attention, you don't play!" Quickly the Dodger players raced from the fence.

In reality, it seemed like everyone but Dominic was nervous. When he entered the dugout, Grayson smacked his shoulder and then ran off to field grounders. Dominic would take his place on the mound. The boy grinned at Jimmy and held up his glove to show the signed ball from the hospital.

"I still have it," he said.

Jimmy said, "Um, you don't want to use that to warm up. It'll get ruined."

"I know." Dominic put the ball down on top of Jimmy's bag. "I brought it for luck. Come on, let's go to the mound!" The boy hurried onto the field.

Feeling butterflies performing a tap dance in his stomach, Jimmy followed.

Despite the Dodgers' players participating in their drills, almost every eye went to Dominic when he started throwing. Mr. Gordon and Mr. Roseburg could've and perhaps would've had a heart attack at so many errors in the drills, but they too were too busy watching Dominic to notice. Mr. Wells stayed outside the field and spoke with Mrs. Roseburg, who had arrived with Brittany. The coach did his best to not watch Dominic throw.

"Start easy," Jimmy said to the pitcher from his crouch. "Just toss it to me."

Dominic ignored him. Rearing back, he threw a bullet that snapped into Jimmy's glove. He'd been waiting for this moment for a long time. He'd also been practicing. Every afternoon at Mr. Wells's house he threw pitching sessions with Mr. Wells. At night he watched instructional videos and did his best to listen to all the advice Mr. Wells gave. Now it was payoff time.

After five more throws Jimmy's glove hand was starting to sting. Mr. Wells called for them to stop. Having left the stands, he entered the field and trotted to the mound. He waved for Jimmy to join him.

Dominic looked at Mr. Wells and cocked his head. "What did I do wrong?" he asked. He sounded more curious than belligerent.

"Dominic," said the coach, licking his lips. "A pitcher isn't alone. He has a team of fielders behind him and a catcher in front of him. You can't just throw what you want. Remember, you need to work with your catcher. Trust your team, Dominic."

Dominic shrugged. "I know that," he said. "You told me that over and over."

"Dominic," Mr. Wells said calmly, "I've watched Jimmy tell you to slow it down. You haven't been doing that."

Dominic blinked. "Oh. I've tried to. I just can't help throwing hard."

Mr. Wells looked at Jimmy and raised his eyebrows. "What do you think?" he asked.

Jimmy grinned ruefully and shook his glove. "If he throws like this in the game we're going to win easily. He's hit every target I've given him so far."

"In that case," Mr. Wells said, smiling, "let's shut it down and wait for the game."

25

The first inning of the championship game started with a bang when Grayson took the first pitch for an opposite field double. Jimmy followed with a clean single in center. Only a strong throw from Joey kept Grayson from scoring. He scored on the next pitch when the overwhelmed pitcher landed a fastball in the dirt a foot from home plate. The ball ended up at the backstop as Grayson raced for home.

Immediately, the coach of the Cardinals barked for time and he called for a pitching change. The starting pitcher kicked the mound in disgust, but gave up the ball without argument. This was the championship game and there would be no messing around. The new pitcher was Nate Dyson.

After Nate's warm-up tosses, Shawn walked to the plate with a swagger in his step. The small Cardinals' pitcher on the mound just stared at him coolly. His first pitch was his arcing changeup that caught the outside corner for a called strike. The next pitch zipped in almost immediately after Nate got the ball. It hit the inside corner for another strike. Shawn frowned and choked up on the bat. Another arcing changeup finished him off. He swung too early and caught nothing but air.

This set off the loud Cardinals coach and got the fans going.

As Chase went to bat next, Mr. Wells motioned for Grayson to sit by him. Instead of taking his usual seat on the bucket away from the players, the coach sat in the dugout and paid more attention to his players on the bench than the game.

"Okay, Gray," the coach said pleasantly. "We're going to play a game. What will be the next pitch?"

Grayson licked his licks and shrugged. "Fastball?"

"I'm guessing it'll be his falling changeup," the coach said.

Sure enough, after taking the sign, Nate wound up and threw a slow falling pitch that completely fooled Chase. He swung too early and too high.

"Now it's a fastball," Mr. Wells said just before Nate indeed threw a fast one. This one Chase almost caught up to. He fouled it back into the backstop.

"How do you know?" Grayson asked, his eyes wide with even more respect for his coach.

"Easy," Mr. Wells said, grinning. "Nate is a great player, but he's tipping his pitches. Watch. When he throws his changeup he always first pauses to grip the ball in his glove. He grips it about three times before he even starts to wind up. On his fastball he doesn't pause at all. He gets the ball and fires it right back without even pretending to windup."

Once keyed to this, Grayson easily saw his coach was right. Excitedly, he rushed to share the information with Phil, who waited on deck.

Mr. Wells sighed with pleasure as the game continued. His eyes twinkled with mischief. Nate got Chase to popup for an out. Then Phil swung on the first pitch, a fastball right down the middle of the plate. With a loud clang, he sent a low sizzler straight back to the mound. The Dodger crowd started to roar, but it turned into groans. Somehow Nate managed to pivot his body and backhand the scorching grounder into his glove. He calmly threw to first for the final out.

Grayson threw his head back in disbelief, but Mr. Wells gave him a pat on the side. "You can't always beat talent," he said with a smile. "Now get on out there." The coach then turned his attention to his starting pitcher.

The moment had arrived. Dominic would make his pitching debut. Grabbing his glove, he stumbled from the dugout, ignoring his teammates' pats on the shoulder. Mr. Wells wished him luck and he grunted in return. His mind blank and heart pounding, the boy barely heard his instructions from Mr. Gordon as he headed for the mound.

In the stands, Sara stood and yelled, "Let's go, Dominic!"

Then Rose's tiny voice was clearly heard. "Which one is Jimmy?" she demanded. "Dommy said Jimmy the best baseball player in the world is here. And he has a sister Rose. I want to see Rose!"

"You're Rose," his mom said, sounding confused. "Sit down and watch your brother."

"Go Jimmy and Dommy!" Rose screeched before complying.

Dominic's face burned—with embarrassment and pleasure. For the first time, his entire family would be watching. His mom had promised to take off work to be there and must've brought his sisters during the top of the first…

He didn't dare look toward them as his eyes settled only on the mound. His heart started to beat a mile a minute.

Then suddenly a dull thud struck his back—not hard, but definitely firm.

"You okay, Dominic?" Jimmy asked him, his catching mask pulled down.

Dominic swallowed and nodded. "Just nervous," he admitted. "I've never really done this before in a game."

Jimmy pushed up his mask and put his arm around Dominic's shoulder. "Just relax," he said in a friendly tone. "This is just like before. I'll show you my glove and you just throw the ball there. Okay?"

Dominic nodded and took a deep breath, feeling some of his tension leave. "It's just I don't want to mess up."

"Trust me, Dominic," Jimmy told him. "We all mess up. I did with you, remember?" He gave Dominic's back a final pat and trotted toward home plate. "Remember, just aim for my glove," he said over his shoulder. He stopped just before reaching the plate before turning again. "And you can tell me about 'Jimmy the greatest baseball player in the world' later," he added. He grinned. "I definitely want to hear about it!"

Dominic's eyes narrowed, but then he smiled and felt relaxed. "Yeah," he muttered. "He's the one with the big mouth."

Sara's voice cheered again, this time joined by a host of other Dodger fans. Somewhere in the midst of it, he knew he heard Bud's voice. His dad had to be watching…

Taking another deep breath, he settled on the mound and started into his first warm-up pitch.

The Cardinals came up only down a run, something their loud coach made sure to remind them about.

"We're down!" he hollered as he watched Dominic intently as the pitcher got loose on the mound. "But we're not out! Far from it!"

Dominic's first throw had sailed high over the catcher's head and clattered into the metal mesh backstop. The next one went well wide and caused Jimmy to make a diving catch, stretching out to his left.

The Cardinal coach's mouth curved into a wicked smile. "Remember, these guys once led us by five runs," he barked loud enough for the Dodger side to hear him, "and we still won! Easily! Let's force their pitcher to throw, got it?"

This turned out to be bad advice. While Dominic finished his warm-up pitches, the third-base coach, a pencil-thin man with a serious face, walked up to Nate, the Cardinals' leadoff batter. Not as belligerent as the Cardinal head coach, he still eyed Dominic with cool, calculating eyes.

"Take some pitches," he told Nate, loud enough for Jimmy to hear. "Let's let this pitcher walk you. Give him a good show, but don't swing. We'll make him a little wild. Trust me."

Knowing the strategy, the head coach roared loudly in from the dugout. "Let's get an easy base here!" he yelled.

The umpire settled in behind Jimmy and called for the batter.

Feeling a little mean, Jimmy called for the first pitch to be slow and down the middle.

In the warm-ups, Dominic had started tight and come out throwing all over the place. Now he was starting to settle in. Concentrating on Jimmy's call and wanting the pitch to land on target, he went into a slow windup, carefully lobbing the ball straight into Jimmy's glove.

Nate kept the bat on his shoulder and watched it go by for a strike. His eyes bugged out as the lollipop pitch went by untouched.

Jimmy could feel the batter's frustration at missing the inviting pitch. He grinned from behind his mask.

"One more!" called the third-base coach. "Let's make this guy consistent." He clapped his hands together.

Jimmy again called for a pitch down the middle. This one came harder, but almost begged to be hit. Once again Nate let it go by and he quickly fell behind 0-2.

Loud groans rained from the crowd in red. The fans for the Cardinals were incensed. They'd never seen Nate let two good pitches go by without swinging.

"You got to swing to get a hit!" yelled a father. "Come on, Nate! What's going on with you?"

The third-base coach bit his bottom lip and made the motion to swing away.

The loud coach of the Cardinals stood in his team's dugout and banged the fence in front of him, clearly not happy.

Jimmy only grinned more broadly as he saw it. The next pitch he asked for was a high heater. Dominic delivered, right on target.

Nate chased it and went down on strikes. He didn't look at his coaches as he trotted back to the dugout.

Jimmy glanced to the Dodger dugout and smiled. He knew Dominic had it. Just like that, the pitcher and catcher were playing a game of high-speed catch.

After two more batters, Dominic had three strikeouts. Not a single ball touched a bat. Seeing the first strikeout had sharpened his focus and he did everything Jimmy asked. He seemed shocked when the inning suddenly ended.

As the last batter flailed helplessly at his inside heater, he saw Jimmy roll the ball toward the mound as he got up and trotted toward the Dodgers' dugout.

The crowd cheered loudly and started chanting his name.

"What just happened?" Dominic asked, a little surprised.

Shawn, coming in from third, smacked the back of his pants with his glove. "You just threw lights out, Dominic!" he crowed. "You took down the side, man! One, two, three, bang!"

"Already?" Dominic asked. Sweat ran down his face and his arm suddenly burned. But a smile crossed his face. "That was fun."

Just like that, all the nervous tension evaporated from the Dodger dugout. It became a party that proceeded with a hit parade.

Poor Nate tried his best on the mound. After striking out, he went back out determined to return the favor. It didn't work out for him. Somehow all the Dodger hitters knew what he was throwing before he even started his pitch.

After an entire season of hitting, the Dodgers were locked in and ready with their bats. Armed with the knowledge of Nate tipping pitches, they were primed and eager. Tom started the inning with a single—rifling a changeup between first and second base. Draymond batted next. He'd been sick a lot during the season and missed some games. He didn't miss Nate's first pitch—a fastball that he turned on in a hurry. The third baseman was in position to make the play, but his glove wasn't fast enough and the ball zipped right under him and into the outfield.

The crowd started to buzz and Nate bit his lower lip as he got the ball back. This did not seem possible. Taking a deep breath, he glared toward home plate.

Will batted next. He sent his first pitch high in the air for a popup to the second baseman. Still, the fact that Will had swung and made contact unnerved Nate. All his pitches were being hit by weak batters. His next three pitches were in the dirt. One squirted by and advanced the runners to second and third.

In the Cardinals' dugout, the thin, serious coach just looked bewildered and confused. "I don't get it," he muttered.

Next to him, the loud coach was just irate. "They're stealing our signs!" he yelled. "Don't use them anymore. Just throw the ball, Nate!"

Nate did just that. The next four pitches were nothing but fastballs. Mike got a piece of one, but went down swinging for the second out. The third out took a while to come.

Xavier, as Jimmy predicted, had turned into a pretty good ballplayer in his first year. He'd developed into a pure fastball hitter. It was the off-speed pitches that messed him up. Poor Nate hadn't done his scouting. He fired in more fastballs.

Letting one go by for a strike, Xavier drove the next pitch deep into centerfield. The fielder misjudged it and the ball ended up well over his head. Xavier ended up on third and the Dodgers had two more runs.

Liam followed with a grounder up the first baseline that got into the outfield. Another run made it 4-0. These were supposed to be the weaker hitters of the Dodgers.

The Dodger fans were on their feet and the Cardinals' loud coach's hat was in the dirt. Batting last, Dominic entered the batting box next. He carried his new bat and wore Jimmy's batting gloves. It was only his second official at bat all season. But earlier he'd shown he could pitch on his pitching debut. This made the Cardinals nervous.

Nate wiped sweat from his brow and kicked the dirt on the mound. It was the first time all year he looked nervous when pitching.

Jimmy started the clapping in the dugout and the entire team joined him. They even started chanting Dominic's name. Jimmy didn't go that far, but he did yell for Dominic to hit a home run. Only he had heard Mr. Wells's orders to Dominic before the boy went to the plate.

"Act like you're going to knock it out of the park," Mr. Wells had said softly, "but don't take your bat from your shoulder. Trust me. You'll be on first." Then he'd smacked the back of Dominic's shoulder. "I'll see you safe at home."

Dominic had nodded and strode to the batter's box like the descendant of Babe Ruth.

The first pitch went into the dirt for ball one. Ball two was called on the next for being too high. Finally, Nate got a strike on a generous call on an outside pitch.

Swallowing hard, the pitcher started fingering the ball in his glove again. This didn't help him because Dominic, looking cool and confident, didn't chase any pitches. Nate threw the next two pitches in the dirt.

Without lifting his bat, Dominic reached base on a walk. He nonchalantly flipped his bat to the dugout and sprinted to where Mr. Roseburg waited at first. Mr. Wells had done a lot of coaching at his home and Dominic had proven to be a good listener when given the chance. Mr. Roseburg greeted Dominic with a pat to the back and then started telling when and when not to run.

The Dodgers moved to the top of the lineup as Grayson trotted eagerly to the plate. The Cardinals coach found his hat and clapped his hands together. "One more out, boys!" he roared. "This is the guy, Nate! You put him down before, do it again!"

That had been in a different game. In this game Grayson watched Nate throw quickly and knew another fastball would be coming. Watching the seams spin toward the plate at shoulder height, he stepped into his high swing and was rewarded with solid contact. A hot liner sizzled off his bat and shot over the shortstop. Only a good play by the centerfielder kept it to a single. This loaded the bases for Jimmy.

The Cardinals' loud coach yelled for time. Muttering about sign-stealing thieves, he stalked to the mound and called for a new pitcher. Joey Carter would take the mound next.

Jimmy stood and watched the warm-up. Joey had a smooth motion and a hard delivery. He didn't tip his pitches. Shrugging, Jimmy swung the bat and tried to time the pitches as the Cardinals' pitcher threw. Then the umpire announced it time to play ball.

Seeing Jimmy settle in the batter's box, Joey curled up his upper lip and bared his teeth into an ugly smile. Then he spat before looking for a sign.

Breathing easily, Jimmy took a practice swing, crouched low, and waited. He took the first pitch high for ball one. The next pitch he swung and missed to even the count.

Stepping out of the box, he looked toward third at Mr. Gordon.

"Hit me home!" yelled Dominic from second. "Come on, Jimmy!"

Mr. Gordon grinned and pointed to Dominic. He said, "Just do what he said."

"It's the best player in the world!" shrieked a young girl's voice from the stands. "It's Jimmy!"

Rolling his eyes, Jimmy stepped back into the box. He did a few more practice swings and then stared at the pitcher, trying to find the ball. The last pitch had been low and away. He decided to hope the next one would be the same. Lucky for him, it was.

Jimmy reared back and delivered all his power into his swing. He got the ball cleanly and solidly. As soon as he hit it, he knew where it would end. Dropping the bat, his eyes never left the ball's flight as he started for first. It kept going, going, and gone…over the fence. A home run—the first in his life…and it was a grand slam.

Unfortunately, it counted as a two-run grand slam. As soon as the ball cleared the fence, the loud Cardinal coach launched from his dugout, demanding the five run per inning rule.

The umpire looked at him, but then nodded as he waved the runners around. "Only two runs count," he called out. "I know it's a championship game, but we're playing the five-run inning mercy rule."

The Dodgers didn't care. They were too busy screaming and leaping up and down in glee.

Joey tried to glare at him from the mound, but finally just shook his head in respect. Nate, playing at shortstop, put his glove under his arm and gave a sullen clap. Then the loud Cardinal coach hollered for his team to get off the field. They were batting. But first they had to watch the runs score.

As Jimmy trotted to first he kept his head low, but inside he burst with joy. His dad greeted him at first with a knock on his helmet and swat to his pants. "Nice one, kid," he said gruffly. "Go finish your bases anyway. It's your first."

As Jimmy calmly continued to second, he watched Dominic charge around third, his face lit up with joy. Jimmy couldn't stop smiling then. The second run, the fifth run for the Dodgers that inning, came from the foot of Dominic Lewis.

His cleat print remained for Jimmy to see as he reached home. Somehow that meant more than his home run.

26

The game only grew worse for the Cardinals after that. The loud coach kept getting angrier and angrier as he tried to steal Dodger signs and get his team back into the game. Chewing gum vigorously, he glared continuously at the Dodgers' dugout while shouting at his players.

The third-base coach for the Cardinals just kept his arms crossed and also tried to find an advantage for his team. Both were clearly frustrated and looking for any break they could find.

Dominic didn't return to pitch in the second inning. He'd thrown so hard and with so much energy in the first that his arm had turned numb and his body felt exhausted. After scoring the run, he happily sat on the bench next to Mr. Wells to watch. Shawn came in as the relief pitcher. Jimmy remained at catcher.

As the two trotted out to the field to warm up, Shawn grabbed Jimmy's arm in the infield.

"Hey, dude, weren't you going to pitch this year?" he asked.

Jimmy stopped to turn to his friend, definitely one of the best. Of course Shawn would remember his big plans before the season. He yanked on his catching helmet and shrugged, glancing back to where Dominic sat with Mr. Wells.

"Nope," he replied. "I just thought I was." He smiled back at Shawn. "Next year or maybe in all-stars I will. Don't worry about that."

"Hey!" Mr. Gordon barked from behind them. "You two going to talk all day, or play ball? Let's get some warm-up pitches! Come on!"

The two jumped into action, but as they trotted to their positions, Mr. Gordon called behind them. "And have some fun out there, boys! This inning is all yours!"

"Whatever that means," Shawn mumbled as he reached the mound. Then he grinned.

After that, once the inning started, every time Jimmy looked for a pitching sign from Mr. Gordon, the coach made a funny face back at him. It was hard to keep a straight face…especially at what Shawn started to do.

Shawn, taking Mr. Gordon's advice to heart, started to "tip" his pitches similar to Nate. For fastballs, he pounded his glove once before firing it from the stretch position. On any sort of changeup, he deliberately gripped the ball multiple times in his glove and then threw from the windup. He was so obvious about it that it took only a single batter before the coaches of the Cardinals called for time and had all their players huddle up.

"I got it!" the third coach said excitedly. "Come in, boys!"

As they did, Shawn winked at Jimmy before kicking the mound in pretend frustration. Jimmy stood from behind the plate and shook his head. He didn't bother visiting the mound…he didn't want to "tip" off the Cardinals that anything might've changed. Being friends with Shawn, he knew what would be coming. Shawn always loved playing games, even when he was already in the middle of one.

Struggling to hide his smile, he put a hand on his hip and hung his glove loosely at his side, watching the Cardinals whisper excitedly in the huddle. They acted as if they just learned a great secret. None dared to look over at the Dodger pitcher.

"Let's go!" yelled the umpire. "Batter up!" he barked. As he did so, the big man in blue patted Jimmy's shoulder and spoke softly. "I've been umpiring for twenty years, kid, but I've never seen something like this…if that Cardinal coach wasn't so loud and foolish, I'd tell him he's in a den of foxes. You boys have his number, his shoe size, and his ball team…all in one giant pickle jar with the lid screwed tight. No air holes, either."

Jimmy glanced back and grinned. "Uh, yes, sir. Maybe."

Grunting, the umpire pulled his mask down. "This ought to be good. No mercy rule is going to save him this time."

Jimmy crouched back down and nodded at Shawn. The coolest pitcher on the mound yawned back, adjusted his hat, and shook out his glove.

Let the fun begin.

The first batter had reached base on a walk. The Cardinals sensed a comeback and their fans were on their feet. Joey Carter batted next. He'd received his "special" instructions from his coaches on the way to the plate and settled confidently in the box.

"Ready to strike out, Joey?" Jimmy asked him conversationally. He rarely spoke to batters, but he couldn't help it this time. When he'd looked for a pitching sign, Mr. Gordon had crossed his eyes and pretended to pick his nose. The whole game felt like, well, a game. It was fun.

Joey merely grunted. He didn't appear to be having much fun. Jimmy didn't blame him. With a guy yelling in his ear the whole game he probably had a headache.

Now Joey meant business and planned to knock all the fun out of the Dodgers in one swing.

"I'm getting my home run back," he drawled softly to Jimmy. "Just you watch." His eyes gleamed as he settled in his stance and cocked back his bat.

On the mound, Shawn deliberately tapped his glove before delivering a fastball in the dirt.

Jimmy managed to block the ball, sliding to his right. Having the ball bounce off his thigh pad, he grabbed it with his bare hand before it could roll away and allow the runner on first to move to second. The runner stayed on first, but clapped his hands eagerly.

Shawn acted like the pitch slipped and he kicked angrily at the mound, but Jimmy knew better. He just wished Shawn would've warned him.

Joey smiled for the first time that night. "Kiss that ball goodbye before throwing it," Joey said back to Jimmy. "I'm going to make your home run look like a popup."

"Good luck," Jimmy said, meaning it. He tried hard not to laugh as he stood and fired a fast ball back to the pitcher.

"Get the next one over," he called.

Shawn snatched the ball in his glove and nodded, as if still mad.

As Jimmy settled back down, he glanced toward his dugout. Mr. Gordon had stuck sunflower seeds under his fingernails and pretended to be anxiously biting them. Grinning, Jimmy set up his glove dead center behind the plate and waited for the payoff pitch.

Tapping his glove, Shawn took a deep breath. From the stretch, he threw a slow changeup right over the plate.

Joey was so sure it would be a fastball that he'd actually sighed with pleasure as he swung. It was definitely a home run swing. It was just way too early and it turned the player completely around. As the ball slapped into Jimmy's glove, Joey ended up sitting down with a thump right on home plate. He wore an utterly shocked expression, completely dumfounded.

Jimmy calmly stood and threw the ball back to Shawn. "Need a hand up?" he asked Joey innocently.

Shaking his head furiously, Joey quickly got to his feet. He glared at the pitcher. This time Shawn fingered the ball several seconds pretending to find his "perfect" grip for a changeup.

"You got this one, Joey!" hollered the Cardinals coach. "Remember what I told you!"

Shawn gave a slight grin. From the windup, he threw a fast ball. Again, completely fooled, Joey swung and missed badly. This time he was way too late.

The Cardinal fans groaned and grew hushed with shock. They'd never seen their batters and pitchers so overmatched before.

Slamming his bat on the plate, Joey glared at Shawn and growled from the back of this throat. He struck out on the next pitch, another fast ball after Shawn had tapped his glove.

The Cardinals coaches howled with agony as Joey stalked from the plate.

"He changed it all!" he shouted as he approached his team. "I didn't know what he was throwing until after he threw it!"

Hastily the Cardinals coaches called another huddle and told their players to disregard everything from the first huddle.

It was way too late by then. The next two batters, utterly confused, struck out. The last slammed down his bat and ducked his head in defeat. From the catcher's position, Jimmy patted his shoulder in sympathy as he rolled the ball toward the mound.

"Tough break," he said. "Maybe next year."

"Yeah," muttered the Cardinal player. "Maybe next year I'll get to play for you guys."

Dragging his bat, he slowly trotted toward his steaming coach, whose face now wore the same shade of red etched on the Cardinal uniforms.

"You Dodger boys are something else," the umpire muttered to Jimmy watching the batter go.

Jimmy could only agree.

The game was pretty much over by then. Cardinals were out hit, out pitched, and out coached from every direction. The Dodgers tacked on five more runs before the Cardinals got another chance to bat.

Grayson, with his two brothers—both fresh home from college—watching in the stands with his parents, took the mound after Shawn. Spurred by a new confidence, he mixed in his knuckleball with his fastball. It completely unhinged the batters, even if it sent Jimmy scurrying to the backstop to retrieve a few wild pitches.

After just four innings, the frustrated Cardinals wearily threw in the towel with the score 16-0. The Dodgers had won the championship with the mercy rule.

"We won?" Dominic asked as the last Cardinal batter went down swinging in the bottom of the fourth with Grayson still on the mound.

"Yessir," Mr. Wells said, clapping a hand on Dominic's knee. "The Dodgers just won the title and you just won your first start, son. Now get on out of the dugout and go celebrate with your teammates."

Dominic staggered to his feet in a daze. Since scoring after his walk on the homer smacked into left field by Jimmy, he'd never lost a wide smile, not even after he'd struck out in his only other at bat.

Now his smile faltered slightly. "You mean it's all over?"

"Nope," Mr. Wells told him, smiling at him mysteriously. "It's just beginning. Now, seriously. Get on out there."

Out on the field, the Dodger players were tossing up their gloves and charging into the pitcher's mound to celebrate. Grayson hopped up and down before running and jumping into Jimmy's arms, nearly bowling the catcher over.

When the team saw Dominic stumble hesitantly from the dugout, the entire team whooped with delight and veered right for the dumbfounded boy.

They ended up piling on top of Dominic in front of the dugout, right where Mr. Wells remained seated with a wide smile spreading across his wrinkled face.

"Hey, come on, guys!" Dominic yelped from beneath a tangle of arms and legs. "We just won!"

"Yes we did!" Chase crowed from on top of the pile. "You're the champion, man!"

The boys cheered louder.

Joey and Nate looked on from the opposing dugout with undisguised envy.

"I hope we join them in all-stars," Nate said, wistfully.

"Yeah," Joey said glumly. "You and me both."

Mr. Wells sat back taking it all in. Years seemed to melt away from his face. The other coaches of the Dodgers moved to stand near him and watch the celebration. They, especially Mr. Gordon, wore similar smiles. Their thoughts unified. Baseball had to be one of the greatest of sports.

Mr. Gordon finally broke up the dogpile by dumping the water cooler on the boys and reminding them they still had to shake hands.

Shrieking from the cold water, the boys gathered themselves and, giddy, finally lined up on the first baseline to face the line of dejected Cardinals.

Any and all ill will between the teams quickly melted away as the players and coaches moved through the line to shake hands and offer congratulations. The season had ended and summer beckoned.

"Great game," the loud Cardinal coach, now speaking in a resigned mutter, said to each Dodger player, slapping their hands.

Near the end of the line, Nate stopped in front of Jimmy and eyed the Dodger boy's spiky wet hair and soaked jersey plastered to his chest.

"Should've been us," he mumbled.

Jimmy grinned and patted the Cardinal player on the head. "Maybe next year, kid," he said gravely.

Nate wrinkled his nose and then looked squarely in Jimmy's yes. "Tell me the truth. Was I seriously tipping my pitches?"

His teammate Joey snorted loudly from just behind him, bumping him good naturedly. "Man," he drawled, "you were tipping your pitches worse than tipping cows on a hot, slow Texas night!"

Jimmy and Nate stopped their conversation and both looked at the bigger boy with raised eyebrows.

"Don't worry," Nate muttered to Jimmy. "If we make all-stars, he gets easier to understand with time."

Joey shoved Nate aside and smacked Jimmy's right shoulder. "Maybe I do, but you sure don't. I couldn't understand a thing out there with you behind the plate. You made us think we were playing in a different league out there!"

Jimmy only grinned and smacked Joey's shoulder in return. "Go talk to Shawn. He's the real joker. Hopefully we'll have a lot of time to teach you in all-stars."

"You bet, man." Joey shook his head. "I still mean to kick your little rear end, even if it's in practice. You got it coming. I won't forget your homer."

Jimmy laughed as the line moved on. "Bring it!" he called over his shoulder. "Just watch out for the fastball down the middle!"

After handshakes and trophies were handed out, the Dodgers went out for pizza and ice cream.

Before leaving, Dominic had run to his mom and dragged her onto the field to introduce her to his friends. She had yet to formally meet them.

Dominic's mom had greeted Jimmy, Shawn, Chase, and Grayson with a huge smile and tears in her tired eyes. She'd seemed embarrassed, but overwhelmingly happy and proud all at once. A tall, slightly plump woman with a gray streak in her otherwise dark hair, she'd looked as if she wanted to hug all the boys at the same time. Clutching a pocketbook awkwardly in front of her, she'd smoothed down her new mint blouse and tan slacks. All she'd said, over and over, was, "Thank you…thank you for helping my boy."

"Uh, ma'am," Shawn had told her politely, "I think he helped us a whole lot more. We couldn't have won without him."

The other boys had echoed these sentiments, but it only seemed to make her cry more.

"Come on, guys," Dominic had said gruffly, clearly more embarrassed than his mom, "come and meet my little sister." The little girl had snuck up on them and had run and attached herself to his leg.

When introduced to Jimmy, the little girl, wearing a brand-new green and yellow sundress, spoiled only by a large ketchup stain in front, had suddenly gone shy. She hadn't said a word, but had hid behind her brother staring at Jimmy with large, dreamy eyes.

Jimmy, who hadn't seen the little girl since the night of the fire, had grinned at her and promised to see her later. "You have a cool brother," he'd told her. "And one thing I learned, he doesn't tell a lie. Ever."

Dominic's face had burned and he'd quickly returned Rose to Sara and his mom before going off with Mr. Wells to the pizza place. Jimmy had offered him a ride, but Dominic didn't want to leave the Dodger coach.

As the boys headed away, Jimmy had noticed his mom going over to Dominic's mom. He'd hid a smile and had no doubt that he'd see her again.

Later, during the ice cream, the teams' all-star players were announced—Phil, Jimmy, Chase, Shawn, and Grayson would join the team, along with Joey and Nate from the Cardinals, and play travel that summer. Mr. Wells would be their head coach…the loud Cardinals coach would be one of his assistants. The surprising news, though, was that Dominic Lewis would serve as the team manager. The other Dodger players all promised to come out and watch. It promised to be a great summer with lots of learning all around.

Jimmy couldn't wait to get back on the field.

27

Jimmy lay flat on his back, drifting lazily on a long inflatable raft in the middle of the pool. Dodger blue and white, the raft matched the other three rafts drifting near him, each occupied by a tired, but contented ball player.

Like Jimmy, they were all in bathing suits with no shirts, including Dominic, who lay in the raft near Jimmy's feet.

Dominic's pasty white skin had been slathered with layers of sunscreen by his older sister Sara before the pool party. Though he still bore faded bruises and cuts from memories that would never be forgotten, he no longer felt ashamed. They were from another life, one that he'd conquered and would be a distant memory, nothing more.

Grayson and Shawn were on either side of Jimmy and both appeared asleep—their bodies limp and their eyes closed.

It was early evening after the big game and Jimmy's parents had invited the boys to an impromptu cookout to celebrate. Even after pizza and ice cream, Jimmy's stomach rumbled as he smelled sizzling steak on the grill, where his dad stood in a group that included Mr. Wells and the dads of Shawn, Grayson, and Chase. Grayson's brothers had been invited, but they had plans with their girlfriends. Dominic's mom was in the kitchen with the other moms preparing a salad and chocolate chip cookies for dessert. Rose and Sara were in the TV room going through Brittany's old dolls that she'd just given to the little girl. Reggae music blared from the speakers of his dad's radio by the grill.

Jimmy sighed in contentment. Everything seemed perfect. The food smelled great and the summer air felt wonderful. He patted his flat stomach and smiled wide. To quote one of his favorite movies, everything was awesome.

"Guys," he said. "This is the life."

"You got that right," Shawn told him, his eyes closed. Then he added, "If only Chase was here to enjoy it."

"Yeah," murmured Grayson, sounding more asleep than awake. "He's so lucky…"

Dominic grunted loudly. "How come? We're the ones floating in the pool. Where's he at?"

Jimmy frowned and lifted up his head. "Yeah, where is Chase? I haven't seen him since we got in the water."

Shawn yawned. "Oh, he's with your sister. She's teaching him French."

Dominic snorted loudly. "She's teaching him *French*?"

Clearly not asleep, Grayson cracked up, stifling giggles.

Jimmy lay still for a moment, his face twisted in a frown.

Shawn made a kissing sound, prompting Dominic to snort. "Oh, that type of French…"

Suddenly Jimmy's eyes widened and he gasped. "Are you serious?! What the—"

He tried to twist his body to face the house, but instead flipped his raft, sending himself flying face-first into the water.

"Whoa! Error on Jimmy!" his dad shouted from the grill. "Can't you control that thing?"

The other dads laughed and turned back to the cooking meat.

At the grill, Mr. Roseburg prodded the steak with a pair of tongs and breathed in deeply.

"You know, Ben," he said to Mr. Wells, "it was a great season, but I'm glad it's over. Man, do I ever need a break."

Mr. Wells nodded. "All-stars will be starting soon," he reminded him.

"Yeah, but we have a week to relax and recover," Mr. Roseburg said, starting to flip the smoky meat. "I need it."

"So do I," admitted the baseball coach. "I nearly lost my faith in the game." He nodded to toward the pool. "Those boys restored it…all of them." Even as he said this, his eyes settled on Dominic.

Back in the pool, Jimmy came up sputtering and wiping his eyes furiously. "You'd better be joking!" he said hotly, oblivious to the adults. Chest deep in water, he started for the side.

Dominic sat up in his raft puzzled. "What's going on?" he asked. "What's wrong?"

Shawn grinned wickedly and also sat up. "Oh, Jimmy just misses his sister suddenly."

"I'm not going to miss you when I ram my fist in your nose!" Jimmy hollered back to him.

He just started pulling himself from the water when from around the corner of the house charged his sister Brittany with Chase right at her side. Brittany wore her pink one-piece bathing suit while Chase had on his lime green swim trunks. Both carried an armful of water balloons.

Jimmy just started to breathe a sigh of relief when the first balloon sailed his way.

"Got you, stupid brother!" Brittany shouted, launching her windmilling softball pitch while on the run. The balloon knifed through the air before exploding with a loud splat into Jimmy's chest.

"I'm already wet, stupid!" Jimmy shouted in retort, biting down from yelping from the stinging pain. His sister had a live arm. Then he ducked, but still got nailed in the shoulder by a balloon fired by Chase. So did Chase.

"Check again, stupid," Brittany said, pulling up at the edge of the pool, wearing a wicked grin. "Chase and I filled these up special."

Jimmy looked down and his eyes went wide. Bright yellow liquid dripped down his skin and pooled around the waistline of his suit, dripping down his trunks.

"Oh, no…" he said. "You didn't—"

His sister's next toss caught him in the face and his head jerked back as liquid exploded against his cheek, going up his nose and into his mouth. He shrieked and flopped back into the water.

Coming up spitting and choking, he glared at his sister, but couldn't help smiling in relief as he tasted sweet lemonade on his tongue. "You two are in so much trouble," he seethed when his mouth cleared of pool water and lemonade.

"I know," Chase told him, cocking back his arm with another balloon ready to throw. "I just asked your sister out. And she said yes."

"No way!" Shawn shouted. "Who saw that coming?

Chase's balloon smacked down into his lap, causing him to sit up sharply only to tilt over and plunge into the pool.

"Saw what coming?" Chase yelled at him when he surfaced. He flung another balloon at Grayson.

Yelping, the smaller boy rolled into the pool as the balloon slammed into the water next to him. "They're throwing toilet water at us!" he cried.

"Get under your rafts!" Dominic shouted, splashing into the water, following his own advice. "Use it as a shield and let's get them!"

He'd made sure to drift in the shallow water and easily stood as he pulled the raft in front of him. He hadn't admitted to his friends that he couldn't swim yet.

Jimmy just stared open mouthed at his sister who smiled sweetly down at him, standing next to his friend…her new boyfriend. Then he closed his mouth and ducked as Brittany launched another balloon at his head.

When he surfaced, he saw his sister standing on the side peering down at him poised with yet another balloon.

"I don't believe this," he groaned. All at once, he turned back, swimming for his raft. A balloon smacked the back of his bathing suit as his sister's deadly aim continued.

The great water fight commenced as the four boys in the pool, led by Dominic, used their rafts as shields and advanced on the balloon throwers, who were quickly running out of ammo. It ended with everyone in the water, shrieking and splashing.

Jimmy tried unsuccessfully to dunk Chase and ended up getting dunked instead.

"That's my man!" Brittany crowed, just before getting a mouthful of pool water thanks to a giant splash from Dominic.

"Leave my friend alone!" Dominic howled, but with obvious joy in his voice.

Shawn took Grayson onto his shoulder and they pretended to be part of the Power Rangers. They ended up toppling back in a splash when Chase dove down at Shawn's knees.

During the ensuing splashing and yelling, Brittany paddled over to her brother and grabbed him around his neck before he could react.

"Listen, stupid," she whispered in his ear. "Chase just asked me on a date to see a movie. It's nothing serious. We're just friends, okay?"

Jimmy squirmed to get free, but his sister held on tight. He tilted his head back toward her. "So you weren't teaching him any French?" he asked.

Brittany reacted by jerking his head back. "Don't be gross!" she cried, just before pulling him under the water and letting go.

Mr. Roseburg watched it all with a blank face and then sighed. "Okay, I know it's only been over for a few hours, but I really can't wait until baseball starts back up," he said, focusing back on the browning meat. He hadn't heard what his kids said, but he'd seen enough.

Mr. Daniels and the other dads laughed.

"You certainly changed your tune fast!" the English teacher said.

Mr. Roseburg grunted. "Hey, I just want to go back to peace and quiet. Baseball is at least something I can predict."

Mr. Wells just smiled. "Don't bet on it," he said. "I have Dominic down not only as the team manager, but also as a possible pitcher."

The other dads groaned, but then broke up into laughter.

"Count me in," Chase's dad said. "I don't think I can miss another game after what I saw today."

Shawn's dad agreed. "You bet. Those boys need to be on the field together." He winced as a tremendous splash erupted in the pool. "It's the only place they're safe."

Mr. Roseburg lowered the tongs and stuck out his right arm to shake Mr. Wells's hand. "I'll never question another decision of yours again—"

A shriek from the pool interrupted him, causing the tongs to clatter on the hot grill. He quickly withdrew his hand and whirled toward the pool to see the commotion with alarm spreading across his face. Of course, Dominic stood in the middle of it.

"You don't know how to swim?" Brittany cried out, sounding aghast. "What are you doing in the water without telling us that?"

Dominic stared defiantly back at her with his head and shoulders just above the water. His bottom lip jutted out defiantly.

The other boys stopped what they were doing and paddled around him.

"I just did tell you," Dominic said, sounding sullen.

"Yeah," Jimmy said, defending his friend. "Besides, we're in the shallow end. It's not like he's going to drown in this."

"Not the point, stupid," Brittany said with a huff. "Everybody should know how to swim before, you know, going swimming."

"Don't worry," Chase said quickly, paddling to Brittany's side. "We'll teach you, Dom. Right—" He suddenly stopped and looked at Dominic with stricken eyes. "Oh, man, I'm sorry. I didn't mean to call you—"

Dominic only shook his head. "It's okay, Chase," he said with a slight trace of embarrassment in his voice. "You can call me Dom now." He grinned crookedly. "We're friends, right?"

Chase relaxed. "Yeah," he said nodding. "We're friends. And friends teach friends how to swim."

The fun quickly resumed—this time with four boys and a girl teaching Dominic the best way to learn swimming—all at the same time.

Back with the adults, Mr. Daniels shook his head as Mr. Roseburg carefully fished the metal tongs from the grill using his bare hand.

"Poor Dominic may have a long summer ahead of him," Mr. Daniels remarked.

Mr. Roseburg yelped and then groaned as he gingerly gripped the rescued tongs. "I may never question you again, Ben," he said in mock seriousness, "but I do plan to get my head examined."

Mr. Wells only smiled wider. "You and me both before this is all over."

In the water, Dominic splashed in frustration. "Okay, quiet!" he yelled. "I can't float on my back, doggy paddle, and start putting my head underwater and kicking my feet all at the same time!"

The other kids stopped and stared. Brittany cracked up first. "You're right, Dominic," she said. "You'd have to turn yourself inside out and drown yourself."

"Let's take turns teaching Dominic," Jimmy said quickly, hopping in front of his sister. "Paper-rock-scissors to see who helps first."

Chase laughed. "This time, I *want* to win."

"Oh, no," Brittany said. She jumped up and came down on her younger brother's head, stuffing him under the water.

Jimmy came up coughing and spitting. "What was that for?" he demanded.

"I heard about that stupid scheme," Brittany said tightly. She turned to Dominic. "Dominic, these stupid boys used paper-rock-scissors to see who had to be nice to you when you first joined the Dodgers."

Jimmy made a face at his sister. Then he turned to Dominic. "Yeah, sorry about that," he said apologetically, ruefully wiping water from his spikey hair. "It was my idea."

An awkward silence settled as Shawn, Chase, and Grayson all stared at the water around them, embarrassed.

Dominic only shrugged. "So what?" he said. "I wouldn't want to be nice to me either back then. Come on, guys. Just teach me how to swim one step at a time."

In an instant the silence lifted and just like that only friends remained.

"Back float!" Shawn hollered.

"Doggy paddle," Grayson chimed in.

"Let Dominic choose!" Brittany cried in exasperation.

Jimmy just splashed her and was immediately splashed back by Chase.

Dominic grinned at all the commotion. Then, closing his eyes, he leaned back in the water and spread out his arms, stretching far from his body. Kicking up his feet and sticking them straight out, he stared up at the sky and relaxed.

"That's it, Dom!" Chase shouted, pausing his splashing.

Dominic barely heard. In his mind, he thought back to where this amazing, wonderful journey had all started—way back, when he was stuck in his mom's bedroom with the Monster Jerk banging on the door, readying to pound him… At the time he'd been a scared, angry kid convinced the world hated him. It was the same day Mack had told Dominic that he'd never have friends…and the same day Mr. Wells had come into his life, changing it forever. As his mind settled, all his anger seemed to drift away and he floated…

"Back float it is!" Shawn crowed.

"Yeah, now it's my turn!" Jimmy cried, shoving water at Dominic's floating form. Then, unleashing a yell, he launched himself up and came down on Dominic's belly.

Brittany screeched. "What are you doing, idiot!"

Dominic went under, his legs and feet thrashing wildly.

"What?" Jimmy asked innocently as he stood, water dripping from his face from his attack. "I'm teaching my friend how to swim."

Dominic burst his head out of the water, coming up with and as a part of the boys...

"That's it," he roared. "I've been playing nice." He went after the closest kid, Grayson. Grabbing the smaller boy under the arms, he lifted him up and tossed him forward.

Screeching, Grayson had his entire body out of the water before he smacked down with a mighty splash.

Then Dominic went after Jimmy.

"No you don't," Jimmy yelped, trying to swim away. "We're friends, remember? I was only kidding!" He kicked water in Dominic's face.

Brittany burst into laughter as her brother's foot was easily caught by Dominic and dragged under.

Another massive splash fight broke out around her. It would be okay, she knew. At the moment Dominic was surrounded by lifeguards. And they had all summer to really teach him to swim.

"Okay, gang!" Mr. Roseburg called out loudly, using his coach voice. "Time to get out and towel off! The food is done!'

Then Mrs. Roseburg poked her head out of the sliding glass door leading to the back of the house. "Dear?" she called, sounding confused. "Have you seen the pitcher of lemonade I just made? I can't find it anywhere!"

"It's in the pool!' Shawn yelled. "At least I hope that's the yellow stuff I just swam into."

Brittany and Jimmy both made eye contact at the same time. Then, taking a deep breath, they both ducked under the water.

It would certainly be a long summer. But it also promised to be a whole lot of fun.

About the Author

Gregory Saur has published numerous middle-grade novels and prefers to be writing safe at home. He understands this is not always an option and many, especially younger people, do not have this luxury. Hopefully this will change. If not writing, he would prefer playing a sport, especially baseball, where he claims to be one of the best players EVER to never play the game. Don't believe him? Just ask his imagination, where he has won multiple World Series, countless batting titles, too many MVPs to count, and more pitching duels than a body can dream of…and nearly all in his sleep. He often wonders, can he make the Hall of Fame for this? He's sure it's possible…in his dreams.